Neil Youn

Love To Burn

Neil Young

Love To Burn

*Thirty Years Of Speaking Out
1966-1996*

Paul Williams

OMNIBUS PRESS
LONDON · NEW YORK · PARIS · SYDNEY

Exclusive Distributors:
Book Sales Limited,
8/9 Frith Street,
London W1V 5TZ, UK.

Music Sales Corporation,
257 Park Avenue South,
New York, NY 10010, USA.

Music Sales Pty Limited,
120 Rothschild Avenue, Rosebery, NSW 2018, Australia.

To the Music Trade only:
Music Sales Limited,
8/9 Frith Street,
London W1V 5TZ, UK.

Cover picture: Jay Blakesberg/Retna

Printed and bound in Great Britain by MPG Books Ltd, Bodmin, Cornwall

A catalogue record for this book is available from the British Library.

For information about Paul Williams's *Crawdaddy!* newsletter, visit Cdaddy.com or write to Crawdaddy c/o Baldwin, 57 Tempsford, Welwyn Garden City AL7 2PA UK, or write to Crawdaddy, Box 231155, Encinitas CA 92023 USA

Contents

Appendices

I'd like to dedicate this book to my old friend
Philip K. Dick, because "Cinnamon Girl" was
his favorite rock song.

And to the Neil Young Appreciation Society
and other keepers of the faith.

And to Zeke, Ben, Amber, Pegi and himself.

Preface

Dear reader/listener:

"You've got to let your guard down."

1

I Sing the Song Because I Love the Man

This essay was written in January 1976. I first became aware of Neil Young in 1966 (see chapter 2) and that interest was continued and indeed increased as each "solo" album came out, 1969, 1970, 1972, '73, '74, '75. So I was already in 1975 very keen to address the question that drives this book: "who is Neil Young and why is his work-as-a-whole so important to me?" A very hip guy I met in Los Angeles named Charlie Haas, later a film writer, had a day job editing an in-house newsletter (cleverly called Circular*) for Warner Bros. Records, and he asked me to write about anything that interested me, and this was it. It appears out of chronological sequence here because it didn't make any sense for me to write a new introduction for this book when I had already written down most of what I want to say, twenty-one years ago.*

I hope you saw Bob Dylan singing "Hurricane" on television (the salute to John Hammond) – he was very good. You couldn't see that performance – I *hope* you couldn't – without feeling and thinking about the *strength* of the man, isn't it incredible, what is it, where does it come from, how does it contribute to or relate to his work?

Every time I see that strength (it has been my good fortune to see it more than once over the years, in Dylan, in Neil Young, in Philip K. Dick and others) and feel the greatness of the music or art that goes with it, I am forced once again to confront the realization that strength in the Emersonian sense (to thine own self be true) is the absolute prerequisite of artistic greatness. God-given talent is nothing without the stamina and the will to use that talent again and again in the

11

face of all odds, in the face of doubts and terrors that other people (those who don't make superhuman efforts of will over and over) can never imagine nor hope to experience.

To me, a great artist is someone who says "I am" more honestly, more powerfully, more beautifully, more straightforwardly, more inclusively than anyone else except other great artists. This is not a yardstick I use to judge people or their works; rather, it is a hypothesis I've been forced to consider after years of reading and looking and listening and saying, "Hey, that's great!" and then wondering why . . . especially wondering why certain people can do it again and again, without really repeating themselves. Why are they great? What are they doing that's different?

My answer, my deduction, my hypothesis is: they are being themselves more completely. That's all.

This is an essay about Neil Young.

Neil Young has made a lot more great music than most people seem to realize. I have all nine of his Reprise albums, and I listen to *all* of them (exception: *Journey Through the Past*, a soundtrack; it was released as an album against his wishes) frequently, with great pleasure and (sometimes) fierce identification. In addition, there are numerous fine songs spread through the CSNY/Buffalo Springfield catalog, and at least one superb bootleg recording variously known as *Young Man's Fancy* or *"I'm Happy That Y'All Came Down."* The bootleg was recorded at a concert in southern California (Los Angeles) in early 1971, and has been continually available on various non-labels ever since. No music-lover should be without it.

In fact, since I don't know where to begin this survey, maybe we should take a look at *Young Man's Fancy.* What a record! It contains fifteen songs, on four sides, plus some talking between songs (and *during* one song, a hilarious version of "Sugar Mountain"). As near as I can tell, it's all Neil alone, accompanying himself on either piano or acoustic guitar. The *sound* of the voice and guitar/piano is extraordinary – as is so often the case on Neil's albums, but this is unlike anything you've ever heard, there's a certain resonance, it's magic . . .

Context: this was months after *Gold Rush* was released, but still a year prior to *Harvest*. The concert includes two songs from *After the Gold Rush* ("Tell Me Why" and "Don't Let It Bring You Down"), one song from Neil's second album ("Cowgirl in the Sand"), two from the last Buffalo Springfield LP ("I Am a Child" and "On the Way Home"), one from the Crosby Stills Nash & Young repertoire ("Ohio"), one legendary B-side ("Sugar Mountain" – it was the flip of "The Loner" and "Heart of Gold" among others), four songs that were to be central to *Harvest* ("Heart of Gold," "Old Man," "The Needle and the Damage Done," and "A Man Needs a Maid"), two songs that showed up on *Time Fades Away* and one that surfaced on *On the Beach* ("Love in Mind," "Journey through the Past," and "See the Sky about to Rain"), and finally one song so far unreleased ("Dance Dance Dance," a classic, identical in melody and rhythm to the Young-penned Linda Ronstadt hit "Love Is a Rose" except that this early version is much better). A great collection, and certain to turn the heads of those who think only Neil's electric stuff makes it.

One of the songs on this album, "Heart of Gold," inspired me to write a book (it was the bootleg version, not the single, that I heard first and that got me off); there are others that hit me almost as hard, and I hope to get in a word about them later in this article.

Of the "regular" N.Y. albums, the first four are best known, and the most recent, *Zuma*, looks like it will be another big crowd-pleaser (deservedly – whether there's a hit single depends on how well "Drive Back" is edited and promoted, but the whole LP is remarkably appealing and accessible on a lot of levels).

When the first album, *Neil Young*, came out in November 1968, none of the former members of the Buffalo Springfield were "names" to the public yet, and in fact the whole bit of a group member going solo was a new idea and regarded with suspicion. Add to that the fact that the mix was bad (the album was later remixed and reissued) and the material uneven, and you have a career off to a slow start. I am just beginning to get into that album now – maybe partly because my impression of it was based on the earlier mix. Neil has said in several places that the problem with the first album is that it was a lot of overdubs – his general preference is the "live shot," vocals and instruments recorded at the same time. He's also said he likes the record. So do I, increasingly. Lately, "Here We Are in the Years" and "What Did You Do to My Life?" are in my head all the time. My God, the man has such a gift for *melodies* . . .

Each of Neil's next three albums is regarded by many critics and fans as "his best album" or even "his only good album." (The *Everybody Knows This Is Nowhere* contingent won't even speak to the *Harvest* contingent, and vice versa I guess.) This was the period of Neil's greatest commercial success. The second solo album, *Everybody Knows This Is Nowhere* (recorded with Crazy Horse, who got co-billing; Neil and Crazy Horse had only been together a few weeks when they started recording the album), came out in May 1969 and began attracting listeners right away; then in August Neil joined with Crosby Stills & Nash on a part-time basis. Woodstock was their second gig together. CSNY mania swept the nation, as it were, and by September of the following year, when the extraordinary *After the Gold Rush* was released, Neil was unassailably a major 1970s superstar. *Gold Rush* cemented his personal popularity, won him many new friends, and paved the way for the huge success of *Harvest* (released February 1972). Fat years for Neil, at least from the public's point of view. (In 1973 he offered his own view: "Now I'm a pauper in a naked disguise, a millionaire through a businessman's eyes. Oh, friend of mine, don't be denied . . .")

Neil Young. I don't want to put the man on a pedestal. In fact, as the years have gone by and I've grown to like Bob Dylan and Neil Young, and the music they make more and more, I've also found that they've become more human to me, I identify more and more with their actions as well as their words. I was never sure, for example, of Dylan's motivation in writing "George Jackson" – but the reasons for "Hurricane" are unambiguous, self-evident, real. The song is an action. I respect it. I love it.

All of us sitting out here in the audience relate to the person as well as the music. We can't help it. We take things in context. If all we know of the person is the image, we relate to the image. If the music is good enough, and if our ears are open enough, we hear the music and the image is destroyed, and a new more personal relationship takes its place.

Neil Young had problems with image in his superstar years – or rather, his audience had problems – maybe we should say the difficulty was mutual. "What do you want from me?" cries the star, muttering under his breath at an open mike. "We want to eat you raw for dinner, you look so delicious!" his audience responds, though of course they'd be shocked if they could hear themselves. Still, for all the sensitivity of individual audience-members, the mob won't change. So it's the star who has to make the adjustments.

*　*　*

Journey Through the Past, a two-record miscellany which hit the public with all the impact of *Self-Portrait* or early Plastic Ono stuff (except that the ambiguous packaging and Xmas '72 timing made it seem even more of a rip-off), was, accidentally or not, a good step towards lowering the mob's expectations. The next three albums, *Time Fades Away, On the Beach*, and *Tonight's the Night*, each more iconoclastic than the one before, completed the process nicely.

The public gave up waiting for another *Harvest*, and Neil was a free man again. He escaped from the clutches of his hungry fans by giving them more truth than they wanted.

Which is not to say the post-*Harvest* stuff isn't terrific. At the moment, *Time Fades Away* is my favorite Neil Young album.

Like *John Wesley Harding*, it starts with a title track that happens to be the least important song on the album, lent dignity by having the record named after it. "Time fades away." The phrase – not the song – suggests that this guy is a has-been. It's a self-deprecatory gesture. The real message of the album is more along the lines of "you can live your own life" – but it took me dozens of listenings to realize that, to open up, to feel it.

I couldn't get into the record at all at first. I didn't even like "Journey Thru the Past," a song which used to make me almost cry every time I heard it on that Rita Coolidge album. I guess the whole thing was just too raw, too unconnected with my idea of what it was I liked about Neil Young. I passed. A year later, *On The Beach* came out, and I listened to it, and liked it, and that plus some intelligent words by Robert Christgau on *Time Fades Away* sent me back to the earlier album. And I discovered "Don't Be Denied." Also around that time I heard Neil perform "Don't Be Denied" live (on the CSNY tour) and the intensity of that moment just burned into my brain, electric guitar like a rivet gun, human being like a human being:

> "The punches came fast and hard
> Lying on my back in the schoolyard."

And I listened to the album more and more, especially for that one song (ooh, such guitar), and eventually I began to hear the whole thing, the melodies, the rhythm, the perform-ance, even the words and intentions . . . And one day I realized that there was a song for this decade even better than "Don't Be Denied," and it was on the same side of the same album.

* * *

What I have to say about Neil Young is in no way simple. It's as hard for me to get to him in words as it is for me to get to

16

me. I've been writing this essay for months, maybe years – I've wanted to write it very much, kept asking different editors for the assignment – and still it's difficult, still I have to fight my way forward, trying to release my passion, trying to make my peace.

Trying to learn something, I guess.

I don't write about music. I write about listening to music, which is an experience, which is personal, and also about as universal as sex. Nine and a half years since I first heard "Nowadays Clancy Can't Even Sing," and I'm still reaching towards Neil's music, and he's still making new music that reaches me, and that's got to mean something (and it isn't something you'll ever read about in *Newsweek*).

It means him and me are both alive. There are probably only about twenty-seven of us on the whole planet, so that's not a small thing at all, if you know what I mean.

*   *   *

After *Time Fades Away* and *On The Beach* (I really loved "Ambulance Blues") came *Tonight's the Night*, which some suggested shouldn't even be released. But in addition to his amply expressed self-doubts, the kid's got real courage-of-his-convictions – very rare, surprisingly rare in this and all businesses. "Great works of art have no more affecting lesson for us than this," says Emerson. "They teach us to abide by our spontaneous impression with good-humored inflexibility then most when the whole cry of voices is on the other side." A (you should pardon the expression) transcendent album. (Almost any quote from "Self -Reliance" would fit nicely into an essay on Neil Young.)

Tonight's the Night is what I mean by good music. I've heard some people call it sloppy. To me, slick is sloppy (I'm dead serious about this). When I hear *Tonight's the Night*, every note is in place, is exactly where it should be – the hard work

17

it takes to make a record like this is of a kind that the people who lay down 183 splices and overdubs can't even imagine. But it is in fact harder work than that other kind, and truer, and the music that results is far, far better.

Slick is sloppy because it's superficial. The real work of writing a story is largely done before one sits down at the typewriter. The same is true in making a record – however much effort may be required in the studio, the quality of the finished work is limited by what the artists brought into the studio in the first place.

I'm sick to death with producers – and critics, and fans – who think great guitar playing comes from the fingers rather than the heart.

Tonight's the Night (especially first track, first side) is about as high as recorded music can be. The only recorded perform-ance I can think of that's as immediately alive and communi-cates as much of the human beings playing it is "Please Mrs. Henry" on *The Basement Tapes*.

Everybody has their own aesthetic. Mine is something like, "and the truth shall make you dance." I can even listen to *Tonight's the Night* in the morning.

* * *

Zuma is Neil's ninth. It's not as personal, not as intense, as his best stuff, but it's encouraging because it suggests new worlds of wonder beyond the old exhaustions. I like to listen to it, especially side two, especially "Drive Back," which has a great build-up-and-release structure, the sort of thing that rock 'n' roll is all about. And "Cortez the Killer" is a fine laconic dream & nightmare, slightly science fictional (did his girl-friend leave him and go to live with Montezuma?), highly effective and timely mythmaking. The hemisphere was raped and pillaged; she waits; is it time yet for redemption? This is where our thoughts are turning . . .

(State of California reports show that Neil Young contributed $5000 to a campaign to ban nuclear power development until reactors meet stringent safety standards. Members of the Union of Concerned Scientists gave at least $11,000; Robert Redford donated $200; Jane Fonda came up with $50. Right on, everybody. Don't forget to vote against the power plants when the time comes, this June.)

Zuma is pleasing. But I think it's a transition. I think there's undreamed-of greatness yet to come.

* * *

"Here We Are in the Years." "Last Dance." "A Man Needs a Maid." "Down By the River." "When You Dance, I Can Really Love." What can I say about these songs?

I can say there has been, and continues to be, no more to the man than meets the ear. He holds nothing back. He lets it all come through.

Melodies, guitars, silly images, awkward, expressive voice, driving rhythm even when it's just him alone with acoustic guitar, it all speaks to me, talks to me of affection for friends, fear of love, need for affirmation wherever it can be found, even in negation, plus loneliness, courage, desolation and a bit of madness and real, energetic joy. So human, human.

I keep listening to these records – each one seems very different from all the others – and I keep finding more of what I'm looking for in them, more of myself. It is nice to have ten years of a man's work to run around in. Consider a song like "Last Dance." I can't hear this one without getting charged up – the *strength* of the playing is so incredible, it always has me punching the air in front of me as I listen, dancing in my chair.

And so much to say! Listen to him in front of that audience ... you have to hear Neil Young in front of an audience, and if there aren't any concerts to get to, the live recordings on *Time Fades Away* are the next best thing. There he is almost begging those kids, everybody, to wake up, and scorning them, mourning them with real compassion, in the same breath. *Da-da* da dom, *da-da* dom dom – it's a *tour de force*, I feel so much from this one, comparable to what I once got out of "When The Music's Over." "Last Dance!"

"See the Sky About to Rain" – as full and gentle as individual raindrops hitting a pond – hits me just as hard at other moments, the bootleg version in particular can unleash a flood of emotion. There's no similarity at all between this and "Last Dance" and yet somehow the magic is the same, that intensity of impact . . .

Music/creativity is a clue to something bigger. "I sing the song because I love the man; I know that some of you don't understand. Milk-blood to keep from running out . . ." Basically, we just have to keep at it.

"Oh no, oh no . . ." Thanks, Neil, for everything.

2

Buffalo Springfield

This chapter was written in January 1967, for the eighth issue of the rock music magazine I had started a year earlier, Crawdaddy! *The album was brand new when I wrote this review (and somehow predicted the difficulty the group would have staying together past two albums). In the previous month I had seen Buffalo Springfield perform in Hollywood and New York, and was quite impressed. I'd also been to live shows by the groups I compare them with (Airplane, Grape, Youngbloods, Doors). It was a good time to be eighteen (or, in Neil's case, twenty-one).*

Let me tell you about popsicle sticks.

To me, a major aspect of rock '67 is the tightness of the new groups. By tightness, I mean the feeling of wholeness a group projects when they're on stage (or in a recording studio), and I'm thinking of Jefferson Airplane, Moby Grape, the Youngbloods, the Buffalo Springfield, the Doors. An individual, an audience, can react to one of these groups as a unit, can feel a group personality reaching out from the stage. I never listen to Neil Young, the way I might listen to Mike Bloomfield or Jeff Beck, because Neil Young isn't on stage; the Springfield is, and the brilliant things Neil does are an inseparable part of the music the Springfield is making. And Neil's excellent playing isn't just Neil soloing away; it's Neil reacting to, working with, each Buffalo, and more than that, feeling a certain way about the gig and the song and the run and whatever because of a sense of his place in things, because

21

of his awareness of himself as a Buffalo Springfield. It's a somewhat different feeling from the feeling of being Neil Young, and as a result what he contributes to the group's communication is different from what he'd contribute were he in a different group. Basically, tightness is a matter of finding the right people to work with, people who can form a tight emotional unit with you as well as a musical unit; a group must have a stable personality, and its personality must relate well to the type of music it works with, for that group to be tight. That doesn't mean everyone has to be best friends – it means the members of the group have to be interacting creatively toward a common goal, a certain sound, for the audience to be able to interact with the group as a whole. Conflict – competition – destroy wholeness.

Tightness comes in many flavors. Jefferson Airplane has a dark solidity to its sound, as though each member were a thick black line and the six so close musically that all you see/hear/feel is a deep solid rectangle of sound and personality. The Youngbloods, perhaps the tightest group in the country, are nonetheless four very distinct musicians. You hear four separate things, but you feel one feeling. They are four quarters, working in perfect unity but with a very different oneness from that of a dollar bill. The Buffalo Springfield resemble neither of these groups in their tightness; more distinct as personalities than the Airplane, they are at the same time not as separate as the Youngbloods. If you see the Airplane as a solid rectangle, and the Youngbloods as four separate lines standing together, then the Springfield is/are a criss-cross, a popsicle stick construction held together only by the force of each stick on each other stick, a subtle and seemingly delicate wholeness which nonetheless communicates itself extremely powerfully to a receptive audience.

Buffalo Springfield (italicized because that's the name of their album, Atco 33–200) is, a lovely, moving experience. You have to be into it, however; chances are you won't even like it on first hearing. All the songs seem to sound alike, and the group sound is quite thin. These are valid criticisms. There are certain samenesses in the Springfield's material, and if you hear them on one of their rare off nights, you'll be quite bored. But what the Springfield do is rise above these samenesses, employing beautiful changes and continually fresh approaches within their particular framework. The more you listen to this album and become familiar with it, the more you'll hear in each song. As for the thinness, the production job on this LP is sadly amateurish. The bass is under-recorded, the drums misunderstood, and the guitars tend to tinkle when they want to ring. On stage, the Springfield have a deceptively full sound: they're not as loud or as solid as the Airplane, but because every note each man plays is so perfectly directed – like the popsicle stick construction – they project a richness and a fullness which is more satisfying than one could possibly imagine. It's a delicate balance, how-ever, and it wasn't achieved in the recording studio. This is partly for production reasons – poor miking, poor mixing, and the wrong studios for the Springfield's sound – but it's also because the group wasn't completely on when they did these sessions. Much more can happen to these songs on a good night than did happen in the studio.

But the album, despite it all, is beautiful. Every track on it will entrance you, at one time or another. "Clancy" will prob-ably be first – both melody and lyric hit very hard, and once the rhythm changes and the phrasing sink in, you're done for. The objectivity of the song is heartbreaking: "Who should be sleeping that's writing this song, wishin' and a-hopin' he weren't so damn wrong?" Straightforwardness – with a sort of implied understatement – is characteristic of the Springfield. Consider the titles of their songs: "Flying on the Ground Is Wrong"; "Sit Down, I Think I Love You" ; "Leave." They love to come right out and say it, with a shrug of the shoulders and an innocent look.

But it's not so much innocence as openness. Honesty, warmth – these are key words in describing a Buffalo Springfield performance. They present themselves to the people, offering

23

nothing but giving everything. There's love in their music – not the driving, evangelical love of Jefferson Airplane, but a straightforward take-it-or-leave-it love, all yours if you want it and will share in it. If the Springfield leave you cold, it's probably because you want to be left cold; once you get into them, you'll be stunned by their warmth. It's the extraordinary amount of honest emotion conveyed in this LP that makes it exceptional.

"Flying on the Ground" is the song that knocks me out the most just now. It's an unassuming little love song that walks all around the edges of rock's oldest clichés and comes away quietly fresh. "Baby Don't Scold Me" plays with some more recent clichés – mostly Beatle stuff – but still manages to sound 100% Buffalo Springfield. The Springfield – no matter what they play – are too much themselves to resemble anyone else; every noise the group makes is riddled with the uniqueness of their personality. This very fact may work against them. At present, the Springfield are an excellent and exciting group, and I would go far from where I am to hear them. But unlike many groups who aren't as good, the Springfield do not strike me as a growing unit, one that will branch out into new fields of musical expression as it finds itself overfamiliar with the field it's in. Right now the group could release another album in much the same style as the first and still show us new tricks – but another LP after that would be pretty draggy without some major changes. What worries me is that the Springfield are so tight and so spontaneous in what they're doing now that whatever new things they approach they seem to approach in relation to the past. They know what they can do and they do it excellently. But that's not enough; to remain as good as they are, they must get better – they must grow. And while each individual in the group is probably capable of further musical growth, the group as a whole – though it is a brilliantly tight performing unit at present – may not be a tight growing unit as well. I hope I'm wrong about this; meanwhile, it should be remembered that groups, people, must and do change . . . and a fiercely whole musical unit today cannot even count on

24

being together a year from now.

I've purposely avoided discussing the individual Buffaloes; they're all talented – Richie's phrasing is extremely fresh and effective; Dewey is an excellent drummer, comparable to the Hollies' Bobby Elliott; Bruce is surely the secret master of the group; etc. – but to me the group can only be thought of as a unit. I don't want to overlook, however, the songwriting talents of two of the Buffaloes: both Neil and Steve are exceptional quite apart from writing for a specific group – their songs would surely be recorded, though not the same way, if there were no Buffalo S. Steve's "Sit Down, I Think I Love You" is already a West Coast hit in a cover version by the Mojo Men; almost every other song on this LP has the potential to be a single. In few cases could a cover version be better than the Springfield's; but it might well be more commercial. Both Neil and Steve are capable of unusually clever lyrics, song structures and changes that work well, and light, effective melodies. But they never seem to write a song together, though their styles are quite related; it is characteristic of the Springfield that each man does his part, independently, and the parts just fit together.

This album was recorded early last fall; since then the eternal war between Past and Present has broken out anew, this time in open battle on Hollywood's Sunset Strip. Battles tend to beget songs; November's clashes moved Stephen Stills to write the first major topical song since "Hard Rain." "There's something happening here; what it is ain't exactly clear. There's a man with a gun over there, telling me I've got to beware. I think it's time we stop, children, what's that sound? Everybody look what's going down . . ." The title of the song is perfect: "For What It's Worth." There is no bitterness, no dialectic; just description, and a word of unspoken advice: hold back from the battle – look around – we've already won the war.

"For What It's Worth" is the first Buffalo Springfield single to make the charts. It should be at least a million-seller; we owe ourselves that much.

25

3

Rock 'N' Roll Cowboy, Disc 1

So today is November 19, 1996; a week ago Neil Young turned 51, still on the road, still making new albums that are never quite whatever we expected, and still four and a half years younger than Bob Dylan. Also, after 28 years, still performing and recording with Crazy Horse. Quite an accomplishment. Sure makes up for not being able to stick it out with Buffalo Springfield.

Who is Neil Young? The author of an extraordinary body of work (songs, recordings, performances). A body of work I love, and can hardly begin to make sense of. Oh well. A glance at other people's writing about Neil – the books and also the letters from true fans in *Broken Arrow*, the journal of the Neil Young Appreciation Society – tells me I'm not alone. I sing the song because I love the man, yes. But who is he? And *why* do I love his songs so much? And why does there seem to be so little agreement among Neil fans as to which are his best works or even as to what are his prime virtues and strengths as an artist? Really, it is not at all difficult, if you interview your friends, to find two people who both consider Neil Young one of the finest artists to come along in their lifetime but who each keenly dislike or disparage Young albums that the other considers his very best work.

So I've been working on this riddle, and this book, for thirty years, okay? And what I want to say is, hello Waterface. Welcome to Miami Beach.

Like many of the other chapters in this book, this will be a personal essay in the form of a record review – kind of a musical diary entry. The record in this case is a four-CD set, a bootleg from Great Dane Records in Milano, Italy, called *Rock 'N' Roll Cowboy, A Life on the Road, 1966/1994*. Okay, so we have *Decade* and *Rust Never Sleeps*, and a someday forthcoming ten-CD "career anthology" of mostly unreleased material that Neil and his friend Joel Bernstein have been preparing for years . . . but for a retrospective that you can hold in your hand and that successfully articulates a lot of the essence of Who Neil Young Is And What He Has Accomplished, I do earnestly recommend *Rock 'N' Roll Cowboy*. Not that I advocate breaking the law. But hey, maybe Neil, like the artist formerly known as Prince, could bootleg the bootleg and sell it through his website and we'd all be the richer. Let the music flow.

* * *

Hello Waterface. I know that some of you don't understand. These two words are for me an embodiment of Neil's aesthetic. When *Tonight's the Night* originally came out, there was a little pamphlet, actually a sheet of paper folded in fourths, included in the sleeve that holds the record. I hope this has been a part of the experience of everyone who's encountered this haunting *tour de force* album, but I suspect it sometimes gets lost along the way. It explains everything. In Dutch. That's the Neil Young aesthetic. You tell your listeners everything they need to know to understand this fiercely personal and radically idiosyncratic album, and you do this by including with the album a reprint of a magazine article that looks like a two-page spread from *Rolling Stone* and is peppered with tantalizing subheads like TONIGHTS THE NIGHT, SOMETIMES I FEEL LIKE I'M JUST A HELPLESS CHILD, DANNY WHITTEN, NIXON, and FILM . . . but the text is unreadable. "It's Dutch. It's an article about the 'Tonight' stage show and a complete account of the facts and events leading to the record. It seemed a good idea to print it in Dutch because in the U.S. nobody would be able to understand any of it. Because I didn't understand any of it myself, and when someone is so sickened and fucked up as I was then, everything's in Dutch anyway," Neil explained in an interview in Paris in March 1976.

On the insert itself he explains, on the outermost fold in white typewritten words on a black background, "Hello Waterface: Welcome to Miami Beach. Everything is cheaper than it looks. As you know, the Santa Monica Flyer is the longest train around. It's so fast and straight with its up to date. I'm just down here working on BB's plane crash album and it sure looks good to me.

"Tonight's the night. We're gonna get loose in the caboose with our backs to the tracks. Yes, we're all on vacation and we deserve it. Waterface, I sincerely hope you can make it back in time.

"It all feels so strange. This train is just too fast. It never stops you know. Unless you get off. But I remember BB. He called my name. He said, 'tell Waterface to put it in his lung and not in his vein.' "

Go in one fold and you read, in Neil's handwriting, "This album was made for Danny Whitten and Bruce Berry who lived and died for rock and roll." (Both died of heroin overdoses.) And other info, including that that's the late Danny Whitten singing (live, with Neil and Crazy Horse) "Come On Baby Let's Go Downtown." Open the last fold and there's the 1973 Dutch article, headed by a photo of Neil almost as classic as the "preacher" shot on the album cover, and the handwritten heading "Welcome on Miami Beach, Ladies and Gentlemen!" Issue #12 of *Broken Arrow* included Mark Lyons' translation of the article, which speaks empathetically and very frankly about Neil's depression and heavy alcohol use during and in the months before the London concert the journalist attended. He quotes Neil's stage monologs that night: "According to some rumors I'm dead already, but I'm standing here . . . I'm not Catholic but I believe in a sort of confession. Here tonight, ladies and gentlemen, I want to sing a song for Danny Whitten who can't be with us tonight. I can feel the Jose Cuervo but I think that what I want to say is getting across. I'm talking slowly about a good friend of mine and I don't want to discredit his name. This is a song for him. Perhaps I'll sing fifty songs for him this evening. You never know . . ."

* * *

That was the Tonight's the Night Tour, September – November 1973, represented on *Rock 'N' Roll Cowboy* (end of Disc 1) by "Tonight's the Night" and "Tired Eyes." *Cowboy* is a wonderfully designed album that you can hold in your hands like a book (a very handsome book). The four CDs are on the inside covers, two in front two in back. Between the covers is a tall slick booklet with terrific photos and clear information about each song on each disc, including a fascinating and very thoughtful selection of quotes from Young illuminating the circumstances of the composition of the song or of its performance. There is also an ongoing well-organized (but not always perfectly accurate) listing of tours and concert dates and locations. Every song is from a live performance. Many are unreleased or otherwise unusual ("Birds" sung with Graham Nash at the Big Sur Folk Fest a year before it appeared on an album, "Out on the Weekend" solo at a BBC TV studio, "Southern Man" with the short-lived Stills-Young Band). Altogether there are 63 songs, with selections representing 22 different years out of the '66-'94 era, and five full hours of music.

The only aspect of the package that doesn't fully resonate for me is the title, though it helps when I remember that "cowboy" has a different connotation for European fans of a North American singer than it does for me. Probably it connotes freewheeling individualism, the loner riding the rock range. The album starts absolutely perfectly for me (because this is how my awareness of Neil started, thirty years ago) with "Nowadays Clancy Can't Even Sing," live with Buffalo Springfield at Whittier High School in 1966 or 1967. And in a lovely expression of the album's theme, a snippet of Neil's voice, the tail end of his spoken introduction to the song, is the first thing you hear on the album: "THE THING IS, JUST NOT WANTING TO BE WHAT EVERY-BODY THOUGHT I SHOULD BE." Not the loner but the individualist. That's who Neil Young is, and that is the message conveyed by this song, which happens to be arguably his most important song (though not best-remembered) in terms of the impact it had on his career.

The first three songs, first twenty-one minutes, of *Rock 'N' Roll Cowboy* are superb examples of what is best in Neil Young's work, and why he is so loved and so influential (his impact on other musicians and other creative contemporaries). The three tracks combine to make a fine pocket retrospective, an efficient history and exposition of what Young's work, and his soul, his spirit, are all about. "Nowadays Clancy Can't Even Sing." "Birds." "Cowgirl in the Sand." Thank you Erik Lafayette and cohorts in Milano. You have made the case for Neil Young as convincingly and compactly and eloquently as it could possibly be made. Wish your compilation was more easily available. *This* is the answer to my "who is?" question. And the other 3⅔rds discs and 60 songs are almost as well-chosen and often close to as pleasurable. As it stands, one of the albums of the decade, or the half-century. Bravo. And I'm not kidding. Just as I thirty years ago confidently urged my contemporaries to check out an album by a new group they'd never heard of, I now urge the same folks or whoever's out there to open yourselves to the possibility that *Rock 'N' Roll Cowboy* is in fact a devastatingly effective (and appropriately imperfect) summation of the work-as-a-whole of one of rock and roll's all-time greats. It is. He is. And not just for his image (never mind that "Godfather of Grunge" hooey). For his artistry, his body of work.

* * *

The impact of "Clancy" on Neil's career? I'll explain, and at the same time I hope to get in a word or two about the beauty of the song and this (ragged) performance. Neil Young hereby asserted his power as a songwriter, and his commitment to his art. "Clancy" made such an impact on Richie Furay when he and Neil first met, and so affected Stephen Stills and others involved, that as a result each participant (musician, manager, record company guy etc.) fought off his doubts and came to believe in the strength and potential of this band. So because of the song, there was a band.

And "Clancy" also was to become (as a Buffalo Springfield single in July 1966) Neil Young's first widely released song, after he'd been playing in bands continuously since age fifteen (1961) and had been making recordings since 1963. The breakthrough. Cute contradiction. The chorus "can't even sing" is what started him singing before the public. Further twist: that's not Neil Young you hear singing, except on the harmonies, on the single of "Nowadays Clancy Can't Even Sing" included on the first Buffalo Springfield album, or on the first track of *Rock 'N' Roll Cowboy*, live from Whittier High School (or so we believe) in southeast Los Angeles, sometime in 1966 or 1967. It's Richie Furay. So Neil's illicit cowboy compilation starts with another man's voice. Yet I think almost any fan listening will agree with me that it sure sounds and *feels* like Neil Young. The voice of his heart. Via this song and this group (including Neil on guitar and vocal harmonies) and Richie's wonderful lead vocal. Yeah, on this track Neil "can't even sing" because the record company people don't think the world is ready for the rawness and eccentricity of his voice. But he sings anyway, doesn't he? "Who's trying to act like he's just in between?" "Singing the meaning of what's in my mind . . ." Wow. Thirty years later I still get gooseflesh.

The text that accompanies the song listing in the *Cowboy* booklet demonstrates the strengths and weaknesses of the booklet (presumably written by "Erik Lafayette" who is credited on the bootleg – unusual, but because of quirks of Italian law this is a semi-legal bootleg – with "concept and executive production"): "Written by Neil Young for Clancy Smith, a schoolmate stricken with multiple sclerosis. Recorded in 1965 as a demo at Elektra Studios, then re-recorded one year later with Buffalo Springfield at Gold Star Studios in Los Angeles, this song finally made it to record in August 1967. This live BF version features Richie Furay on vocals." *Those were really good days. Great people. Everybody in that group was a fucking genius at what they did. That was a great group, man. There'll never be another Buffalo Springfield. Never."*

The quote in italics is from Neil Young, of course. We're not provided with sources (what year, who published the interview) for these quotes, but what do you expect? At least it's not in Dutch. "August 1967" is a misprint, a screw-up resulting from careless proof-reading or fact-checking. What they mean is July 1966. "BF" presumably is a misprint for BS. The name of Neil's high school schoolmate and his medical condition are correctly and helpfully provided, but to say the song was "written for" him is slightly misleading. John Einarson's well-researched book *Neil Young, The Canadian Years* paints a clearer (and very illuminating) picture. The song was written in late summer 1965, and "was born out of his frustration and hopelessness following the break-up of his band and his failure to garner any interest for what he was trying to say musically." Einarson also notes Neil saying in later interviews that the song is also about his feelings after breaking up with a girlfriend. He quotes Neil on Clancy Smith: "He was a kind of persecuted member of the community. He used to be able to do something, sing or something, and then he wasn't able to do it any more. The fact was that all the other problems or things that were seemingly important didn't mean anything any more because he couldn't do what he wanted to do."

So the song wasn't "for" Clancy but rather used him in a kind of personal symbology, a figure whose situation, in Neil's memory, embodied Neil's own feelings of frustration and loss and determination to persevere. Good insight into the songwriter's process (how a name or an image takes on a resonant meaning). Einarson tells us that shortly after writing the song, Neil took part in another unsuccessful band audition, and then went to New York City (the audition had taken him from Toronto to southern Vermont) and looked up Stephen Stills, whom he'd met in Canada when a band Neil was in had opened for a band Stephen was in. Stills wasn't home, but Richie Furay answered the door, and Neil played him "Nowadays Clancy." Furay liked it, taped it, wrote down the lyrics, and was soon performing it himself. Furay: "I remember thinking, 'this guy's a pretty interesting guy.' The song had a haunting melody to me, maybe it was the way Neil sang it. It was certainly not a typical song like the kind I was used to listening to. The song was really unique. It had metaphors and allegories about this classmate named Clancy who was just one of those guys everybody picked on."

It's an inspired song. To understand Young's power (over us) as a songwriter and performer, we must focus on his gift for melody, his ability through his use of melodic progressions and lyrical fragments to evoke and express strong feelings, his evident sincerity in relation to whatever he's expressing. His conviction. His intensity. His commitment to a personal vision. This song is about that commitment. An anthem, forerunner of "Don't Be Denied" and "My My, Hey Hey." Oh, and we must also focus on his use of rhythm, of musical tension and counterpoint, balanced tensions, and the vivid colors he paints with the sound of his guitar playing and the sound of his voice.

"Who's that stomping all over my face?" "Before I can take home what's rightfully mine." "Who's got the feeling, yeah, to keep him alive?" Fragments of thoughts, feelings, images.

34

Inspired songwriting technique. And clearly inspired in the sense of spontaneous, intuitive (guided by spirit), not calculated at all.

The beauty of the melody and the way it fits with the words. And the surprising ways the words seem to break the rules of syntax and normal storytelling, and manage to tell the listener a story anyway, a story that turns out to be (maybe because of all the space left to the imagination) especially relevant and powerful for me or you personally, this particular listener. Bingo. Connection. Great song. The power of rock 'n' roll.

The Whittier live performance makes a nice start for the compilation because it's so early – Neil similarly included live Buffalo Springfield recordings in his first (slightly awkward) retrospective, the soundtrack to his 1972 film *Journey Through the Past*. The iffyness of its sonic quality (not so bad for such an early live rock recording, but there are uncomfortable moments) is also very helpful at the start of the compilation. After all, this is gonna be 63 live tracks of various origins, nothing polished in the studio. So this rough but very rewarding recording serves as a timely reminder of Neil's aesthetic, a breaking down of resistance, an initiation. I refer to the aesthetic, expressed on *Tonight's the Night* and many other albums, that authenticity and spontaneity, preservation of rough edges and of cool sounds, take precedence over any considerations of "cleanness" or "professionalism" or even "prettiness."

Not that this isn't pretty. When you are in the right mood (more on this subject soon), it's gorgeous. A real gift. Because as sentimentally attached as I am to the original recorded version, this one (if you can get past the lo-fi sound) is much better. The band has grown into the song more (or maybe the studio made them stiff), and especially with Neil's decorative lead guitar notes the total sound is now hugely more expressive of the song's *feeling*. Along with which, not surprisingly (because musicians spark each other), there's a lot more feeling in the vocal. And all the stunts, the shift into waltz time in the middle of each verse, the great withhold-and-release hook in the chorus ("can't .... even sing!") and the resolving melody fragment that follows, work so much better here and seem so intrinsic to the song. Very pretty. Gosh, with the right producer this could have been a huge hit back then, but maybe it's just as well . . .

* * *

Track 2 on *Rock 'N' Roll Cowboy* is "Birds." This is still not Neil Young as a solo artist but him as a member of the only other group he's been part of between 1966 and the present (he quit both groups while they were still active performing bands). Yeah, this is Crosby, Stills, Nash & Young, at Big Sur September 13, 1969 (though *Cowboy* mistakenly calls it 1968), less than a month after they first performed together.

Five weeks earlier, Neil had recorded this song for his patchwork masterpiece *After the Gold Rush*. That version was piano-based (Big Sur is strummed guitar), and Neil was accompanied in the choral parts ("when you see me *fly away* without you . . .") by two or more of the following: Danny Whitten, Nils Lofgren, Stephen Stills, Ralph Molina – whereas at Big Sur he's singing with Graham Nash. Just two guys wailing this farewell to a lover. Must have been quite a sight. And for sure it's a wonderful, indeed very moving, sound. Preserved for us on *Rock 'N' Roll Cowboy*.

"When you are in the right mood." When you're in the right mood for it, you can really connect with a Neil Young performance. And not if you're not in the right mood. And it's possible to be in a mood for one type of NY song but not for another. This I think helps explain how true fans can differ so radically in their evaluation of particular albums or performances. Young's art is very feeling-based. So we listen with our feelings, our emotional presence, and the mystery is how he manages to encourage us in this rather rare or difficult sort of attentiveness. The listener has to be open, and we like the artist

36

because he or she is consistently or frequently able to open us. But by the same logic, we can't expect ourselves or our fellow fans to always be open to whatever he's doing or whatever way he's doing it. Nah. He either blows us away or he bores us or he irritates us or he draws us in remarkably. And this recording of "Birds" is a good example – it's quite possible to be left cold by it, either because you're not in the mood (happened to me) or because you're attached to the excellent original album version (happened to my sweetie). And I'm here to report that it's also possible to fall in love with it, to be surprised at how this very simple performance (repetitive strumming and one long verse/chorus twice with just two lines altered in the second go-round) can be so attractive and can pull forth such emotional response as you hit the repeat arrow and listen to it over and over. If you are open to it, this two-and-a-half-minute performance can put you into a heck of a mood.

Just a month after Big Sur David Crosby, if he'd had a tape of this, could certainly have heard it as his lover Christine trying to comfort him with a tender goodbye from the spirit world after her car crash. Or one can hear it the way it was presumably intended, a man acknowledging to his lover (in this case probably his first wife) that they're splitting apart, and instead of guilt or anger offering her his loving and protective feelings towards her, wishing her well as one does one's mate or one's child. Projected onto images of bird mates, as humans often do in their love poetry. An amazingly tender song and performance, neatly representing another side of Neil Young that can't be passed over when speaking of his power and impact and accomplishments as an artist.

* * *

And then there's a third, equally vital, equally central side of Neil Young, and so of course we come to "Cowgirl in the

Sand," live with Crazy Horse at the Fillmore East, March 6th or 7th 1970. If you're not in the mood for this, too bad. This is the meaning of life. This is the apotheosis of Danny Whitten and Neil Young and Crazy Horse. This makes the short list of all-time great long rock tracks, up there with "Sister Ray" and with the original *Everybody Know This Is Nowhere* album version of "Cowgirl," which this take equals, believe it or not. It's as alive and beautiful, and more live, and utterly reinvented in the moment as great live rock performances should be, and infuckingcredible. This is the heart of the matter. This is it. I'm not kidding. Hard to believe Neil and his record company had a good recording of this (they used Danny singing "Downtown" from these same shows on *Tonight's the Night*) and never released it, so far. The guy have an attack of modesty or something? This is the proof of all that Godfather of Grunge signifying. This is like a recording of Charlie Parker and band inventing what jazz was to become and getting it about as good as it would ever be gotten. Some night in New York City. Wow.

Five and a half years later Neil told Bud Scoppa (*Creem*, 11/75): "We thought we had it with Danny Whitten – at least I did. I thought that I had a combination of people that could be as effective as groups like the Rolling Stones had been . . . just for rhythm, which I'm really into. I haven't had that rhythm for a while and that's why I haven't been playing my guitar; because without that behind me I won't play. I mean you can't get free enough. So I've had to play the rhythm myself ever since Danny died. Now I have someone who can play rhythm guitar, a good friend of mine." Bud reasonably guesses, "Nils Lofgren?" and Neil answers, "No, Nils is a lead player, basically." The conversation veers in another direction so Neil never names the player, but no doubt he's referring to Frank Sampedro, now in Crazy Horse and now in the process of recording *Zuma* with Neil and CH – the return of the Horse after the release of *Tonight's the Night* pacified Danny's ghost and Neil's troubled heart. Anyway, this quote of Neil's about rhythm and what he had with Danny is the absolute key to

"Cowgirl in the Sand," especially this *Cowboy* live version.

Before I say more about that, there's a couple of fascinating quotes in the *Cowboy* booklet that I want to share with you (the quote above is from my own files, which is why it comes with source info). I realize I'd been exposed to some of this history before, like in Neil's *Decade* notes, but it didn't sink in until I saw it in this form. So pay attention, class, you can expect "circumstances of the writing and arranging of 'Cowgirl in the Sand,' 'Cinnamon Girl,' and 'Down by the River' " to show up on future quizzes.

"I wrote 'Cowgirl in the Sand,' 'Cinnamon Girl' and 'Down by the River' all in one afternoon in Topanga. I had 103° temperature and I was sick in bed." (NY)

"Neil wanted me and the rest of the band to come up to his home studio and record some 'strange songs' he'd written while being laid up with flu. In a single day we did 'Cowgirl in the Sand,' 'Down by the River,' and 'Cinnamon Girl.' There wasn't much need to discuss it." (Billy Talbot)

So – thrown by the potter in bed with a fever. And then (days or hours later?) fired in the oven of Neil Young & Crazy Horse (Danny Whitten rhythm guitar, Billy Talbot bass, Ralph Molina drums) playing Neil's music together for the first time. Legend days. Mythic moments in modern/western perform-ance art. The birth of a sound. And more than that. Of an art form.

March 1969: "Cowgirl in the Sand" and those other master-works recorded at Sunset Sound in Hollywood for inclusion on *Everybody Knows This Is Nowhere*. (No, as far as I can tell, the album versions were not recorded that day at Neil's that Billy talks about. Just shaped, explored, discovered.) March 1970: "Cowgirl in the Sand" performed live by NY & CH at the Fillmore East (one month into their second tour together) and recorded by the artist, and hopefully due for inclusion, someday, on his "from the vaults" multi-CD anthology. But for now, one of the reasons *Rock 'N' Roll Cowboy* is worth whatever outrageous price you have to pay for it.

"Cowgirl," "River," and "Cinnamon Girl" all finished in the top ten in a 1995 poll of Neil Young fans to determine their favorite NY songs of all time. All songs about being a male and being aware of the power of the right (or even wrong) female: "She could drag me over the rainbow, send me away . . ." "Can I see your sweet sweet smile?" "I could be happy the rest of my life with a cinnamon girl." Romantic? Yeah. And in pain. And having feelings. That's what this music is about. Having feelings.

The purpose of the words is to point in a direction. And the purpose of the duelling guitars (lead standing, dancing, on the ground built by rhythm) is to color in the spaces. You want to know how it feels to be a man (young – he was 23 when he wrote them – or otherwise)? Listen to these songs, any versions. Listen to the guitars. Lots of emotional information inside.

It would be a mistake to think, logically enough, that since the lead lines are most identifiable, most poetic, most impressive, they must be the home of all the information. What thrills us, awakens us, and transforms us by so powerfully articulating our feelings here is not just what we hear in the foreground. It's the extraordinary ceaseless dynamic created by the way these instruments are playing together. In a sense, some of the music and a lot of its complex emotional content is being created in us, the listeners, as we respond to and identify with the passion of the driving rhythm lines at the same time that we're dazzled by the soloist's free and expressive outbursts. We also feel how much each element of the sound is shaped moment to moment by what the other half is doing. Rhythm generates outburst and vice versa, and the whole (inside us as well as out there) becomes hugely more expressive and full of information than the separate parts could be if they weren't feeding off each other. We fall in love with the *sound*. And all the things it says (which can't be found anywhere else) about who we are and how it feels and why it fucking matters.

What is that lead guitar saying (egged on by that implacable rhythm section)? Same thing he always says: "Feelings, I'm having feelings." They're creating an environment in which he can see (feel) himself, and he's doing the same for them. And together they're doing it for us, and as we listen every cell in our bodies is singing along.

Fourteen minutes and twelve seconds of trance music. It's liberating. Absolutely ecstatic. Such an emphasis on instrumental music (more than twelve minutes) as opposed to instruments-playing-behind-vocals (less than two minutes) is unusual for such a song-based genre as rock and roll. Neil Young and Crazy Horse are masters of the form, and experientially you absolutely feel like what you just heard is a *song*. There's a verse-chorus structure (every verse beginning "hello," addressed to a different woman or different name for the same woman). And tight purposeful instrumental breaks (one just over three minutes, one almost eight minutes) stringing those verses together and absolutely never a dull or wandering moment. A triumph. It's interesting, considering this very important aspect of his music, to remember that for Neil Young's first three years as a rock and roller the kind of music he and his bands were making was almost exclusively instrumental. The first songs he wrote and recorded were instrumentals. Words came later. He certainly has a gift for words. But melodies, and speaking your heart through your guitar and through the interaction between guitar and other rhythm instruments, were there first.

"I thought I had a combination of people that could be as effective as groups like the Rolling Stones had been . . . just for rhythm. Without that behind me, I . . . can't get free enough." This 1970 live "Cowgirl" is definitive evidence that NY & CH were indeed capable of the exalted "effectiveness" of the early Stones or for that matter of John Coltrane with Elvin Jones, Jimmy Garrison and McCoy Tyner. What a treasure. I can't begin to tell you what an endless pleasure this is to listen to, over and over and over. (And no doubt there are many more such treasures out there, on bootlegs or tapes I haven't encountered yet.) I just have to be careful not to wake the neighbors by pounding along to the beat with my foot or fist.

*   *   *

Three months later Neil was back at the Fillmore East, not with Crazy Horse but with Crosby, Stills, Nash & Young. The next two *Cowboy* tracks are said to be from the June 3, 1970 show (second show in a six-night stand at the Fillmore), both *After the Gold Rush* songs (already recorded, not yet released to the public): "Tell Me Why" and "Only Love Can Break Your Heart." All of the Fillmore East shows were recorded by Atlantic Records and two were filmed for a projected CSNY documentary. So a few performances from these shows can be heard on the live CSNY album *4 Way Street* or seen in Neil's film *Journey Through the Past.* And for the record, Pete Long's excellent reference work *Ghosts on the Road* asserts that the "Tell Me Why" on *Rock 'N' Roll Cowboy* is actually from June 28 at the Los Angeles Forum.

The *Cowboy* booklet notes that "Tell Me Why" features Stills on upright bass and Crosby and Nash singing harmonies. There's a quote from Neil: *"I never really fit into CSNY as well as Joe Walsh did with the Eagles. Everybody had a different viewpoint on what's happening and it takes a whole lot to get them all together. It's a great group for that. Four totally different people who all know how it should be done, whatever it is."* The note under "Only Love" just indicates that the song was written for Graham Nash (not for him to sing, but to make him feel better).

These are extremely likeable and pretty songs and performances. What's not to like? The live harmonies are delightful, varied and even subtle in their application. Two terrific tunes with provocative words and instantly appealing melodies. Wasn't it bold of Neil to keep the title "Tell Me Why" even knowing we might think Beatles comparisons? Well, he could stand the comparisons. His new songs, and his "weird guy next door" persona, didn't set the world on its ear, but they certainly made a lot of friends very fast, with the help of radio play and Neil's new CSNY celebrity. "Only Love Can Break Your Heart" became his first hit single as a solo artist, peaking at #33 in the U.S. (just enough to be top 40), and helping spur *After the Gold Rush* to platinum sales status.

In any case, these two *Cowboy* tracks are rewarding listening. "Wooden music," in the descriptive phrase CSN (and C especially) favored. Acoustic instruments, and three-part harmonies. Nice that these surprisingly modest and quite excellent examples of CSNY at work have been captured for posterity (and our personal collections). I enjoy hearing them.

Neither differs hugely from the *Gold Rush* versions, but both are different enough (and of high enough quality) to make worthy additions to the canon. And just about as loveable, if this year finds you in a mood to love this sort of thing.

"Tell Me Why." This kind of sound, and the marvellous and intriguing vocal persona created by the three voices combined, invites us to listen to the words. Okay. What we get is maybe not *great*, but a very good example of what we'll call Neil Young's Intuitive Narrative style. That means you can feel there's a story, and so you have to listen to the words and guess what the story might be. At best you can even write it yourself, to fit your present emotional circumstances. With these stories you don't just choose your own ending; you choose everything. You thread it together. Or your subconscious does.

Basic songwriting strategy, country or rock or pop: come up with a mind-catching chorus phrase that many listeners will be able to apply to their own situations or dreams or fears. And if you're a singer-songwriter, it's better if it doesn't sound like you sweated over it, if it sounds like this is probably the way you really talk and think. Authenticity. Well, that one's easy for Neil. "Is it hard to make arrangements with yourself/When you're old enough to repay but young enough to sell?" I always liked that, and could easily imagine it applying to a musical career or to my own life. And there's a lovely edge of sarcasm or anyway self-mockery in it. Plays nicely against the sweetness of *"tell me why!"* Which is a great line, quite different from the Beatles' usage; here it conjures up the three-year-old in each of us talking to his/her parents. But that's not the narrative, just a passing (and powerful) image. The narrative can be quite variable depending on what we want to hear. But if we do listen closely, what story can we put together from this? We notice the first verse speaks of "the searcher" and identifies him as "he" ("alone in his fright"). So the singer could be speaking to himself or to a male friend. Second verse has a strong suggestion of the familiar Neil Young "boy speaking to girl" set-up: "I am lonely but you can free me/All in the way that you smile." This could be addressed to himself, but that takes a leap – which is how intuitive narrative works. Or if it *is* to a girl, doesn't the chorus come across a little snotty? No, he must be mostly talking to himself. And so the listener, it could be said, makes arrangements with himself . . . and hopefully has fun with what he (or she) hears as a result . . . and finds this composite voice and this durable melody quite expressive of it! I do, again (26 years later), with this new-to-me version.

"Only Love Can Break Your Heart" avoids the riddle of who-is-the-second-person-lyric-addressed-to? because it is so evident that this is one of those songs that must be heard as speaking directly to the listener, any listener. Not just Graham N, no matter what Neil has said. If the persona is a man talking to a friend, what's this "I have a friend I've never seen" stuff? Makes good sense if it's just Neil talking to you or me, telling us a story that doesn't have any need to be related to the childhood recollection of the first verse. Let me also say, in praise of the songwriter's craft, that the (childhood segment) line "trying to make the best of my time" is quite felicitous. And the structural trick of repeating and condensing the second verse as a kind of coda is clever and effective. Good songwriting. And good performing – I think at least in terms of the conditions of their voices these guys had a number of off nights, but this wasn't one of them. And it's fitting for this anthology that Neil is the lead voice in both cases. And finally let me point out that the reason this was a hit single is that "only love can break your heart" is a perfectly universal clever phrase, and with this melody it instantly takes on personal resonance, regardless of what the rest of the lyrics may say. Bingo.

*　*　*

"Everybody's Alone" is the first of many unreleased songs on *Rock 'N' Roll Cowboy* – "unreleased" meaning you haven't heard this song (in any form) if you only have his legal albums. There are a great many songs Neil has written and recorded but not included on an album, plus others he has performed at concerts but never yet recorded. Kind of the "underground" part of his body of work as a songwriter. (Prince and Picasso are two examples of other artists who've kept similar private archives.)

The note in the booklet says: "Originally scheduled to appear on a Neil Young & Crazy Horse aborted double album, whose original track-list also included 'Bad Fog of Loneliness,' 'I Need Her Love to Get By,' 'Big Waves,' 'Oh Lonesome Me,' 'Wondering,' 'Winterlong,' 'It Might Have Been,' 'Dance Dance Dance.' " The booklet also reports: "recorded during rehearsals at KQED TV, U.S., December 1970." Pete Long in *Ghosts on the Road* adds that KQED is in San Francisco, but "the date and venue of this performance remain unconfirmed." The tentative date he provides is February 19, 1970, which seems more likely than December. The rest of what I know about the song is Neil also recorded it in a recording studio on August 10, 1969, which suggests he might have written it around the time he wrote "I Believe in You" and "Birds" and "Helpless" (no, it's not in that league, but still worth a listen). And he performed it in concert at least once, in Santa Monica,

California, March 28, 1970, at the last Neil Young & Crazy Horse concert until December 1975.

The first couple of times I heard "Everybody's Alone," I thought it was nothing special. A little throwaway. Later I noticed the six-note chorus was stuck in my mind, haunting me, singing in my inner ear "everybody's a-*lone*," and it felt good. Since then it's been growing on me. A terrific perform-ance, for one thing. Sometimes when Neil Young sings alone, accompanying himself on guitar, the sound of his voice is quite magical. When that happens the recording quickly becomes an old friend; you look forward to hearing it again. His guitar strumming here also seems full of feeling, simple but moving. The song is also simple, but not a downer or a whiner as you might suppose from the title. Actually, in a simple or unpretentious way, he's being philosophical. The message of the repeated title phrase (the chorus) seems to be: "you're not alone in your loneliness." The first verse is friendly ("If you're looking for me/You'll find me resting in the shade/Of the mountains and the trees/And I don't mind if you stay"). The second verse continues the meditative mood and comes up with one very clever line: "Someone saying that I'm not the same/That's not so easy to be, but . . ." And then the conclud-ing verse surprises when he sings (soulfully, simply): "All I want you to know/Is that I love you so much/I can hardly stand it/ And everybody is alone." Sounds like he means it. I think he's singing to his audience (the person who eases his loneliness by being willing to listen).

The next track (disc 1, track 7) reaffirms my idea (based on long experience of listening to concert tapes of Bob Dylan and others) that the same song can differ tremendously from one show to the next in the amount of feeling put into the per-formance, and that the important variable from show to show is not the technical quality of the playing and singing but something about the mood the singer (or the whole band) is in. This is confirmed backwardsly because this track, "A Man Needs a Maid/Heart of Gold," is technically okay and

46

pleasant, but not one third as powerful as the performances of the same songs ten days later, as captured on the *Young Man's Fancy* bootleg I praised in chapter one and as described in chapter four in an essay I wrote when *Harvest* was new and "Heart of Gold" was on the radio around the world.

The *Cowboy* track is from a solo concert January 22, 1971 at the American Shakespeare Theatre in Stratford, Connecticut. At that point in the tour he was playing both songs on the piano, and they can be called a medley because their melodies are quite similar in these arrangements, and Neil segues from "A Man Needs a Maid" to "Heart of Gold" and at the end of "Heart" he repeats the tag line from "Maid," "When will I see you again?" By the concert that appears in its entirety on the double LP *Young Man's Fancy* (which Pete Long describes as "possibly the most famous Neil Young bootleg"), February 1, 1971 at the Dorothy Chandler Pavilion in Los Angeles, things have changed. The songs are still together, but now "Heart of Gold" is first and it's played on guitar and harmonica; then after some entertaining talk (Young has a very good conversational rapport with his audience at this show) he plays "Maid" on piano.

If you want to hear Neil Young give one of the best performances of his life, you have to find *Young Man's Fancy* or the equivalent, with particular emphasis on "Heart of Gold" and "Cowgirl in the Sand" (yes, solo acoustic – and shortened) and "Journey through the Past." Track 7 of *Rock 'N' Roll Cowboy* sounds good and is historically interesting ("H of G" on piano and without harmonica, two weeks before he recorded the official version in Nashville – with Linda Ronstadt and James Taylor – which went on to become his first and only #1 single), but it is no match for the astonishingly intense Feb. 1 versions of these songs.

The first quote accompanying this track in the *Cowboy* booklet is actually (uncredited) Young's spoken introduction to "A Man Needs a Maid" from Feb. 1st. Here it is (I've restored the charming last sentence, which they dropped): *"This is a song I*

47

wrote under weird circumstances. I usually don't write too many songs too fast, but all of a sudden I found myself not being able to move around too much, and in a bed a lot. And, um, my mind started wandering. And when I got home I kept hearing this song over and over in my head. And I didn't know what it meant when I first started hearing it. I'm starting to see what it means now."

When he sings, in "Maid," "I was watching a movie with a friend/I fell in love with the actress," it's a true story. The movie was *Diary of a Mad Housewife* and the actress was Carrie Snodgrass, who was to become the mother of Neil Young's first child, Zeke.

Another interesting note is that the live recording of Neil singing "The Needle and the Damage Done" included on *Harvest* is from January 30, 1971, between the shows at the Shakespeare and at the Chandler.

The second quote about the medley in the booklet is from a *Rolling Stone* interview published August 14, 1975 and conducted by Cameron Crowe: *"A lot of it was my back. I was in and out of hospitals for the two years between* After the Gold Rush *and* Harvest. *I have one weak side and all the muscles slipped on me. My discs slipped. I couldn't hold my guitar up. That's why I sat down on my whole solo tour. I couldn't move around too well, so I laid low for a long time on the ranch and just didn't have any contact, you know. I wore a brace. Crosby would come up to see how I was, we'd go for a walk and it took me 45 minutes to get to the studio, which is only 400 yards from the house. I could only stand up four hours a day. I recorded most of* Harvest *in the brace. That's a lot of the reason it's such a mellow album. I couldn't physically play an electric guitar. 'Are You Ready for the Country,' 'Alabama' and 'Words' were all done after I had the operation. For the most part, I spent two years flat on my back."*

* * *

Rock 'N' Roll Cowboy continues with three more solo acoustic winter 1971 tracks: "Out on the Weekend," "Love in Mind," and "Dance Dance Dance," all recorded on Feb. 23rd in London for a BBC TV broadcast. The set list for the broadcast is noteworthy because at a time when Young had a new album recently released in the U.K., he chose to play one song from that album and nine unreleased songs (six of which would surface on *Harvest* a year later).

"Out on the Weekend." There's a weird hum on this track (maybe it's that bad fog of loneliness, or a fluorescent light at the BBC) that interferes with this listener enjoying it as thoroughly as he would otherwise. In any case, if we did not have any other recording of this song, this would be a great treasure, because the essential spirit of the tune is here, and it's a good one. And again the track is of historical interest (for the Neil Young scholar or student who perhaps lurks inside most fans), because in comparison with the *Harvest* version recorded five weeks later, it seems a kind of rough draft, a clue to the songwriter's process. The words are essentially the same. But they're in a different order, and in the shifting around I'd say the songwriter has succeeded in establishing a continuity and therefore an effective, powerful, narrative, where before there was only the promise or hint of such a thing. You can hear "Out on the Weekend" in this BBC performance yearning to make a certain statement, to really be the excellent song that it threatens to be (that it might even be already, without the hum and to a sympathetic listener and if there were no other, better-realized version).

The changes have to do with verse sequence. This is a song without a chorus (the early, BBC, version repeats the line "See the lonely boy, out on the weekend" three times, but it can't be the chorus because it's at the beginning of the verse, not the end). Often in Neil's (and other people's) songs, the absence of a chorus is compensated for by repeating verses or parts of verses in a way that helps give a song a sense of motion and structure and pleasing symmetry. So watch what's happened here. The early version starts with the verse "See the lonely boy, out on the weekend/Trying to make it pay/Can't relate to joy, he tries to speak and/Can't begin to say." This is followed by "I think I'll pack it in and buy a pick-up, take it down to L.A . . ." and then the third verse: "The woman I'm thinking of, she loved me all up/But I'm so down today . . ." Next the first verse is repeated, there's a soulful harmonica break, and we get the verse that starts, "She got pictures on the wall, they make me look up/From her big brass bed." After "bed" he sings, "Oooh, ooh ooh ooohh . . . Somewhere in her head," as if he hasn't finished writing this verse or else forgot that line. The "ooohs" are great, however, so I'm not complaining. And then the last verse is the first ("See the lonely boy . . .") yet again.

So that's a structure, yes. But the structure of the finished song is hugely more successful at setting a mood (the right mood) in the beginning, the middle, and at the end. With the effect that the song truly casts a spell. Intuitive Narrative gets us all writing scripts with ourselves in them. Which in this case, since this is the first track on the album, has the added virtue of setting a mood and relationship between listener and artist that can endure for the whole album. Especially since there is a core of songs on the record that make up a song cycle, that clearly seem to be about the same relationship or life situation ("Out on the Weekend," "Harvest," "Heart of Gold," and "A Man Needs a Maid").

So in the March edit, Neil took the second verse ("Think I'll pack it in . . .") and started the song with it. Very good. Second is the former third verse, "The woman I'm thinking of." The verse that starts with the title line is now third. "She got pictures," with the missing line filled in, is now fourth, and then the song is wrapped up by a repeat of the second and third verses. "See the lonely boy" is much more effective coming in the middle and then ending the song. And the repetition of "The woman I'm thinking of" also does a lot to settle for the listener the question of what this song's about. Just suggestive enough now. The elements were all in place for a powerful song. And then some artful reshuffling worked wonders.

The other thing I notice about this "rough draft" is how well Neil's guitar playing lays out a blueprint for the unique and delightful bass line and drum part that Tim Drummond and Kenny Buttrey added to this song (unforgettably) in the recording session.

So I like it that *Rock 'N' Roll Cowboy* offers us not just enjoyable alternate (live) performances of songs, but sometimes also fascinating insights into how a song or arrangement took shape. More clues for the "Who Is N.Y.?" riddle.

Since I'm bootlegging the bootleg here by sharing with you most of the quotes they put in their booklet, the "Weekend" one is: *"It's just my outlook. I guess my outlook is just bleak or desolate or something. I don't know. But even when I'm happy it sounds like I'm not. And when I try to say I'm happy I disguise it. Like I really say I'm really happy in the second part of that verse. I say I'm completely happy by saying, 'can't relate to joy . . . tries to speak and can't begin to say.' That just means that I'm so happy that I can't get it all out. But it doesn't sound happy. The way I wrote it sounds sad, like I tried to hide it or something."*

"Love in Mind" gets another inside-the-songwriter quote: *"I used to call this girl up from the road who I was in love with, but I'd never actually met. I used to talk to her all the time on the phone, usually late at night because of the time difference. And I'd wake up in the morning feeling so good."*

The official release of "Love in Mind" is on *Time Fades Away,* a 1973 album with the radical premise of a live album made up entirely of new (previously unreleased) songs. "Love in Mind" is the only track on the album that isn't from Neil's 1973 tour with the Stray Gators. Maybe *Cowboy*'s compiler forgot that, because otherwise I don't know the rationale for including the BBC 2/23/71 solo piano version when there's an almost identical (or slightly more powerful) version on an official album, recorded at an L.A. concert 1/30/71 (same show as the official "Needle and the Damage Done").

Finally from the BBC taping there's "Dance Dance Dance," with this informative note: "Written by Neil Young, and recorded by Crazy Horse on their 1971 album *Crazy Horse.* Performed solo by Young in 1969, 1970 and 1971. Revived in 1983 and performed regularly that year. Also performed occasionally on 1987 USA tour and on 1992 acoustic tour."

So all I have to add about "Dance Dance Dance" is I like the *Young Man's Fancy* version better because I like the baroque sound of the audience being the rhythm section. Good song, anyway, and one of Neil's more "rhythmic" solo acoustic songs. The same melody and rhythm (i.e. different words) became the better known "Love Is a Rose," a hit in 1975 for Linda Ronstadt. Neil's version of "Love Is a Rose" is on *Decade.*

* * *

The next three tracks on *Cowboy* are from a Jan. 21, 1973 concert at Carnegie Hall in New York City. What happened to 1972? Well, the back trouble may have been a factor, but Neil Young didn't tour from March '71 to Dec. '72. He did make some guest appearances at Crosby & Nash shows in fall '71 and spring '72. In November 1972, a couple of months after the birth of his first son, he started putting together a touring band. He'd announced back in May 1970 that he wasn't going to work with Crazy Horse any longer, apparently because Danny Whitten's worsening heroin dependency was interfering with his ability to make music. So in fall '72 he needed a band. He started rehearsals with Kenny Buttrey (drums), Tim Drummond (bass), and Ben Keith (steel guitar), experienced session musicians who'd played on the *Harvest* sessions – and added his old friend Jack Nitzsche on piano (Nitzsche had arranged "Expecting to Fly" and "A Man Needs a Maid," and had played piano on Neil's tour with Crazy Horse in early 1970). Neil christened the resulting band "The Stray Gators," and played more than 60 shows with them between Jan. 4th and April 3rd, 1973. Johnny Barbata replaced Buttrey on drums for the second half of the tour.

The *Cowboy* Carnegie tracks and the accompanying comments and quotes:

"Cripple Creek Ferry." "Rarely performed live. Originally written for Dean Stockwell's unreleased movie *After The Goldrush.*" Neil: "*After The Gold Rush was kind of the turning point. It was a strong album. I really think it was. A lot of hard work went into it. Everything was there. The picture it painted was a strong one.* After The Gold Rush *was the spirit of Topanga Canyon. It seemed like I realized that I'd gotten somewhere.*"

"L.A." "*This is a song I wrote in 1968. Out on the West Coast people were beside palm trees, living by the ocean, worrying about earthquakes.*"

"Soldier." "*Recorded for my first film,* Journey Through the Past, *in a sawdust burner at a Northern California sawmill to the accompaniment of a roaring fire. There was an unfortunate sequence of events surrounding my movie. The record company told me that they'd finance me doing it only if I gave them the soundtrack album. They took the thing* [the soundtrack] *and put it right out. Then they told me that they didn't want to release the movie because it wasn't . . . well, they thought it was weird. But they took me for the album. That's always been a ticklish subject with me.*" (Source: first sentence from Neil's *Decade* notes, the rest from the 1975 *Rolling Stone* interview.)

Disc 1 continues with two more early 1973 performances: "Harvest" from Washington D.C. 1/28, and "Sweet Joni" alone at the piano from Bakersfield CA 3/11. The note under "Harvest" says, "written in London, the day before a gig at the Royal Festival Hall, but recorded in Nashville." The source for this info is a comment Neil made on stage in London. The booklet then provides us with a quote from Tim Drummond: "*One day I was walking down the street in Nashville when a photographer friend stopped me to tell me Neil Young was in town to be on the Johnny Cash TV show. He was also trying to do some recordings at the Quadrophonic Studios and needed a bass player. So I showed up and we cut most of the songs on* Harvest. *Later we went out to Neil's ranch near San Francisco and finished the album in this old barn, with bird shit*

all over and holes in the ceiling and a remote truck parked outside."
(Drummond was the first white musician to play with James
Brown's Famous Flames. He played on Bob Dylan's album *Slow
Train Coming* and toured with Dylan from 1979 to 1981. He has
turned up on Neil Young albums as recently as *Harvest Moon*.)

We don't know when "Sweet Joni" was written. It's an undistinguished song, lyrically or musically, but since it seems likely
it was a very early composition, it's interesting he decided to
drag it out for a few shows in 1973. The booklet quote reads:
*"I've known Joni Mitchell since I was 18. I met her in one of the
coffee-houses. She was beautiful. That was my first impression. She
was real frail and wispy looking. And her cheekbones were so beautifully shaped. She'd always wear light satins and silks. I remember
thinking that if you blew hard enough, you could probably knock her
over. She could hold up a Martin D18 pretty well, though. What an
incredible talent she is."*

* * *

Neil Young recorded two albums in 1973. The first was the
aforementioned *Time Fades Away,* all recorded live in early
1973 with the Stray Gators (except "Love in Mind") and
released September 1973. The second was *Tonight's the Night,*
recorded in a makeshift studio with "The Santa Monica Flyers"
in August and September 1973, and not released until summer 1975.

A few other significant dates: In February 1972 *Harvest* was
released and immediately became a huge success. In November 1972, the very night Neil sent him away from tour rehearsals because it wasn't working out, he couldn't do the job,
Danny Whitten died of a heroin overdose. Summer 1973,
Neil's friend Bruce Berry also died of a heroin overdose.

The last two tracks on *Rock 'N' Roll Cowboy,* Disc 1, are
"Tonight's the Night" and "Tired Eyes," both performed live
with the Santa Monica Flyers November 15, 1973, at Queens

College, New York City. Before I share with you the useful quotes attached to these songs in the *Cowboy* booklet (wish I could share the music itself, but all I can do is write about it and hope you'll seek it out or petition the artist to release it), I have two other quotes I think offer necessary and vital insight into the artist's process.

From the *Decade* notes: " 'Heart of Gold.' This song put me in the middle of the road. Travelling there soon became a bore so I headed for the ditch. A rougher ride but I saw more interesting people there."

Question from Cameron Crowe in his 1975 interview: "*Time Fades Away*, as the follow-up to *Harvest*, could have been a huge album . . ." Neil: "If it had been commercial." Crowe: "As it is, it's one of your least selling solo albums. Did you realize what you were sacrificing at the time?" Neil: "I probably did. I imagine I could have come up with the perfect follow-up album. A real winner. But it would have been something that everybody was expecting. And when it got there they would have thought that they understood what I was all about and that would have been it for me. I would have painted myself in the corner.

"The fact is I'm not that lone, laid-back figure with a guitar. I'm just not that way anymore. I don't want to feel like people expect me to be a certain way. Nobody expected *Time Fades Away* and I'm not sorry I put it out. I didn't need the money, I didn't need the fame. You gotta keep changing. Shirts, old ladies, whatever. I'd rather keep changing and lose a lot of people along the way. If that's the price, I'll pay it. I don't give a shit if my audience is a hundred or a hundred million. It doesn't make any difference to me. I'm convinced that what sells and what I do are two completely different things. If they meet, it's coincidence. I just appreciate the freedom to put out an album like *Tonight's the Night* if I want to."

From the booklet: " 'Tonight's the Night.' Written in August 1973, this song debuted live in the same year, then became a hard rock number in 1978 during the *Rust Never Sleeps* Tour and a slow piano ballad for the 1992 Acoustic Tour." *"The whole* Tonight's the Night *album is about life, dope and death. When me, Nils Lofgren, Ralph Molina and Billy Talbot played that music we were all thinking of Danny Whitten and Bruce Berry, two close members of our unit lost to junk overdoses. The* Tonight's the Night *sessions were the first time what was left of Crazy Horse had gotten together since Danny died. It was up to us to get the strength together among us to fill the hole he left. Bruce Berry was CSNY's roadie for a long time. His brother Ken owned Studio Instrument Rentals, where we recorded the album. So we had a lot of vibes going for us. There was a lot of spirit in the music we made. It's funny, I remember the whole experience in black and white."*

Also from the booklet: 'Tonight's the Night *didn't come out right after it was recorded because it wasn't finished. It just wasn't in the right space, it wasn't in the right order, the concept wasn't right. I had to get the color right, so it was not so down that it would make people restless. I had to keep jolting every once in a while to get people to wake up so they could be lulled again. I don't think* TTN *is a friendly album. It's real, that's all. Either you'll want to hear it or you won't. A lot of records don't even make you think that much. Then after that it will take you somewhere if you want to listen to it. I'm really proud of it. It's there for me. You've got to listen to it at night when it was done. Put on the Doobie Brothers in the morning. They can handle it at 11 am. But not this album. It's custom-made for night-time."*

"Tired Eyes." *"A bleary view of a drug murder in a Los Angeles canyon. Out of pitch, but still in tune. This song puts the vibe right there."*

"Tonight's the Night" and "Tired Eyes" live in Queens are good performances, and good to have. But hey, if you want to know who Neil Young is, get copies of *Time Fades Away* and *Tonight's the Night* and listen to "Don't Be Denied" and "Tonight's the Night" (Part I, first track on the album). Okay. Now you've got the complete picture.

4

Searching for a Heart of Gold

This essay, my first record review in more than two years, was written in February 1972 at the request of the editors of Japan's New Music Magazine. *I had just met the woman who was to become my first wife and the mother of my children.*

That heart of gold he's searching for – that heart of gold *I'm* searching for – that h. of g. you're looking for – it's not some other person. It's me – it's you – it's Neil Young – it's the heart of gold inside. The untapped vein. I know it's here somewhere.

For me to like a record it has to scratch the back of my brain (never mind the front – I can reach that myself) – it has to touch my heart and it has to move my blood. That's all.

I like this record.

I've been all over hell and back – what else can I say? – I been to Hollywood, I been to redwood, I crossed the ocean for a heart of gold – and here I am in Tokyo, Japan, listening to *Harvest* on my Sony cassette recorder, taking it off and spitting it out for you my friends in various corners of the globe – I don't know why – it doesn't matter.

Yes it does.

It's such a fine line . . .

For me to like a record it has to speak to me, personally, from inside, in such a way as no mere hunk of plastic can; sweat of human brow is not enough, you got to speak for me, you got to speak for me stuff I can't verbalize myself, "it's these expressions I never give," you got to give them for me to call yourself an artist, you got to give them with me, nothing less will do.

Thank you.

I've learned a lot about love since you saw me last – Neil Young has learned a lot about love since we saw him last – what we know we can't tell – only share.

And you know it too, babe.

That's why we're here.

I first heard "Heart of Gold" when my friend Bill Berkson (whose neighbor Tom Clark wrote the picture/poem *Neil Young*) played me the *Live at L.A.* bootleg, just after Ellen's baby was born, the day I left Bolinas.

Then when I finally got to Berkeley (mid-November), Pat and Dick Lupoff took me in. I had my Sony by then. I made many great tapes from Dick Lupoff's record collection, including one, my favorite, that starts with the bootleg version of "Heart of Gold." At first I thought H of G too heavy to begin with, but nothing else worked. Finally I took the risk. My best tape. "Heart of Gold," "Suzie Q" (Creedence), "Section 43," "New Morning," "Won't Get Fooled Again," "Where Do the Children Play?", "Hard-Headed Woman," "Wild World," and "Daydream" (the original Lovin' Spoonful recording, remember?). Try it and see.

Raymond (Mungo, my partner) and I travelled all up and down the coast playing "Heart of Gold" to disbelieving ears before jumping off the edge in February, crossing the ocean etc. Our boat came in February 12th, Lincoln's birthday. When we arrived in Kobe, H of G was on the radio. I had looked for the album before leaving Vancouver, not out yet, there it was in the Sogo Department Store when I set foot on Asian soil. Warner-Bros/Pioneer Record Company (a joint venture). Made in Japan.

Wow.

And it's just a record about how hard it is to love. Hard

because of who I am, not who everyone else is. "See the lonely boy, out on the weekend . . ." It ain't a plea for sex. It's a plea for salvation.

A plea to the gods. Women or men can't save us now. (Can't even imagine the perfect mate any more, now that you've met her – him – and run away.) We must save ourselves.

Help.

But it's all about men and women. Right on. It's the only story I know, the broken heart, don't try to sell me no mystic enlightenment. Will I only harvest some? Yeah, but a little more each year. Deeper sorrow and greater joy. And there's no turning back. I've been loving you too long to stop now.

This album is about the pain of becoming increasingly conscious. As we go through life we either fall asleep – die – freeze in position – or we keep on going and it just gets rougher and we find out a lot of things we never wanted to know. Awareness is pain. But every junkie's like a setting sun. I mean, some of us are just too proud to die.

"I sing the song because I love the man. I know that some of you don't understand."

Neil (you) (me) complains that he can't love, doesn't know how, but his real problem is that he can't stop loving. He is one of that small company of great souls who stand all the taller as the going gets rougher. And when you stand tall other brave souls can see you, and it gives them strength.

Bless the artist who finds himself unable to betray his respect for the human spirit. Bless the man who fears no evil in the valley of the shadow of death, the hope-less mad man who lives on faith and follows his inner light.

Bless you. Are you worthy of the music you listen to? Have courage. Pain released is joy. These songs are a step in the right direction. Praise the Lord.

Harvest as a whole is not as fine as *After the Gold Rush – Gold Rush* had a wholeness, a depth of character that took a while to get to know, and takes almost forever to get tired of . . . *Harvest*

59

in many ways is just Neil Young's new album. Okay. But a little overdone. What's this gatefold crap, anyway? Why two sheets of gaudy cardboard (multiplied by two million) when one would do as well? What's with these photographs and six-foot posters? Still trying to sell yourself, kid? You should be old enough to repay by now.

Opulence ain't pretty in a depression – why make an aesthetic of it? Something is rotten in Hollywood, lay off Alabama for a while.

Some of the songs are overworked – "There's a World" has been cooked to a veritable pulp – vegetables are better a little on the raw side. The album for all its soul and beauty lacks the cold steel ring of utter necessity, it was made by a bunch of rich dudes, the singer sounds desolate but rather well-fed, only the songwriter/composer still seems absolutely alive.

I'm writing these words as a warning to myself. Look alive, here comes a buzzard.

"Words. Words. Between the lines of age." It's hard to make this change. This collection of songs contains some great work by a man whose stature on the century scene increases by the moment. Neil Young distrusted fame and made loud puzzled looks at his audience ("Hello Mr. Soul" "Out of My Mind" "Broken Arrow") long before he had the misfortune to sell a million records. Our hopes and fears are always the same things (we're afraid of what we want; we want what we're afraid of) and we make them manifest (i.e: songs of fear of fame strike a common chord and achieve much success).

Oh Lord I sympathize with this singer so much. He's *me*. That's why I love this record.

It's also why I hate it at times. Too flawed. It's hard to make this change. Oh why can't I just love me with all my heart? Because then nobody else would. Okay.

It's such a fine line.

This is an album about how hard it is to be loved. The singer never speaks of loving in the active sense (the most he offers is to "fill your cup with the promise of a man"), at times he'd like to give up the struggle ("A Man Needs a Maid"), but he knows what he wants ("I need someone to love me the whole day through"). ("Just one look in my eyes and you can tell that's true.") (I wonder.)

So again it's the theme of "Hello Mr. Soul" (what am I going to do with these women?) and "I Am a Child" (look how helpless and pretty I am, please love me). ("Coming to you at night I see my questions, I feel my doubts; thinking that maybe in a year or two we could laugh, and let it all out." And the most beautiful words of all, how can we thank this man for saying them? "Now that you've made yourself love me, do you think I can change it in a day? How can I place you above me? Am I lying to you when I say, that I believe in you?")

But maybe the great realization that you made yourself love me (and what can I offer you but faith?) must always be followed by the even greater, far less pretty realization that I made you love me in the sense that I asked for it – even knowing I couldn't accept it – and even as I'm running down the road away I'm still asking for it, still need love and want to live up to what you see in me, but baby I've got to escape, I'm sorry . . .

And the fine line that keeps us searching is ultimately what I want to call your attention to. It's the line between good and evil, the line between sky and sea, the thin edge on which we walk over the infinite, belief in ourselves, the fine line of faith in the face of doubt. God bless us all who continue to dare to love.

"A may-ay-ay-aid . . . man feels afraid." That's the way I often hear it in my head, and ain't it the truth? And if you can understand how I fear (and want) you, and I can face your fear of and desire for me, maybe we can go on trying to love each other anyway.

Neil Young is a Scorpio man and I am a Taurus man and I

can feel the opposition and the sameness. And if we all are to become mere myths, and subjects for each other's essays and songs, I hope we can keep our sense of humor and walk through myths like butter. We are not so helpless. We are not so old.

I like the harmonica playing, and Ken Buttrey's familiar drumming (*Blonde on Blonde*). I like the whole schmaze of "A Man Needs a Maid" and I love the way the album opens, the *sound of* "Out on the Weekend" is perfect, magnificent. "Heart of Gold" is just what it should be, really haunting and punchy . . . but my heart belongs to the bootleg recording of the song, which is more personal and powerful. Best of all would be any real person (not a record) singing this song in a real situation. Flesh is the home of heart.

(Don't forget to throw away your phonograph when the time comes.)

And so on.

Thank you for your patience.

I like this record.

5

On the Beach

This is another quick ("live") response from a listener to a brand-new album by a favorite artist. In those days, albums by certain groups and individuals were like tribal news, seemingly direct broadcasts from the collective unconscious. Thanks to Jaakov Kohn, a wonderful man who edited the scruffy and very visible Soho Weekly News, *I felt free to write as if I were talking to a hip and trusted friend, not as though I were writing for a New York City newspaper. God bless him. This appeared in* SWN *August 1, 1974. Please note that I do in 1996 consider* Time Fades Away *an unquestionably good album. But I've chosen not to make any changes to these "time capsule" pieces, even when I'm wiser than that now.*

Neil Young has done it. He has put out an unquestionably good album, his first in two and a half years. He sure needed it; but then, so did we.

"Rock music" means a lot of things; I think I like it to mean "contemporary music," which in turn means music for my contemporaries (I don't give a damn about anybody else's contemporaries). In which case, two vital attributes of rock music are honesty and relevance, or, to put it another way, the sensitivity to know what the times are, and the strength to embrace them or rise above them.

Neil Young, despite the two forgettable albums he released before this one, and despite or maybe because of the self-conscious effort that went into this new record, is one of the very few rock artists who has had anything relevant or honest to say about the 1970s. *On the Beach* is a suitable sequel to *After the Gold Rush* and *Harvest,* and together these three albums tell

63

us more than any other source about the current self-image of the American male between the ages of 20 and 40.

There are eight songs on *On the Beach,* and all but two of them are blues. Musically, this is a delight. When I first saw Neil Young on stage in 1966 I was extraordinarily impressed with him as a *lead guitar* player, not as a singer or songwriter (his best efforts in those areas came later). And *On the Beach* contains the best lead guitar work by Neil since "Cowgirl in the Sand." It also contains some lovely work from many of Neil's favorite sidemen, including Ben Keith on slide guitar, steel guitar, dobro, bass, piano and even drums (he's on every track, on an album which went through three co-producers), Tim Drummond on bass, Ralph Molina on drums, and Rusty Kershaw on slide guitar, fiddle and liner notes. All sounding good, sounding like this one came out the way the author heard it in his head.

Emotionally, the blues on this album are the expression of an introverted person who has to sing to earn his supper, who *needs* to sing to feel like a person, but who can only sing about his feelings, and who fears that what he feels has become too personal to share. He evaded the issue for a while, and now on *On the Beach* he suddenly (he threw out a whole other album he'd prepared for release) and effectively comes to grips with it. "I'm deep inside myself, but I'll get out somehow." "Though my problems are meaningless, that don't make them go away." Saying this stuff in public, it must be pointed out, is not weakness but strength.

The vocals on *On the Beach* are all good, though the ones on the second side of the album are by far the most interesting and moving. Neil's voice can be extraordinarily effective on his own material, but it has varied greatly from record to record, so the overall quality of the singer's voice and of his use of his voice is another pleasure of this career-redeeming album.

"Walk On" is the first song, an uptempo guitar duet with bright, caustic vocal, and it introduces the dominant themes of the record. "I remember the good old days/Stayed up all night getting crazed." And "I hear some people been talking me down" – these words actually open the album, and clearly one of the chief things on Neil's mind is the criticism he's gotten from reviewers and "friends."

It's tough to be overly sensitive – even if you're not a star – but perhaps this has more universal applications, insofar as the entire generation of which Neil is a member and spokesman has watched itself, on TV and in the other media (including, especially, pop music), all its collective life. We are as self-conscious and paranoid as our President and his press secretary and most of our other leaders. And we must face up to this paranoia before we can hope to undertake any public activity effectively.

Cutting a record is a public activity, especially when you are or have been a success; and so Neil Young's record of his own doubts and of his renewed self-confidence ("Some get strong; some get strange; sooner or later, it all gets real – walk on") touches all of us in that sensitive place where we – even if it's only to walk down the street – expose ourselves to public view .

And exploring and affirming collective reality is, I repeat, the primary purpose of good rock music.

The most important and most characteristic songs on the album are those that open and close side two, "On the Beach" (title tunes always *seem* more meaningful) and "Ambulance Blues." Both pieces are long, moody, deceptively simple . . . very effective contemporary adaptation of the traditional blues form. Both songs portray the old folkie from the sixties, somewhat hung up in the glories of the past and deeply afraid that the present is somehow getting away from him.

"On the Beach" is confessional. "I need a crowd of people, but I can't face them day to day." "The world is turning – I hope it don't turn away"; "Now I'm living out here on the beach/But those seagulls are still out of reach." No conclusions are offered, it's all just statements, descriptions of the situation, and oh so down (compare "I think I'll get out of town" with "Are you ready for the country, because it's time to

65

go?" 2½ years ago). But – very important – not pessimistic. This is a hopeful album, despite its gloominess, because it so brilliantly explores the fine line between resignation and struggle, and then unambiguously opts for continued struggle every time. The only unclear moment for me is "Revolution Blues," definitely a put-down of every "revolutionary" from Charlie Manson to Patty Hearst. I don't disagree with the put-down, but the song is weird, I'm not sure why it's here.

"Ambulance Blues" recalls the folk music days in Toronto in the early '60s (a superb vocal; the sudden transitions between verses are especially nice; I also like the harmonica – can't be an old folkie if you don't play a mean harmonica). But it also seems to suggest an escape from the past, redemption:

> "I guess I'll call it 'Sickness Gone'
> It's hard to say the meaning of this song
> An ambulance can only go so fast
> It's easy to get buried in the past
> When you try to make a good thing last."

Neil Young has always had this ability to write silly stuff (like "Sugar Mountain," what a beautiful song!) and have it reach me in a profound way. It's a real magic trick, and I want to testify that he's still got the power.

"Ambulance Blues" is also a straight-out attack on commentators like me – "All you critics sit alone/You're no better than me for what you've shown" – and it's certainly as true as anything I've said attacking rock stars. The final verses tell a story about the singer sitting up till morning in some café, brooding about a "friend" who told him, "You're all just pissing in the wind/You don't know it but you are." After a long instrumental meditation, the singer strikes back – "I never knew a man who could tell so many lies" – saying, in effect, I am *not* pissing in the wind! And though the level of debate may seem odd to some, truer words were never spoken, and I want to thank Neil for saying them for all of us.

There are other fine songs on the album, a haunting one

called "Motion Pictures" and an old favorite of mine (from bootlegs and a great recording by the reunited Byrds), "See the Sky About to Rain," which isn't as soulful as I remember it, but this arrangement does make it fit the album (which is good; on albums, the whole should take precedence over the parts). And as a final example of how perfectly, in its low-key way, this record has captured the spirit of the times as I perceive them, this ditty (from "Vampire Blues," which seems to be about the energy crisis):

"Good times are coming, I hear it everywhere I go.
Good times are coming, I hear it everywhere I go.
Good times are coming, but they sure are coming slow."

On the Beach is must-listening for those who have survived this far.

6

Crosby, Stills, Nash & Young

Two more stories written for the Soho Weekly News. *The first is about a large outdoor rock event I attended. Can you imagine finding out President Ford has just pardoned President Nixon when Neil Young announces it from the stage? The second is a review of some record company "product," a CSNY greatest hits album. Originally it was combined with a review of Roger McGuinn live and on a new album.*

Soho Weekly News, Sept. 12, 1974:

Sunday September 8th, as one punk President forgave another (for unconfessed sins) and Evel Knievel parachuted gracefully into Snake River Canyon and Hurricane Carmen slammed into Louisiana and then turned merciful, 90 or 100 thousand people gathered in the dust and mud of Long Island's Roosevelt Raceway for one more huge outdoor rock concert, the biggest this year in the New York area and, surprisingly, one of the best ever: glorious proof of what is possible when professionalism is combined with heart (and a bit of luck on the weather).

September's a good time for a rock concert, the harvest is in so there's joints enough for everyone, and that old back-to-school energy even affects the musicians. Roosevelt Raceway was the last stop of a valiant, all-summer, cross-country American tour by the Crosby, Stills, Nash, Young & Mitchell quintet. Joni Mitchell has been backstage at a lot of the CSNY concerts this summer, but this time she was actually put on the bill, appropriately enough since she's more of a solo star these days than any of those other guys. Joni performed with her back-up band, Tom Scott & the L.A. Express (a good pop-jazz group who did a fine set of their own while tens of thousands of adolescent women waited expectantly for Joni). Also on the bill were Jesse Colin Young, who has opened all the CSNY concerts this year, and the Beach Boys – an unbeatable line-up of talent. Add the fruit of the harvest and hot September sunshine (in place of the widely anticipated clouds and rain – it had been cold and miserable all week) and you've got the makings of a very fine eleven hours . . . if you don't mind crowds.

The crowd was pleasant – mostly high school kids (and young college-age) from Long Island, New Jersey, The Big Apple, and Westchester – especially if you stayed away from the relatively small section of ground from which it was possible to actually see the performers; naturally enough the population density was quite high in that area, and there was a certain amount of jockeying for position ("Don't stand on my blanket!"). This was no Woodstock, there was no special sense of collective identity (the audience was too homogenous to find itself interesting), but everyone was having a good time.

The music was excellent. Jesse Colin Young's disembodied voice and music started floating through the air on that superb sound system shortly after we arrived (12:30), turning on everyone in sight. In late 1966 the Youngbloods were a magnificent live band, and then there was a slump when the expected commercial success didn't materialize, and then another great period in 1969, gradual dissipation after that until I forgot about them, and now here's Jesse on his own with that same old mellow fire, only better and more tuned to his audience than ever. A delight.

The Beach Boys are exuberant performers who happen to have some of the best material ever written by anyone; their set (which I squeezed up close to the stage for part of – it's a toss-up, fun to be up front watching but the sound is better further back) went from one peak to another, "I Can Hear Music," "Sunny California," "Long Promised Road" (Carl just incredible on keyboards), "Don't Worry Baby," "Sail on Sailor" . . . it was religious, ecstatic, the whole crowd seemed in love with the Beach Boys, singing along, dancing, not letting them off the stage. James Guercio (producer of Chicago) played bass, and Mike Love wore a green Caribou Ranch shirt, white pants, a silver belt, Panama hat with multicolor brim, and a double string of puka.

Joni Mitchell was in great voice, much better than the Avery Fisher Hall concert I saw in January, every note vibrating gloriously through the air to every corner of the racetrack. She asked us to imagine we were 50 people in a club in Philadelphia. The crowd right in front of the stage, which had been evenly mixed for the Beach Boys, suddenly became almost entirely female. Joni's music needs intimacy, and she couldn't quite create it – she's still self-conscious on stage. But her audience could identify with that, too; and her songs and the strength and beauty of her voice carried the day.

At 7:45 CSNY came on, and the crowd, which was already well-satisfied, just fell apart with pleasure. The performers got real happy, too – amazed at such a good feeling coming from so massive a crowd. The music just got better and better. Early highlights were "Immigration Man," "Almost Cut My Hair" (terrific ensemble guitar playing), "Walk On," and "Only Love Can Break Your Heart" (Joni coming on to join in the harmonies, as she did many times during the evening, most notably during a remarkable five-part "Judy Blue Eyes"). The format of the show – CSNY played for four hours, switching from acoustic instruments to electric, from one solo performer to another with all combinations of voices and instruments supporting him when appropriate – was very very effective. They kept the crowd up, kept

71

themselves up, and tempered all personality excesses. All energy went into the music. Every one of the singers was in excellent voice and spirit, more than fulfilling the promise implied by their superstar status and past achievements (a more satisfying concert, in its way, than either Clapton's or Dylan's 1974 show). Consistent standout was Neil Young ("Don't Be Denied"). CSNY's music is about survival – the audience may have been too young to fully dig it, but they could certainly feel the intensity.

Neil had two beautiful songs I'd never heard before: "Sonrise" and "Long May You Run," both surprisingly up. He played more fine songs than I have space to list; and I could have stayed for many more.

It all climaxed with bonfires spotting the field, people singing along (as they did for all the familiar songs), dancing, letting their hearts loose, a final encore of "Ohio" and a terrific rush of collective energy that zapped audience and performers alike and left one and all satiated and grateful to have been there.

Large outdoor concerts have a tendency to be uninspired and uncomfortable and generally more hassle than they're worth. Famous superstars staging comebacks can be damned tedious if you're listening for music rather than for nostalgia. But there are exceptions; and they're enough, when they happen, to make everything else worthwhile.

A good show's a good show; that's all. Next week Jerry Ford will dive into the Snake River Canyon, without a parachute. Don't miss it if you can.

Soho Weekly News, Oct. 3, 1974:

I guess I believe in common denominators; anyway, I've always half-assumed that if you took the music that sounded so great to me in 1965–1968, and divided it by my own youth at the time, you'd get something roughly equivalent to what's around today as heard through the ears of an open and enthusiastic eighteen-year-old.

Not so. I begin to realize that, unfair as it seems, my adolescence (that period in one's life when popular music is most meaningful) coincided with a brief era of quality and growth in rock music beside which 1973–74 (for example) is boredom incarnate. I never really believed this, always figuring it was just my getting older and out of touch, but recently I've been asking whatever teenagers I meet to tell me who their favorite musicians are. Invariably they say, "Jimi Hendrix" or "the Who" or "the original Byrds" – people who were on top seven years ago. Only a truly imaginative person would have predicted in 1967 that the most popular rock groups in 1974 would be composed almost entirely of the same people who were making hits in '67. Yet it seems to be the case.

Worse still, it is very hard to think of an artist who has actually *progressed* since the late sixties, turning out better music now than he or she did then. Joni Mitchell, maybe. But most of the former greats, those who are still alive, are doing stuff that ranges in quality from not-quite-as-good-as-before to terrible.

Has the muse deserted us? Is she hiding? I know that these record reviews I'm writing now are not as exciting as the ones seven years ago, and I'm not too happy about it. I don't think it's correct to say we're all old men at age 26 or 30 or whatever – that doesn't explain the absence of monstrously energetic younger musicians and writers to knock us all on our asses.

Roger McGuinn was in town recently [deleted section in which I talk about his excellent show with some hired young musicians, and his recent solo album] . . .

Crosby Stills Nash & Young are another good old band who are sounding better now, live, than they ever did in their heyday. In case this seems to contradict my earlier statement that none of these artists have progressed since the '60s, let me explain that many have progressed as professional performers, entertainers, within the confines of having to perform for huge audiences and being limited to mostly familiar material – but they have not progressed as productive artists, either in terms of new songs, sounds and ideas, or on the simple level of producing exciting new recordings.

This presents a marketing problem, one which the record companies have solved by means of reissue packages, such as *So Far,* which purports to be CSNY's Greatest Hits on a little sticker that cleverly disappears when you take off the cellophane. *So Far,* consisting of material drawn from the three CSNY group LPs (all of which are still in the record stores), is already a Top Ten album, presumably because people who have felt no urge to purchase the first CSN album, or *Déjà Vu,* suddenly rush to the stores to grab the material when presented in the guise of a *new album.* Consumer psychology: don't buy anything old (i.e., anything with an old package around it), new is always better, even when, as in this case, the new package is a musical disaster compared with the albums it's drawn from. It doesn't hang together right, mixes styles and moods in such a way as to emphasize the group's weakest aspect: its slickness and artificiality. The wholeness of the original albums, their integrity, is missing.

The answer from an aesthetic point of view is for the record companies to devote new and more intelligent efforts to promoting backlist. Old wine in new covers might sell, but please spare us the new programming unless the original programming can be improved on (a good example of creative packaging is the Beach Boys' *Endless Summer,* now the number one album in the country thanks to good TV promotion, and in many ways the best musical package released in America this year).

It still seems a little sad to me that today's teenagers have to listen to the music that turned me on, instead of some brave new world of their own. But as long as there's a '60s resurgence – hardly a revival because the '70s in a musical sense

74

have yet to express themselves as anything more than a continuation of what has gone before – let's get it right. Let's find a way to sell these new customers the music at its best, instead of at its shiniest. Just a matter of polishing the proper apple, methinks – does the a&r department speak to the promotion department?

7

Rock 'N' Roll Cowboy, Disc 2

Here we go. Another disc, another 17 songs. And more than that. A whole new era in the artist's work. 1974–1978. Well, you've got a start on this era if you read my summer '74 responses to *On the Beach* and CSNY live. The second *Cowboy* CD consists of six performances from 1974 (solo or with CSNY), six from 1976 (with Crazy Horse or the Stills/Young Band or solo), three from 1977 (with the Ducks or the Gone with the Wind Orchestra), and two from 1978 (with Crazy Horse). No, nothing from '75.

What this serialized-inside-a-book essay is about, what bootlegs like this are about (with artists like this) is *the hidden side of the iceberg*. The rest of the artist's oeuvre. Hidden in public, in live performance. Who is Neil Young? The guy who showed up and sang these songs in these particular ways on these nights. And a guy who makes it clear (for instance in "Love Art Blues," track 5 of disc 2) that his purpose in life is to do exactly this.

On *Cowboy* 2 he does it very well. Attention 21st Century! You wanna have a grip on this guy Neil Young's body of work as a major "rock and roll" late century artist? You need to listen to these illicit-at-the-time recordings. There's more to the picture than meets the eye (or ear), and Neil knows it, which is why he's preparing his own box set.

Track 1. "Pardon My Heart." Wow. Oh my God. The *Zuma* version a year later is a likeable and forgettable song, but this May 16, 1974 solo performance is a revelation. What a voice, what a guitar player, what a great song. A major work. Where did this come from?

Pete Long explains (in his invaluable *Ghosts on the Road, Neil Young in Concert*): "On May 16, Ry Cooder and Leon Redbone played solo sets at the Bottom Line in New York City. Taking advantage of the convivial atmosphere, Young asked if he could do a guest set when the show was over. After Ry Cooder's encore, the audience was invited to stay but no clues were offered as to the identity of the next performer. A few minutes later Neil Young was introduced and proceeded to play an acoustic set that must rank as one of his most relaxed and communicative performances ever."

Long further notes that "nine of the ten songs that he performed during his hour on stage were at that time unreleased, although four of them would shortly feature on *On the Beach.*"(Indeed, had been recorded the previous month.)

The *Cowboy* booklet says of "Pardon My Heart": "this autobiographical song is about Neil's relationship with his second wife, the actress Carrie Snodgrass." This is surely true; they separated (though I don't think they ever married) before the end of '74. And now I want to share with you the 1975 interview quote that the booklet places under "Love Art Blues":

"Joni Mitchell writes about her relationships so much more vividly than I do. I use . . . I guess I put more of a veil over what I'm talking about. I've written a few songs that were as stark as hers. Songs like 'Pardon My Heart,' 'Homefires,' 'Love Art Blues' . . . almost all of Homegrown [the album he cancelled and replaced with *Tonight's the Night*]. *I've never released any of those. And I probably never will. I think I'd be too embarrassed to put them out. They're a little too real."* (Later that year he did include "Pardon My Heart" on *Zuma.*)

Neil's May 16 performance of "Pardon My Heart" (and of track 2, "On the Beach," also from that Bottom Line set) is absolutely mesmerizing. So much musical presence (his

78

acoustic guitar communicates rhythm and bass notes and melodic texture as if his fingers were a whole band) (not to mention the beauty of his voice this night) . . . and, using this sublime musicality as a vehicle, so much immediate, recognizable *emotional* presence. You can reach out and touch his situation. Stark, indeed. As much because of the performance as because of the words. (A different performance, and the passage of time, made the same words safer for *Zuma.*) This one is so gentle, so relaxed (as Pete pointed out), and so scary in its immediacy. Communicative indeed.

What does the song (performance) say? It says a lot by what it doesn't say. No bitterness. No defensiveness. The pain is felt but not dramatized. And the song, while it laments a "fallen situation" that "feels so wrong," is also (without attempting to deny the finality of the situation) a genuinely loving celebration of what's good in the relationship. "It feels so good, when the love flows the way that it should." He treats it, properly, like one of the seven wonders of the world. Real love. We had it, babe. He doesn't say that, but he gets it across. And he says he loves her in the present. "I love you more than moments we have or have not shared." (Nice choice of words, arguing that his love in the present is bigger than such past moments as his transgressions or their golden memories of falling in love.) "Pardon my heart," indeed. It has something it wants to say. About the curious coexistence of feeling so good and feeling so wrong.

After which track 2, "On the Beach," is no disappointment. It's a fucking epic. I always liked the album version, but this solo acoustic performance is proof that it really is as great a song as its advocates (hi, Johnny!) claim. My God. Again, like the Fillmore East "Cowgirl," it sounds to me like a great transcendent jazz track. The night the Coltrane band really got out there. Except this time it's solo acoustic, so maybe Monk's a better comparison. Or maybe Skip James?

Sure, you can make fun of it as "I've got the rich rock star blues . . ." But he really does, and he gets across the humanness of his situation and his feelings regardless of his circumstances. So naked. It could be hilarious, but all the more reason to admire his honesty and his courage. Way to go, Neil. "The world is turning; I hope it don't turn away." He really does care about our attention. "All my pictures are falling from the wall where I placed them yesterday." Nice reference to "Out on the Weekend." ("She got pictures on the wall, they make me look up, from her big brass bed.")

Besides, the universality (and timelessness) of Neil's blues was established by Jack Logan's marvellous recording of it (on his album *Bulk*), back when buying a house on a Malibu beach was certainly not a possibility on Jack's mind.

Meanwhile, back in Greenwich Village, check out that guitar playing! His touch. His humor. His attack. The moments when the soundboard resonates like a piano. And those deliberate little blues runs so eloquent and exploratory between the verses. The colors. The interplay of guitar and voice. The cool pulse that runs through the whole performance. Heck, even the lady coughing reminds me that this is an audience tape and how fortunate we are that this moment was captured.

And, being me, I can't help being reminded of Bob Dylan one year later a few blocks away at the Other End, coming up on stage after a Jack Elliott performance to spontaneously share a new song he's just written in the second person about a collapsing relationship (the parallel, you see, is with "Pardon My Heart," not "On the Beach," though the two are certainly related) called "Abandoned Love." ("But me, I can't cover what I am . . .")

"On the Beach" and "Pardon My Heart" from May 16, 1974 are keepers. Cornerstones in the body of work. And we'll encounter a few more ("Love Art Blues," "Shots," "Like a Hurricane") before this disc is over.

*   *   *

Tracks 3, 4, 5 – "Traces," "Human Highway," "Love Art Blues" – are all from the same show, the opening concert of the Crosby, Stills, Nash & Young summer '74 tour, July 9 in Seattle. These were shows in front of huge audiences (50,000 and up) who'd paid high prices to see the superstars, so it was bold of Neil to continue the approach he'd explored on his last two tours, of packing his performances with songs the audience hasn't heard before.

"Traces" and "Human Highway" sound like they were written for CSNY musically; indeed there's not much to either song past the quite attractive melodies and chord changes, very suited to the CSNY vocal sound, indeed quite lilting. To my taste, this "Human Highway" is enormously more enjoyable than the (dumb) later version that ended up on Neil's 1978 album *Comes a Time*. I enjoy "Traces" too, and do appreciate the inclusion on *Cowboy* of both tracks. But I must also report, just to keep things in focus, that these two are certainly not great performances, nor particularly successful or memorable songs. Both songs seem to have been written in 1973. "Human Highway" was going to be the title track of a second CSNY album that the quartet rehearsed in May '73 and started recording the next month, and then abandoned (because of personality conflicts within the group that often prevented them from completing projects they'd begun). "Traces" seems to date from the same period, and was definitely recorded by Neil (possibly a demo) sometime that year.

For a change of pace, let me point to what doesn't work (especially lyrically) in these two songs. I think we may be able to get some insight into what gives Young's best songs their power by dissecting a couple of failures. By the way, my hunch as to the reason for the failures is that it's connected to the writer's ambivalent feelings about being in the group. So he's not sure what audience or aesthetic he's writing for. Such uncertainty is often an obstacle to inspiration. A shame, though, because there *is* something inspired about the melodies and basic arrangements. It's almost as though both

81

the singer and the listener want the songs to be saying something and feel like they almost know what that something is. Tantalizing.

The song structure of "Traces" is promisingly weird: a distorted sonnet, fourteen lines arranged in three mostly non-rhyming verses, and then repeated in full (two and a half minutes total). The first verse says, with that disarming NY direct address: "Believe me when I tell you, that a love true isn't hard to find." (Some of the directness is in his tone of voice, and in a certain melodic and rhythmic emphasis on each word that is engaging.) Is it a verse or just a charmingly long line?

The beginning of the next verse is, "Cause I found mine . . ." This to me is a poor payoff. We're supposed to believe him (he's testifying) and trust that there's a "love true" for each of us, because – And the reason he gives is that he's just found his. Not much of a reason. Yes, this could be a very sweet beginning to a love song, but neither the performance nor anything else in the lyrics makes me feel that he actually is in love ("love true"!) at this very moment. Actually what the song mostly is is vague. Which makes the title intentionally ironic. "Let's make a song that sounds like just a trace (or vague traces) of itself!"

Well, a game effort is made when the third verse (the remainder of the song's only stanza), seemingly changes the subject (a trick Neil has tried in other songs, sometimes quite successfully): "None of the neighbors remember names, they only see the faces." This has no discernible connection with the love true he found or the one we're supposed to believe is easy to find. Finally, the best I can do is to imagine that in a kind of dream-logic, "hard to find" segues into an actual search, complicated by the poor memories of the neighbors the detective tries to interview. Nice conceit. But does it work? No, not in my opinion, a fun game but it never rises above its collapsed narrative. No I don't believe you. I do like the fact that the "neighbors" line quoted above turns out to be the first half of the song's only couplet, ending in the title word ("traces" rhymes with "faces") so the stanza feels like it ends in a chorus. And then the whole stanza is repeated. The verse-segments as segments have some real motion and charm. They just don't have content. This lack of payoff helps illuminate how significant the payoff in some of Neil's other lyrics is to the power of their respective songs. "It's these expressions I never give that keep me searching for a heart of gold." That's a hell of a payoff. "It's hard to leave the traces for someone to follow" isn't. It's even hard to say, and therefore hard to hear. And at least for my clever mind it isn't easy to make it seem Meaningful. Anyway, not in this love song. Easier for me to imagine it a line that's fallen out of "Human Highway," which I think is about the superstar's relationship with his/their public. In which case "With destinations still unnamed, it's hard to leave the traces for someone to follow" becomes the complaint or excuse of a "spokesman for his generation," that if I/we don't know where we're going, how the hell can I write a great anthem laying out guidelines?

"Human Highway" has an autobiographical feel (quite effective, for example, in several of the *Harvest* songs), at least to my ears ... but not a very enticing one (though there are some nice phrases, good choices of words), and once again no payoff. On the good songs, the closer (or more) you listen the more you are rewarded. "Traces" and "Human Highway" don't pass that test. "I come down from the misty mountain, I got lost on the human highway," the opening line, feels to me (when they all sing it together) like it could refer to Neil coming down from Canada, David and Graham coming down from their very successful hit-single-making early groups, Stephen maybe coming down from a folkie dream or from his own youthful hit single. And the human highway a rather good description for the trail of concerts full of lively flesh. Could also describe their fame, in which each arguably got lost. The lines that continue the first verse (which is also the third/last verse, each six lines long) are attractive and striking ("take my head refreshing fountain") (maybe an attempt at a "lay down your weary tune" message) . . . but again the payoff (also the last line of the stanza and of the middle verse, so also a kind of chorus) is disappointing, and in my opinion downright dreadful. "How could people get so unkind?" Very victim-y, Neil. And not much of an anthem.

I do like the start of the middle verse (in Seattle and on *Cowboy*): "I come down from the crooked mansion, and I married the DJ's daughter." In my understanding of Neil-speak, I imagine this is a reference to the house he once lived in up Topanga Canyon, and a coy "explanation" of how he happened to get such a big hit record after he left there. Quite cute, if you think of it as similar to Dylan's marvellous "explanation" (written in mid-'74, so Neil's 1973 song anticipates it) of his own success, in "Idiot Wind": "She inherited a million bucks and when she died it came to me. I can't help it if I'm lucky." But this clever humor is spoiled when Neil whines, "Now my name is on the line, how could people get so unkind?" This is not very clear or inspiring, but in context I take it to mean that people spoke contemptuously of him because he'd become a rock star . . . and that hurts his feelings. Okay, "On the Beach" has related sentiments. But in that song they work, very well. So I can't like "Human Highway" half as much as I'd like to. Anyway, the *Comes a Time* version muddies the water even further by changing it to "I went looking for the D.J.'s daughter" – no marriage, which certainly spoils my fantasy that he's "explaining" his unseemly success.

* * *

And then, from the same Seattle CSNY show, we get track 5, "Love Art Blues," which is practically a solo performance by Neil on piano and harmonica with one of the others (Stephen?) strumming acoustic guitar and adding a fairly discreet second voice for some lines or words ("Traces" and "Highway" are full rock band sound and three- or four-way lead vocals). Likely written 1974 not 1973. And this one has a superb payoff. And guess what? It's a particularly successful Neil Young song (in my opinion) and a *great* Neil Young performance.

Recall that this is one of the three songs from the aborted *Homegrown* album that Neil described as comparable to a Joni Mitchell song in terms of starkness on the subject of one's relationships and "*too* real, I'd be embarrassed to put them out." "Love Art Blues," like "Pardon My Heart," does not contain language that reveals any private matters; it's only embarrassing for the writer because he knows the specifics of incidents that are described very obliquely. "Homefires," on the other hand (performed on the CSNY '74 tour but we'll come to it on *Cowboy* when we get to disc 4 and 1992), is so revealing I can imagine Neil thinking of the three songs together and wincing because they deal with the same personal history. But only "Homefires" spells it out: "I'm not the same man I was a while ago." "I'll walk these borders in search of a line/Between young lovers who live separate lives." "How long can this go on? Late at night when I've been drinking/Substitute comes at me winking." Yes. We *think* we know what he means in "Love Art Blues" when he says, "I went and played too hard." But we can't know for sure (songwriter offers no further information), and indeed there's a nice double entendre on the word "played," so I wouldn't call "Love Art" embarrassing. Just poignant. And honest. And powerful.

The thing I find surprising about these three songs is that none of them makes any reference that I can pick up, not even an oblique one, to the third party in Neil's relationship with Carrie Snodgrass. I don't mean a winking third party. I'm talking about a very young person who does make an appearance in another new song, track 6, "Hawaiian Sunrise": "In the morning when you rise, will you look in my son's eyes?"

In any case, "Love Art Blues" very successfully articulates its primary message, which is not that boys will be boys. It is the undeniable and very relevant fact in any artist's life that love and art can at times pull you in very different directions, thereby causing suffering. The premise is clearly and charmingly stated: "I've got the love art blues/Don't know which one to choose." And then the payoff is simple and perfect and devastating, a couple of verses later: "Why must I choose between the best things I ever had?"

"I spilled my promise cup, I really don't know why" probably refers to infidelity. The rest of that verse ("now the distance lies between you and I") is quite effective, because it is the only place in the song where he speaks in the second person, only mention of "you." Otherwise he's talking to us, the boys in the bar (I guess I get that image because his blues piano playing is so evocative), in the third person about his problems. "There's really something to lose/With these love art blues." Amen, brother. I hear you. Tell it like it is.

And if you're really paying attention, you might ask, what does infidelity have to do with a conflict between love and art? The answer is not given outright, as is usually the case with Neil's song lyric riddles. Instead, the song is structured so that it climaxes in the answer, which is itself a riddle: "I went and played too hard." Since his art is making music, then in addition to sowing wild oats doesn't this also refer to putting too much energy into his guitar playing, his singing, the performance side of his life? Yeah, and I'm sure it's ironic. The thing is, his aesthetic (part of it, the Crazy Horse side) is the harder you play, the better the music. But that also takes him away from his girlfriend – geographically, because playing hard includes loving the road, and also in terms of his attention.

But I assume the real issue can be found in the double meaning of "the distance between you and I." She's home with the kid. He's travelling around the world playing his rock and roll, with lots of opportunities for playing around. This is contradicted slightly by a note in John Robertson's *Neil Young:*

The Visual Documentary that says of the summer '74 CSNY tour, "Young elects not to travel by plane from show to show with the rest of the entourage. Instead, he drives from town to town in his camper-truck, accompanied by Carrie Snodgrass, one roadie and his dog." Intriguing. But what about Zeke? Oh well, whatever the biographical facts may be, the song says what it says. And it certainly says love and art can give you the blues when they start competing with each other. And says it with humor ("my songs are all so long . . .") and very little self-pity and lots of soul. Says it awfully goddamned well.

That is, it does on this *Rock 'N' Roll Cowboy* track, which is from opening night, July 9, 1974. Great piano. Excellent harmonica. Superb vocal. Good accompaniment. Great timing. A magnificent performance, clearly at a moment when the songwriter/performer absolutely feels the song's subject matter and is totally committed to getting it across. Totally relaxed and totally committed both at once. So he gets in a groove with himself, and we can hear it, feel it, to the point that we can believe that this art of performing might indeed be one of the best things he ever had, and hard to leave for his beloved partner (or vice versa).

The songwriting is excellent, even though it's "just a blues" and blues songs look simple. But in fact the choice of words and the ways the words are highlighted by the rhythm and the tune are very skilful. And effective. And the very simplicity of blues song structure lends itself to marvellous inventions any poet could be proud of. As is often the case with Neil's songs, the verse-chorus structure offers no chorus in the usual sense; nor is there a musical bridge, an elegant changeup in the middle. So what is there? Six four-line verses, with rhymes between the second and fourth lines. The first verse and the last verse are the same, and this repetition combined with ending lines one and four with the title phrase and rhyming all four lines with each other, makes the whole verse feel like a chorus. So the structure is chorus, verse verse verse verse, chorus. More nuances: verses three and five are the same. So

87

the six verses can be described as: A B C D C A. The repetitions affect the way you feel about the song and what it says. And a particularly nice nuance is that the first line of verse B, "I went and played too hard," is repeated after A is repeated, so that it becomes the last line of the song. The climax. Dug into by the singer(s) as if they were just about to do the whole song over again. Instead they stop short after this line, and it's a glorious ending.

This conflict between taking your art on the road (almost the only place it can exist for you as a performer) and pleasing and keeping the woman you love, is a primary theme of Bob Dylan's film *Renaldo & Clara.* In writing about Dylan, I've called attention to the extent to which the content and effectiveness and even beauty and intelligence of a song can be determined by the particular performance it is given, and therefore for the performer every performance is a separate statement and a distinct artistic creation. Neil Young and Bob Dylan are performing artists, and it is incomplete to consider their song-creations as pieces of writing that express the intention of the songwriter. They also express the intention (presence) of the performer, at the moment of performance. We can discuss this aspect of the art form thanks to the miracle of (legal or illegal) live recordings.

So I happen to have an illegal recording of another performance of this same song a month later, August 15th, at an indoor venue on Long Island, New York. The bootleg in fact is named *Love Art Blues,* a good title. But the performance of "Love Art Blues" thereon is a thudding disappointment compared to the brilliant July 9th performance. It makes you wonder if one could really appreciate how good a song this is if it were only delivered in this uninspired package. I don't think so. The words and tune and arrangement are exactly the same, but they don't add up to anything. The performer's not in the mood, his piano playing is leaden, the audience is beating time loudly with applause and it's competing with the singing rather than supporting it. Why did these same Great Dane bootleggers include this lifeless performance on their *Love Art Blues* album, when they could have used the great one they stuck on *Cowboy* a year later? I don't know. But I feel certain that which version you hear is going to make a huge difference in one's relationship with this song. The August 15th performance has nothing to say. It's not technically bad, just uninspired. This is apparent even before the slow hand-clapping starts. It might have been a good night for some other songs, but the singer definitely sounds like he's not into the content or the feel of this one this time. Ditto the piano player.

Which is to say, don't take the performer's art for granted. The songwriter may have been inspired (or not). But the most important thing now is whether the *performer* is inspired (in relation to this song, this performance) tonight.

"Love Art Blues," then, July 9 1974 version, is in my opinion a major work. I can imagine Bob Dylan doing a fabulous cover of it (as he did with John Hiatt's "The Usual").

*   *   *

Cowboy 2, track 6, "Hawaiian Sunrise," is from Sept. 8, 1974, the last U.S. show of the CSNY tour, the one I wrote about in chapter six. Another song that has never been officially released. This version is quite pretty, all acoustic instruments, ethereal group vocals soaring over the stand-up bass. This is a performance where the CSN three-part harmonies interact particularly well with Neil's lead vocal. If you like CSN at their best (first album), this recording will delight you. Even if you're not tickled by the goofy "Hawaiian" melody. And the performance is moving to me when I hear it (as I must, given the lyrics, regardless of John Robertson saying Carrie was on the tour) as this man in a hotel room thinking of his estranged mate on a far-off island waking up and looking into the eyes of his almost-two-year-old son. The song consciously echoes "New

Mama" ("got a sun in her eyes"), written almost two years before, a song that is deliberately echoed once again in Neil's 1996 song "Big Time": "I'm still living in dreamland." Some themes don't fade away.

* * *

Track 7 jumps us forward to 1976, and "Like a Hurricane." As the *Cowboy* booklet explains: "written in a bar in Redwood City, California, in 1975. Neil started playing this song during the December 1975 Northern California Coastal Bar Tour with Crazy Horse." This was the return of Crazy Horse. In '74 Billy Talbot and Ralph Molina met Frank Sampedro and eventually discovered he was the rhythm guitarist they'd been looking for since Danny Whitten died. Neil was impressed with the new Horse and asked them to accompany him at sessions for the *Homegrown* album. Then in July '75 they recorded *Zuma* together. The next month they recorded a new song called "Like a Hurricane."

Then Bob Dylan in October launched his Rolling Thunder Revue tour of mostly unannounced shows at small venues in New England. Neil was inspired to try a similar anti-superstar stunt, and took Crazy Horse on a set of unpublicized surprise shows at the end of '75 he called the "Northern California Coastal Bar Tour." The version of "Like a Hurricane" included on *American Stars 'N Bars* in June '77 and *Decade* in Nov. '77 was recorded with Crazy Horse in November '75 at rehearsals for the Northern California Coastal Bar Tour, also known at the time as the "Rolling Zuma Tour." These were the first Neil Young/Crazy Horse shows since 1970, although Talbot and Molina had been part of the Santa Monica Flyers for the Tonight's the Night Tour.

In March 1976 Neil and Crazy Horse played 22 shows in Japan and Europe. The exhilarating performance of "Like a Hurricane" included on *Rock 'N' Roll Cowboy* is from the third show of this tour, March 5th at Festival Hall in Osaka, Japan. On this tour, a huge electric fan was set up on stage to "blow away" Neil and the Horse while they played this song.

"Like a Hurricane" has so far appeared on five officially released Neil Young albums (the other three are *Rust Never Sleeps, Weld,* and *Unplugged*), more than any other song. Johnny Rogan, in his *Complete Guide to the Music of Neil Young*, says, "for many this is the apotheosis of the Neil Young/Crazy Horse partnership." Pete Long says, "It can comfortably be considered as a prime candidate for most people's Neil Young Top Twenty All-Time Greats." Brian Keizer, in his 1996 book *Neil Young*, writes: " 'Like a Hurricane' is Young's grand formal iconic masterpiece, like 'You Really Got Me' and 'Louie Louie' a unique, instantly distinguishable formal model of rock and roll music." Keizer continues: "On 'Like a Hurricane,' Young used the melody line as an instrumental intro and then a modal springboard for euphoric crescendoing guitar histrionics. If its dynamic contour is less fungible and identifiable than Chuck Berry and Bo Diddley's work, it is that guitar tone, the instrumental melodic statement and restatement of theme as it pulls against the lumbering rhythm section of Crazy Horse, that are most often being referred to when over the last fifteen years someone has said they hear a 'strong Neil Young influence.' "

Finally Neil Young says (to interviewer Mary Turner in 1979): "A lot of people think we play so simple, there's no finesse. But we're not trying to impress anybody. We just want to play with a feeling and none of us can play that fast . . . We can play it very slow, extremely slow; but not fast, we just can't do it." Turner: "But 'Like a Hurricane' gets cooking pretty good." Young: "Yeah, but if you listen to that, I never really play anything fast. And all it is is four notes on the bass. It just keeps going down. Billy plays a few extra notes now and then and the drum beats the same all the way through. It's like just a trance we get into. But if you try to analyse it, figure out why it sounds . . . Sometimes it does sound like it's real fast, like we're really playing fast, but we're not. It's just that everybody starts swimming around in circles and it starts elevating and it transcends the point of playing fast or slow. Luckily for us because we can't play fast."

It's a song about sex and romance, about the extraordinary feelings and projections one can experience when looking at a stranger in a bar, given more power because it's in the second person, a passionate and sincere love song addressed to a stranger. It could be considered a restatement of that other cornerstone NY/CH song, "Cinnamon Girl." "I could be happy the rest of my life with a cinnamon girl." The point is that whether or not it's true love, these are very real feelings. An important part of the singer's experience. In both songs he identifies himself as "a dreamer (of pictures)." So maybe this sexual restlessness is also central to his creative process. In the *Decade* notes he says of "Cinnamon Girl": "Wrote this for a city girl on peeling pavement coming at me through Phil Ochs' eyes playing finger cymbals. It was hard to explain to my wife."

From the booklet: "*Crazy Horse brings out a part of me that's very primitive. We really put out a lot of emotion – which is easy for a kid to relate to. So it's very childlike. I've had great times with them.*"

*   *   *

"Stringman." (Track 8.) Way back in chapter three, I mentioned that whether you like (or connect with) a Neil Young song seems to depend on whether you're in the right mood for it when you hear it. If so, this presents a problem for critics who want to be perceived as having "objective" reasons for their judgements and evaluations. But when it comes to the relationship between the audience and a work of art (let's say, for example, a painting, or a performed song), objective standards are much less reliable than subjective ones. Undeniably, many people immediately liked "I Want to Hold Your Hand" and "Heartbreak Hotel." That's the information: the potency of the response these peculiar-at-the-time recordings provoked in their listeners. And since Neil Young's achievement rests on his ability to express feelings and on the strong feelings his songs, his performances, inspire in his listeners, I believe the only real information Johnny Rogan or Paul Williams or Brian Keizer or any other commentators can provide you about the relative value of Young's recordings (artworks) is, in effect, "this one makes me feel a lot." Or, "this one, observably, makes a lot of people feel a lot." Or, "this one probably would if more people got a chance to hear it."

And another side of this equation is that the quality of the song can depend enormously on whether the singer/ performer is in the right mood when he delivers it. Garbage in, garbage out. You can't transmit feelings you're not having at the moment. The "Stringman" on *Rock 'N' Roll Cowboy*, recorded live in London March 31, 1976, and later overdubbed with electric guitar and vocal harmonies for inclusion on a never-released "live" album, is the version most NY collectors had heard, and which caused them to rank it in the top 30 in a *Broken Arrow* poll of favorite Neil songs. This version is an excellent example of the power of Neil Young as a performer when he is perfectly and intensely in the mood for this song he's singing and what it says and everything it has to give. This performance conveys the song so clearly and with such conviction one feels as though one has just spent a truly rare and memorable moment of closeness with a good friend. Okay. But seventeen years later Neil Young recorded the song again for a live album, and this time the album was released, and as a result many people heard this song for the first time (on *Unplugged*). But he absolutely wasn't in the right mood for the song that night (indeed, in my opinion it was generally an unconnected night). The officially released "Stringman" is dreadful. Absolutely lacking in anything that sounds to me like a moment of sincere or genuine feeling. Harsh criticism? No, just a listener's honest report. The point is not that a guy can have an off night. The point is that the power of "Stringman" on 3/31/76 rests on how much the singer/songwriter feels and cares about what he's saying. It's a tremendously moving performance. Listen to the 1976 and 1993 versions back to back and I think – I trust – you'll be able to hear quite clearly the presence and absence of spirit, soul, artistic consciousness. Neat opportunity. Now you hear him, now you don't. Compare the two to get insight into who he is when he's in his power.

But please, if you don't have the '76 version, don't listen to the *Unplugged* version just to see what I don't like about it. You can't find out that way. There's nothing "wrong" with Neil's singing and playing on *Unplugged*; what I dislike is the absence of everything in the song that does connect with me elsewhere. And my point is you cannot easily find those things through the words and music alone, the composed components of the song. You find them (directly) in the performance. Some performances. A few very special ones.

I should note that to some extent I'm coming to *Rock 'N' Roll Cowboy* as I did to the albums discussed in the other chapters of this book – fairly fresh. I haven't been a Neil Young bootleg or tape collector, and most of these songs and performances I haven't heard till fairly recently. In the case of "Stringman," I'd heard of it as a well-known unreleased Neil Young song, and then heard it when I got *Unplugged* but wasn't struck by it. The first time I heard it on *Cowboy*, I think I noticed some attractive, seemingly heartfelt moments in the vocal as the song went by. And noticed the characteristic NY weirdness of something about "the sarge who can't go back to war, 'cause the hippies tore down everything that he was fighting for." Yeah, like that song on *Decade* about "even Richard Nixon has got soul." Then after those passing impressions, I got the opportunity, thanks to this book, to really spend some time with the track and focus my attention a little (nice work if you can get it). I was further influenced by a rumor I found in my "research." Johnny Rogan in his book says, "this impressive ballad was allegedly inspired by Stephen Stills." Hmm.

So never mind the celebrity gossip side of this. Intriguing, but what really mattered for me was that I opened myself to what should have been obvious: the singer in the song says he's singing for a dear friend, and the opening lines are to that friend, in response to expressions of depression or more specifically lack of creative inspiration. Again, Johnny's note helped point me in this direction, but what really made me notice the words "no dearer friend" and "on the empty page before you" was the voice of the singer. His affection and compassion, and earnest wish to address the question raised, are so palpable, unmistakable. And then the story line is certainly clear: "You say the soul is gone and the feeling is just not there/Not like it was so long ago." (I immediately think of the Springfield/early CSN days, but this could be a discussion between any two old friends.) And then what else could this be but one songwriter sharing "how to come up with a song" tricks with a friend who feels stuck?: "On the empty page before you, you can fill in what you care./Try to make it new before you go./Take the simple case of the sarge . . ." He's giving examples. Come up with something "new" that's caught your attention or made you think or feel . . . and let that story turn itself into a song.

And then, as in several of Neil's songs, everything rests on an emotional climax in the late middle of the song (so fucking beautiful – makes me cry – because his voice conveys such presence): "I'm singing for the stringman, who lately lost his wife./There is no dearer friend of mine that I know in this life." You have to hear it. Too bad he never, yet, released the projected live album, *Odeon Budokan*, which would have given us among other things this solo piano "Stringman" from London's Hammersmith Odeon and a "Like a Hurricane" from that week in Japan. And, I'm sure, other treasures. And I love the way he gives "string" a different meaning in the last lines. "All those strings" meaning, "all our attachments." Neil Young, philosopher. And caring friend.

* * *

Speaking of Stephen Stills, the next three (particularly undistinguished) tracks on *Rock 'N' Roll Cowboy* are from the brief tour of the Stills/Young Band, June-July 1976. After the CSNY tour ended in Sept. '74, Neil and the others had gone back to their separate lives. In the latter half of '75 Stills toured with his own band, promoting a solo album. When he appeared at UC Berkeley, not far from Young's Northern California ranch, Young visited him on stage. Neil didn't sing because he was recovering from a recent operation to remove nodes from his throat, a recurrent problem for the singer at this time. So he played guitar on a few songs. That was July; Stephen played No. Cal. again in late November, and Neil showed up and they sang together on four songs. Young sang and played with Stills again the next night in So. Cal., and during the electric set Stills excitedly told the audience, "the spirit of the Buffalo Springfield is back!"

They then decided to record an album together, as Crosby and Nash had been doing. The first sessions took place in January 1976, in Miami. Sessions resumed in April after Neil's tour with Crazy Horse.

The album that resulted, *Long May You Run* (released in September 1976) was credited to the Stills/Young Band. Five songs written by Young, four by Stills. I was quite eager to hear the album when it came out – and quite disappointed. I have yet to meet or hear of anyone who is enthusiastic about any part of this album other than the title track (which is included on *Decade* in an alternate mix that adds Nash and Crosby harmonies). So I don't feel alone on this one. And it's not too surprising that the three *Cowboy* tracks from the month-long Stills/Young Band tour are also quite tepid. They are interesting to hear . . . but for historic, not aesthetic, reasons.

Track 9, "Evening Coconut," is interesting because it's an unreleased song not known to have been performed any time except on this tour (no, it's not on the album), and because, like track 10, "Long May You Run," it's a love song for an old (departed) friend who happens to be an inanimate object.

The booklet reports: "Written about Neil's first boat, which – according to Scott Young (Neil's father) – was 'rotten to the core.' Nobody but Neil could string together images of the Statue of Liberty, Atlantis, flying saucers, raging storms, silver wings, crowns of thorns and boats on a bay, and have it all make sense. Well, the boat may have been no good, but the song is a gem."

I'll disagree slightly. The song is very likeable, mostly for its catchy tune and cheerful nature, but it doesn't seem to me that much of a gem in this collection that offers so many priceless jewels, and if the lyrics make sense then I'm afraid I missed the boat somewhere. "The Statue of Liberty is breathing in the air/Atlantis is waiting down below/Late at night flashing lights are sighted in the air/It's no secret what everybody knows." Further clarification is not offered. But the song does have a striking, even charming, "feel" (if you're in the right mood). It is a case however where I doubt I could derive much pleasure from it without the booklet or Pete Long tipping me off that Neil once owned a boat called "Evening Coconut." The closest the song comes to pointing this way is the line, "Have you seen the evening coconut, bobbing on the bay?" Could be a boat or could be a fruit or just more pleasant lyrical nonsense to go with the verse quoted above. Since I don't have a full NY biography to reference, I do have some questions about time and place. Where and when did he own this boat? Sometime when his father had the chance to see it, apparently, so that suggests maybe a lake in Canada? Certainly, Statue of Liberty notwithstanding, he didn't have a boat in New York Harbor. Anyway, I like the song better if I accept it as Edward-Lear-style "nonsense" and don't require it all to make sense. The tune does run in my mind.

The editing of the Neil quote under "Evening Coconut" in the *Cowboy* booklet is misleading. Some comments from the 1975 *Rolling Stone* interview are folded together, and since as usual there's no info as to date of quote, the reader must assume Neil's talking about the Stills/Young Band when he says *"I just couldn't handle it toward the end of that tour. I was going crazy, you know, joining and quitting and joining again. I needed more space."* In fact, however, Neil is talking about why he left Buffalo Springfield. It would be interesting to hear him explain why he quit the Stills/Young Band tour abruptly – he didn't talk to Stephen, just sent him a telegram c/o the venue that he wasn't going to show up that night or at any of the other concerts already scheduled for the next couple of months. Pete Long reports that some attribute this to a recurrence of his throat problems, and others say he felt upstaged by the opening act, Poco.

In any case, we can answer the question ourselves by listening to the album that was stage one of this 1976 collaboration, and by listening to the next two tracks on *Cowboy*, "Long May You Run" and "Southern Man" by the Stills/Young Band July 7th in Providence, Rhode Island, two weeks before Neil's telegram. It wasn't working, folks. The performance of "Long May You Run" is lackluster, not terrible but certainly not up to the modest standards of the album version. The real evidence of trouble in paradise, however, is the other selection. On paper it sounds good: Stills and Young, the original duelling guitars who made Buffalo Springfield such a great live band, reunited in a performance of the Neil Young/Danny Whitten guitar classic "Southern Man," two and a half minutes longer than the original album version. But alas . . . *"Stephen Stills and I just play really good together. We're both very intense and we made some incredible music with each other,"* Neil says in that misplaced 1975 quote in the booklet. But I think almost anyone hearing this 7/7/76 performance would have to agree that this time these two guitar players are playing very poorly together, and what is incredible about the music is its absolute lack of intensity. Rhythm and lead are really limp, just noodling along. A song that was almost nonstop climax in its five-and-a-half-minute version now goes for nine minutes with no climax at all. Even Neil sounds like he's doing a half-asleep run-through of standard arena rock guitar moves. It would seem that these guys were not inspiring each other musically, or maybe they just happened to go out on the road together (Neil cancelled a Crazy Horse tour for this) at a bad moment in each musician's professional life. Too bad. Stills has been quoted as saying, when he got the telegram, "I have no future." This could be considered prophetic of a U.K. single by the Sex Pistols a few months later, which would eventually have an impact on Neil Young's contemplations of the ever present menace of rust.

Two footnotes: Back in '75, this time in the *Creem* interview, Neil said, "In concert, what I play all depends on how I feel. I can't do songs like 'Southern Man,' I'd rather play the Lynyrd Skynyrd song. That'd be great." (He's referring to "Sweet Home Alabama," which includes the line, "I hope Neil Young will remember/Southern man don't need him 'round anyhow.") The other thing is I always liked the line "It was back in Blind River in 1962, when I last saw you alive" in "Long May You Run," and I was pleased to get a full description in John Einarson's *Neil Young, The Canadian Years*, of the day Neil's Buick hearse (nicknamed "Mort," a good Canadian bilingual pun) blew its transmission in the middle of Ontario and was towed to a garage in Blind River. "Neil and Terry stayed on a few more days at the motel in Blind River [waiting for a new tranny, which never arrived]. 'Neil was writing songs all the time there,' recalls Terry. 'I've never met a guy who could write so much.' "

* * *

Track 12, "Give Me Strength," an unreleased song performed Nov. 20, 1976, during the solo acoustic segment of a New York City show with Crazy Horse, has something important in common with "Long May You Run." Both songs were recorded at sessions for the cancelled *Homegrown* album. Those sessions were in December 1974 and January 1975, a bit of information that casts quite a bit of light on "Give Me

Strength" when you listen to it as an autobiographical statement from Neil just after his break-up with Carrie. Listened to
in this light, it seems a perfect example of what he was
responding to when he decided to let *Tonight's the Night* come
out in summer '75 instead of *Homegrown*, as explained in his
comments then to Cameron Crowe:

"I'm sure parts of *Homegrown* will surface on other albums of
mine. There's some beautiful stuff that Emmylou Harris sings
harmony on. I don't know. That record might be more what
people would rather hear from me now, but it was just a very
down album. It was the darker side to *Harvest*. A lot of the
songs had to do with me breaking up with my old lady. It was a
little too personal . . . it scared me. Plus, I had just released *On
the Beach*, probably one of the most depressing records I've
ever made. I don't want to get down to the point where I can't
even get up. I mean there's something to going down there
and looking around, but I don't know about sticking around."

"Give Me Strength" is a good title, but the song it belongs to
is not, to my taste, a strong one. I'd probably like it better if it
felt more like the prayer the title suggests. I've acknowledged
that a listener's response to a Neil Young song is a personal
or subjective matter. So when I report my opinions, it's not
because I think I've been appointed judge over the fellow's
work. No no. But since I reserve the right to be as enthusiastic
as I really am about something as remarkable and enduring as
"Cowgirl in the Sand" at the Fillmore East, it's probably helpful if I occasionally report my other rather personal responses.
I've told you of NY songs that have melodies, chord changes,
lyrics, and structural or performance elements that I find particularly pleasing (and characteristic of the particular, if inter-
mittent, creative power of Neil Young). So for the sake of
honesty or clarity I want to include a few examples of cases like
this where I don't dislike the song and am glad for the chance
to hear it, maybe even like small aspects of it, but don't happen to find the music or lyrics or other elements particularly
well-formed or otherwise seductive and gratifying. Okay?

Autobiographical lyrics: "A lonely man I made myself to be." Nice reference to "Cinnamon Girl": "The picture painted here is not a dream." The sad part: a slightly morose "Give me strength to move along/Give me strength to realize she's gone." Summarizing couplet: "The party ended long before the night./She made me feel alive and that's all right." Yeah, but I'd much rather listen to you say it in "Pardon My Heart."

* * *

As we go into the 1977 section of *Rock 'N' Roll Cowboy* disc 2, I need to say something tangential about this year. One of my favorite Neil Young albums came out in June '77 and, remarkably, was half recorded only two months before, April '77. This is an album that I'm sure gets left off quite a few people's top ten lists of Neil Young records, NY fans being so heterogenous in their NY album preferences. It's called *American Stars 'N Bars*, and although it solidly makes my top twelve it's not represented by a chapter in *Love to Burn*, which is organized partly accidentally, depending on whether I happened to write about an album when it came out – which has largely depended on whether I was doing that sort of thing that year. But no way can I say a few words here about a few live performances from '77 without mentioning that the best live recording of Neil Young in 1977 that I've ever heard is not on a bootleg but is on side one of this officially released album I've been listening to for almost twenty years.

Side one of *American Stars 'N Bars* ("The Old Country Waltz," "Saddle Up the Palomino," "Hey Babe," "Hold Back the Tears," "Bite the Bullet") was recorded live at "rehearsals" (Larson and Ronstadt didn't know they were being recorded) at Neil Young's ranch south of San Francisco, on April 4, 1977, with Crazy Horse plus Ben Keith plus Carole Mayedo on violin plus Nicolette Larson and Linda Ronstadt ("The Bullets") on backing vocals. Great stuff, and at least three of the contradictory

101

sides of Neil Young are united here in one session, the sensitive acoustic guy, the loud raunchy garage band rock guy,
the off-the-wall country guy – and I for one love these five
songs and performances and relate to the "guy" they collectively present. A lot of the Neil Young aesthetic is expressed
here, not as dramatically as on *Tonight's the Night* or *Ragged
Glory* but nevertheless the pure quill. Engaging and honest and
relevant and emotive. Romantic and raunchy. "Bite the Bullet"
is forthrightly and joyously about cunnilingus, as surely as Anita
Ward's "Ring My Bell."

Anyway, '77 was an interesting year. Also released that year:
Decade, and note that *American Stars 'N Bars*, released four
months earlier, calls attention on its inner sleeve to the fact
that it consists of songs recorded in separate sessions in '74,
'75, '76 and '77. Neil and David Briggs created the album as a
retrospective of the past four years to make a statement about
"who I am" before the portentous arrival of the three-album
career summary *Decade*, which was scheduled for 11/76 until
Neil at the last minute asked them to hold it back for a year
('76 being a year when he departed from tours and postponed
retrospectives at the last minute). Besides the Bullets and
Crazy Horse (one day only), Neil in 1977 also performed with
the Ducks and the Gone with the Wind Orchestra.

Who? Well, it was a year of improvising. Tracks 13 and 14 of
Cowboy are from a show at a bar in Santa Cruz, California
8/22/77 by The Ducks with Neil Young. The Ducks were a
local band recently formed by Young's old friend Jeff Blackburn. They knew each other from the L.A. music scene in the
Buffalo Springfield era. Blackburn's Ducks included two guys
who'd been in the re-formed Moby Grape with him. In early
June '77 Neil, whose ranch is a forty-mile drive from Santa
Cruz, heard the Ducks needed a guitar player, and sat in at a
rehearsal. And joined the band. Pete Long, in *Ghosts on the
Road*: "He hired a house near the beach where they prac-
tised for a week and a half. While some may have viewed the
arrangement as simply Neil Young with a different backing

band, the whole venture was actually executed in a much more equitable manner. Young was merely another member of The Ducks and his material was not given precedence over anyone else's. The majority of the songs that the band played were, in fact, penned by (Bob) Moseley or Blackburn."

So for a couple of months Neil Young got to relive the childhood experience of playing in a local bar band. He played roughly 18 gigs with the Ducks, between July 15 and Sept. 2, at a variety of clubs and bars, all in Santa Cruz. Pete Long reports that Young did have some of the shows recorded and contemplated a possible live album. The Ducks renamed themselves High Flight and continued with another lead guitar player. The Neil Young songs performed by the Ducks included "Human Highway," "Mr. Soul," "Long May You Run," "Are You Ready for the Country?", "Little Wing," and five new songs, including the two that show up on *Cowboy*: "Sail Away" and "Comes a Time." Neil would eventually record both songs (without the Ducks) in November. That recording of "Sail Away" turned up on *Rust Never Sleeps* (1979) and "Comes a Time" became the title track of a 1978 album.

The *Cowboy* booklet has a well-chosen quote from Neil to accompany these two performances at which a song is being presented to listeners none of whom has ever heard it before: *"I like to do it backwards. Go out and play the songs first before anybody knows what they are, then you really go to bang 'em down. And they get to either dig it or not dig it, but it's real. That makes it fun even if you don't get the big reaction."*

One is naturally curious to know what the Ducks with Neil sound like. But "Comes a Time" and "Sail Away" don't reveal much. The band, and for that matter the singer, sound almost anonymous. I'm not especially fond of either of these anthemic non-messages (though I will admit the album version of "Comes a Time" is quite pretty, even soothing). These "band" versions sound like the same song, same arrangement, as the familiar acoustic versions. Neil sounds like he's more relaxed, having more fun than he was with the Stills/Young

Band. But he's still not identifiable as that strong musical personality which makes such an impact on us listeners whenever it does make itself felt.

In terms of observing the songwriter at work, it's worth noting that in this early version of "Comes a Time" the first verse is repeated near the end of the song, for a total of three verses and three choruses. The two-verse, two-chorus version on *Comes a Time* seems a clever edit. The words still don't say much, but in the shorter version they *feel* more meaningful. "Sail Away" also gives us a glimpse of song-in-process. It used to start with "Meet the losers in the best bars" (verse 2 on the album), which gives it a different mood than the album version. Maybe the "I could live inside a tepee" verse was moved to the front because he was already thinking of sticking "Sail Away" on an album with "Pocahontas."

Track 15, "Lady Wingshot," was performed in Miami Beach(!!) by the Gone with the Wind Orchestra, November 12 (Neil's 32nd birthday), 1977, at the Miami Music Festival in Bicentennial Park. *Cowboy* doesn't explain what this orchestra is, but does offer the useful information that the song was performed again at a show in 1989. Pete Long reminds us that the Gone with the Wind Orchestra "were to feature on the forthcoming *Comes a Time*." Miami was their only live appearance – they didn't exist as a unit except when Neil Young and Ben Keith brought them together to help him record some tracks in Nashville and Fort Lauderdale that mostly ended up on the 1978 album *Comes a Time*. (Which until spring '78 was going to be called *Gone with the Wind*.) According to the back cover of the album, there were 34 people in the Orchestra, including J. J. Cale and Tim Drummond.

This Miami Beach show was Neil's only known performance in 1977 after the last Ducks show Sept. 2nd. "Lady Wingshot" was first performed here (and perhaps not again for eleven years). It's a love song, singing the praises of a particular woman in a manner somewhat unusual for Neil. And there's no question in my mind that the song is addressed to the woman John Robertson reports Neil began a relationship with in October, a woman who is on stage with him, singing with him, at Miami Beach. Nicolette Larson. The relationship didn't last long (indeed, in January 1978 Young met Pegi Morton, whom he would marry in August '78 and have a son with in November, and stay married to through the coming decades).

Neil met the charming Nicolette in March 1977, shortly before he invited her and Linda Ronstadt to take part in that early April "rehearsal." She sang harmony vocals on six of the *Comes a Time* songs and shared a lead vocal on a seventh, "Motorcycle Mama," at sessions in late October and early November. Near the end of 1978, long after she and Neil parted, she released her first single, "Lotta Love," a Neil Young song from *Comes a Time*, which became a top ten hit for her.

"Lady Wingshot" is a bold and delightful experiment. The first verse, which feels like a chorus when it repeats later in the song, is woven from the melody (and beat and feel) of Young's 1967 song "Broken Arrow" (a very meaningful musical moment for Neil to refer to in any fashion). The second verse presents us with a fascinating shift in tempo and tone, like a bridge but so early in the song, powerfully echoing some familiar hymn. The song's message is the *feel* of these musical elements melded together, and this song and performance do indeed have a message, are heartfelt, have something to say. Now, as often happens with Neil's choices of words and imagery, I can't say I know what he means by "When you see the golden trigger stand before your eyes." But I do like the feel of the language, and the rest of the refrain definitely speaks for me, "By the time you stop to figure, Lady Wingshot flies away."

(Larson was known for her speed on her roller skates.) Good song. Good orchestra. Hope he'll release this track sometime. It would have sounded good on side one of *American Stars 'N Bars*.

* * *

"Shots" is what I've been looking for. I loved "Winterlong" so much when I heard it on *Decade* (and "Star of Bethlehem" and "Will to Love" and "Like a Hurricane" on *Stars 'N Bars*) that then when I'd hear about Neil's cache of unreleased songs, I'd imagine this might mean he could hit us again with stuff this powerful. "Shots" (track 16) is a fulfilment of that promise. And a weird one, because this song *was* released (in 1981, on *RE-AC-TOR*), but in a failed experiment it was done in a manner that gets attention but isn't listenable most of the time, and doesn't allow the song behind the mask to get through. And guess what? It turns out to have been a remarkably moving and intelligent and loveable song. A transformed (before the fact) and very satisfying listening experience. A treasure.

"Shots" (the real "Shots," not the *RE-AC-TOR* pastiche) was performed at The Boarding House in San Francisco on May 24 (Bob Dylan's birthday), 1978. It was a solo performance (backed by a band of three cigar store wooden Indians), the first of ten shows in five nights at a 300-seat club, partly a benefit to help the club stay open. This first night of what Neil's manager Elliott Roberts called "The One-Stop World Tour" was in hindsight a significant turning point. It was the first scheduled Neil Young concert in a year and a half, since the fall '76 tour with Crazy Horse. And the Boarding House stand was his only public appearance in 1978 prior to his legendary (much-praised, much-documented) Rust Never Sleeps tour with Crazy Horse in September and October. It was thus also the occasion of Neil's introduction (first public performance) of several of his best-known songs: "My My, Hey Hey," "Thrasher," "Powderfinger," and (not so famous, but I love it) "Ride My Llama."

And "Shots." This is in fact the unveiling of a major breakthrough in Neil Young's songwriting. "Powderfinger" and "Thrasher" and "Shots" are written like little short stories or films (perhaps he was inspired by how well "Cortez the Killer" turned out). The author consciously creates a setting and situation and then, like a science fiction writer, allows or requires the listener/reader to deduce the circumstances (*why* are they coming up the river in "Powderfinger"?). These songs also show Neil at the height of his craft as a poet (while continuing to demonstrate his sure and inspired hand at melody and rhythm). It's as though he's learned to fictionalize, after writing so much oblique or not-so-oblique autobiography.

"Shots" derives from this narrative approach, but is different in that it is not a particular fictional situation that's described, but instead (in a poet's manner) a general circumstance is described in carefully and cleverly related images, so that we are both watching a scene and contemplating the philosophical observations that arise in our minds from the narrator's comments on the scene.

The first verse (at the Boarding House; the *RE-AC-TOR* version is very different) provides the image, the scene, the mood. Before I quote it, let me also point out that Neil's guitar playing, and the rhythmic pace of the song which the guitar sets and introduces, contribute enormously to setting the mood before the vocal starts, and to giving an edge and a purposeful inflection to everything the singer (narrator) will say. Neil can be a great guitar player in an understated and astonishingly conscious and effective way, and this solo acoustic "Shots" is a good example of that side of his talent.

The song's first words: "Children are lost in the sand, building roads with little hands/Trying to join their fathers' castles together again." Wow. The simple image of children making roads in the sand (at the beach) is vivid and evocative enough, and then how deftly (and, for me, accurately) the poet moves from the associated images of sand castles and parents nearby on a beach to the thought (worth meditating on) that the children's roads are intended to join together the painful separatenesses of the adult world. This in a song which turns out to be very specifically about war and the way concepts of property ("castles") entangle humans in wars. Further suggesting that the natural (innocent, playful) impulse of children is to change this. Very Sixties, man (in a very subtle way). Very Neil Young.

And it wouldn't work so gloriously were it not that the tune and rhythmic setting make that first word – "Children" – stand by itself, followed by a full stop and then an explication of this first and defining word of the verse. The other verses follow the same pattern, with the words "Shots," "Machines," "Men," and "Lust" (until the change-up in the next-to-last verse, when the song which has been entirely third-person becomes second person and changes from philosophy lecture to love song, so this time with a subtle rhythmic shift it starts "But I . . .").

This first verse brackets the song (at the Boarding House), reinforcing the central importance of the children-bulding-roads-in-the-sand image. This is followed by the "shots" verse which clearly establishes the setting of a border war in which shots are ringing out and flying through the night air as a too-normal circumstance, as in Vietnam or El Salvador. And then the road-building image returns: "Machines/Are winding their way along, looking strong/Building roads and bringing back loads and loads of building materials/In the night." Marvellous. Still a child's perspective on adult life (the thrill of your own Tonka dumptruck or steam shovel), and not un-related to images of war in El Salvador. Fourth verse: "Men/Are trying to change the borders on the ground./Lines between the different spots that each has found." This is great. "Men" paired with "machines" and "children." What do men, as opposed to machines, as opposed to children, do? "Bor-ders" echoes "shots ringing all along the border can be heard." So we know he's talking about war, though these could be the same men who were driving the machines. And the "lines between the different spots" for me rings nicely with the image of children playing in sand, making roads (which are lines, as are borders). And it certainly doesn't take a great leap for us to realize that these men are, partly, soldiers, trying to change borders and draw lines between the spot you found (your land) and the spot I found. Playing like children.

It's a powerful meditation, and Neil being Neil has to keep us on our toes by throwing in sex, with a fifth verse that starts "Lust/" and speaks delicately of frustrated suburban wives faking orgasms. This isn't entirely a *non sequitur*, due to the songwriter's use of the words "in the night" to end each verse starting with the second ("shots") verse. So the fourth ("men") verse ended, "But back home another scene was going down, in the night." As we're familiar with rock and blues songs, it's not a leap to suppose he's suggesting the men should worry about what's happening back at home. And indeed the next verse starts, "Lust/Came creeping in the night to feed on hearts/Of suburban wives who learned to pretend/When they met their dream's end/In the night." And well sung. Fabulous stuff.

Then the "I promise to you/I will always be true" verse, which can be heard as the poet's pledge of honesty (and fidelity) to the listener. Or as the sudden introduction of a loved one, as at the end of "Cortez." And finally, the return of the "children" verse to seal the deal . . . no return of "shots" at all, quite different from the recording, the line "I keep hearing shots" isn't in the 1978 version. It's a song about children playing and a contemplation of the human energies that cause war, not a song about urban paranoia in the Eighties as I'd always imagined.

Neil Young can be a very good poet and music maker and performer of songs. Any "Shots" from these ten Boarding House shows is probably worth searching out.

* * *

And *Cowboy* 2 ends nicely with the one regularly-performed song from the Rust Never Sleeps tour that didn't get included on *Live Rust* or in the film *Rust Never Sleeps*: "Come on Baby Let's Go Downtown" from *Tonight's the Night*, with vocals this time by Neil Young instead of co-songwriter Danny Whitten.

"One round baby, let me turn you around, now turn you, turn you, turn you around." Feels good. And sounds great. Like everything one could have possibly wanted the Ducks to be. "The world's third-best garage band," as Neil used to say of himself and Crazy Horse.

8

Tonight's the Night

Friday June 27, 1975, I went to see the Rolling Stones at Madison Square Garden; two days earlier I'd seen the Patti Smith Group for the first time. I was writing a cover story for the Soho Weekly News *on both events, under the title "Rock and Roll '75, State of the Art," and suddenly* Tonight's the Night *was released and I listened and listened and had to add this "bulletin" into the Stones/Patti story.*

This is a bulletin (what an extraordinary week of music this has been!). Neil Young's new album, *Tonight's the Night,* is just about what you've been waiting for all your life. (If it isn't, fuck you. I mean, *chacun à son goût,* you poor slob. You don't know what you're missing.)

It's a "concept album," a disc with a unified theme as it were, so far beyond *Tommy* in thematic cohesion, depth of statement and feeling, and rock and roll vitality that it might even get Pete Townshend to open up his tired eyes.

Even if you haven't gotten off on NY since *Harvest* or *After the Gold Rush* or *Everybody Knows This Is Nowhere* or even "Broken Arrow" (which this album resembles), even if you are completely unaware that "Don't Be Denied" and "Ambulance Blues" are classics of this decade, I think you're gonna like *Tonight's the Night.* It's an experiment, like every record Young has ever put out, and it demonstrates why Faulkner said you can't go on being great at what you do after you stop experimenting – courage is a key virtue for writers, for record-makers, courage to experiment and the clarity of mind to know what it is you want (& recognize it when you get it). Neil Young, by staying true to himself, has not pleased his audience (or rather, his various audiences) every time; but he has kept himself alive, which is a lot more than you can say for many great rock performers, including quite a few who are still breathing.

And I couldn't agree more/empathize more with what this record ("BB's plane crash album") has to say.

9

Decade

Not long after I wrote chapter 1 my friend Charlie was replaced at Warner Bros. Records by another very cool guy (he wrote the book Too Cool, *and was a charter subscriber to* Crawdaddy!*) named Gene Sculatti. After he published "I Sing the Song Because I Love the Man," he asked me to do the newsletter write-up for a Neil Young anthology album that was coming out soon. That was September 1976, and here is the piece that appeared in* Waxpaper *(the new name of the in-house newsletter) that October. There was an official-looking symbol at the bottom of the page that said "SHIPPING APPROXIMATELY NOV. 12," but in fact the release date was pushed forward a year at the last minute by the artist. The album that came out in fall '77 had a few different tracks from the one they sent me information about in fall '76.*

It has in fact been ten years since I first heard a Neil Young song: "Nowadays Clancy Can't Even Sing," the first Buffalo Springfield single. Heard it on the radio late one night and got hooked right away; that wasn't Neil singing lead (which is presumably why the song isn't on this album), but the *sound* of Neil Young came through all the same, grabbed me by the lapels even though I wasn't wearing no coat and clung on for dear life, and one slight decade later I still can't get that song out of my head (or off my chest, as the case may be). The kid has presence.

Matter of fact, there's no one like him, and damn few who equal him. If that point wasn't clear to everyone already, it will be now that this little anthology (a three-record set, *à la* Motown) is in the stores.

It's a very useful album. Kind of like *Hot Rocks,* or *Endless Summer,* pure concentrate of pleasure principle in a single package, stack 'em up. And at the same time as oddball, individualistic, and exhilarating as, say, a three-record set of Keith Jarrett solo piano concerts. Neil Young is Neil Young. *Decade* is essence of the man, face turned out to the great adoring public ("Wanna hear 'Heart of Gold' again?") and eyes turned in staring at a depthless universe that would frighten the most hardened astronomer.

Decade will sell a lot of copies. The price is right, and anyone who ever loved two or three of these songs (which is almost everyone) will want a copy, unless of course they already have all his albums, in which case they'll *have to* buy this one, as it contains five songs never heard before anywhere and two or three never before available on an LP. Should be his biggest disk since *Harvest.* (Cheers from the accounting department.)

Getting specific, *Decade* includes the hits ("Heart of Gold," "Ohio," "Old Man," "After the Gold Rush"), the classic long cuts with Crazy Horse ("Down by the River," "Cowgirl in the Sand," "Cortez the Killer," "Southern Man"), Buffalo Springfield constructions ("Broken Arrow," "I Am a Child," "Mr Soul," "Burned," "Expecting to Fly"), beloved ballads ("I Believe in You," "Helpless," "A Man Needs a Maid," "Cinnamon Girl"), the drug death songs ("Tonight's the Night," "Tired Eyes," "The Needle and the Damage Done"), Neil Young anthems ("The Loner," "Long May You Run," "Walk On," "Time Fades Away"), some odd numbers ("For the Turnstiles," "The Old Laughing Lady," "Soldier," "Don't Cry No Tears" – live version) and those previously unreleased mystery items, one from Springfield days ("Down to the Wire"), one from the first solo tour ("Sugar Mountain"), and five from 1974 ("Love Is a Rose," "Deep Forbidden Lake," "Pushed It over the End," "Star of Bethlehem," and "Winterlong").

There. Now you know everything I know. Due to circumstances beyond our control (a likely cop-out), your humble and obedient servant is writing this notice without having heard the album.

I mention this only to show off my famous honesty. It is also honest to say that I have no doubt whatsoever I'm going to love this record (all three of it). Some anthologies are mere marketing schemes, worse than useless – CSNY's *So Far* is an example that comes to mind. Other collections make a major contribution by redefining and recontextualizing the material therein. This one will do the latter, may even help to free the man from all his self-made myths, leave him a clean easel on which to paint the next ten years of masterpieces while leaving us a suitably weighty memorial of his first fabulous run.

** Love to Burn *bonus: since they gave me the liner notes for the album they thought was coming out soon, here are the notes Neil wrote for three songs that didn't end up on the released album:*

"*Time Fades Away*. No songs from this album are included here. It was recorded on my biggest tour ever, 65 shows in 90 days. Money hassles among everyone concerned ruined this tour and record for me but I released it anyway so you folks could see what can happen if you lose it for a while. I was becoming more interested in an *audio verité* approach to records than satisfying the public demands for a repetition of *Harvest*."

"*Don't Cry No Tears*. Initially titled 'I Wonder,' this song was written in 1964. One of my first songs. This is a live recording from Japan with Crazy Horse."

"*Pushed It over the End*. Recorded live on the road in Chicago, 1974. Thanks to Crosby & Nash's help on the overdubbed chorus, I was able to complete this work. I wrote it for Patty Hearst and her countless brothers and sisters. Also, I wrote it for myself and the increasing distance between me and you."

10

Rock 'N' Roll Cowboy, Disc 3

There's a four-year gap between the end of disc 2 and the start of 3. Neil wasn't touring. More on this below. Then *Cowboy* 3 takes us into the Eighties via two perfs with the Trans Band from fall '82, two with the Shocking Pinks (and a "solo Trans" perf) from '83, two with Crazy Horse from '84, and eight with the International Harvesters from '84 and '85. Okay, got your scorecard? Can't tell the players without a scorecard. Ben Keith was in every one of these bands (even sat in with the Horse at the two dates Neil played with them in the six-year period after '78 and before '85).

Welcome to Miami Beach. Never a dull moment when you try to follow Neil Young's trajectory.

Disc 3 of the 4-CD Italian bootleg *Rock 'N' Roll Cowboy* is a spectacular accomplishment. It makes sense of, or even redeems, a much misunderstood and under-appreciated phase of Neil Young's artistic career and oeuvre. This has been needed. And it also, very surprisingly, manages to be (for me, and I trust I'm not alone) one of those marvellous things, more suited to the vinyl era actually – an album that is an enjoyable listening experience as a whole, inviting many repeat listens to a particular "side" (five or six songs in a row). Not just a record that contains a few very beloved standout tracks – those albums are certainly treasures, but one also comes to appreciate records whose individual tracks may not so obviously be masterpieces, but which seem so profound and satisfying as a whole (or anyway a vinyl side at a time). You know . . . like *Rubber Soul* or *After the Gold Rush*. Or name your favorite examples.

So: *Cowboy* 3 is for me a superb sampler and primer of Neil Young, the Lost Period, the Geffen Years, the early Eighties. And aside from this very useful aspect, it is fun to listen to, with an overall spirit that is attractive and likeable. Adding up to a pleasant and satisfying deepening of the listener's sense of connection with Neil Young and his music.

I like to listen to tracks 1–6 ("If You Got Love," "Transformer Man," "My Boy," "Old Ways," "Kinda Fonda Wanda," "Gonna Rock Forever") and then pick up the (laser) needle and listen to them again. Twenty and a half minutes. And so musically and lyrically resonant with each other, even though they are performed with three different bands, over a period of a year and a half . . . songs representing three albums that *seem* to belong to radically different genres. Thank you, *Cowboy* programmers, for guiding me to an understanding and appreciation of this period that I, like many Neil listeners, had never really connected with, except for a track here or there. I like to listen to this CD. And the transitions, the sequences and juxtapositions, make me smile. Portrait of the artist . . . at a time (not many artists of any kind can say this) when he was being sued by his patron, his record company, for not turning in work truly representative (according to the plaintiff) of who he is and who his public wants him to be. That ornery Neil Young. Well, this group of six makes him sound like a sweetheart. A childish one, maybe, but that's consistent with the guy he used to be who sang, "I am a child." Okay. This is fun music. Of various kinds that all turn out to be related. Musically and lyrically. "Sure looks like we're all gonna rock together." "It's hard to teach a dinosaur a new trick." "Why are you growing up so fast, my boy?" "If you got love . . . can't live without it . . . ." "Sooner or later you'll have to learn . . ." "Transformer man . . ."

What was happening to the transformer man between 9/78 when he sang "Come on Baby Let's Go Downtown" and

10/82 when he sang "If You Got Love" and "Transformer Man"?

His second son, Ben, was born (11/78) and soon diagnosed as suffering from cerebral palsy. The same as Neil's other son! Who wrote this script?? It's not a genetically carried illness; the doctors say this was coincidence. Well, in any case, Neil wrote himself in as a loving, patient, and courageous (and not-absent) husband and father. After his highly acclaimed (career-restoring) Rust Never Sleeps tour, he stayed home for four years and didn't tour or perform, focusing instead on being with Ben and Pegi as they all worked at the very demanding task of communication across a gulf few of us have confronted.

The first Neil-quote on this subject I want to share with you appears in the *Cowboy* booklet under the song "Computer Age" on disc 4 (a song from the 1983 album *Trans* that shows up on disc 4 in a 1987 version). The quote, unattributed as usual, seems to be from a radio interview. "Trans *was about all these robot-humanoid people working in the hospital and the one thing they were trying to do was teach this little baby to push a button. Read the lyrics, listen to all the mechanical voices, disregard everything but that computerized thing, and it's clear* Trans *is the beginning of my search for communication with a severely handicapped non-oral person. People completely misunderstood* Trans. *They put me down for fuckin' around with things I shouldn't have been involved with. Well, fuck them. But it hurt, because this was for my kid."*

Neil did not perform live or do any recording in 1979. And then in March 1980, a year and a third after Ben was born, Neil's wife Pegi was found to have a potentially fatal brain tumor. In May 1980 she underwent brain surgery, which was very successful. In June Neil wrote a song called "Stayin' Power" ("We got stayin' power, you and I/Stayin' power through thick and thin"), which he then recorded with four other songs – the five together became side two of an album released later that year, called *Hawks & Doves*. In October he played eleven songs at a festival in Berkeley, California, with another once-only performing troupe, "The Hawks & Doves Band." End of that year and beginning of the next, he and Crazy Horse started recording *RE-AC-TOR* at his home studio. In March 1981 he played three songs at a New York City tribute to guitarist Mike Bloomfield. The festival and the tribute were his only known live performances between October '78 and July '82.

And while noting the calamities that must have had some effect on the artist other than preventing him from leaving home to perform, I suppose it should also be noted that shortly before Ben's birth, the night of the next-to-last show of the Rust Never Sleeps tour in Oct. '78, Neil's house at Zuma Beach in Malibu (not his primary residence at the time) was destroyed in a large Southern California brush fire.

By 1982 things had begun to stabilize after the challenges of '78, '79 and '80. Early in the year Neil and Pegi decided to discontinue their son's participation in a very demanding (of parents as well as child) daily routine called The Program, which they had been practising since October 1980. The new approach seemed to work for Ben, and it also left Dad free to go back to being a live performer. And to write and record a new album called *Trans*, released in December 1982.

* * *

In July and August, '82, Neil and his new Trans Band (familiar faces from different Neil Young milieus: Ben Keith of the Stray Gators, Bruce Palmer of Buffalo Springfield, Ralph Molina of Crazy Horse, Nils Lofgren of the Santa Monica Flyers, Joe Lala of the Stills/Young Band and, briefly, Bob Mosely of the Ducks and Moby Grape) played seven shows at venues within sixty miles of Neil's ranch. At the end of August they began a European tour, 31 shows in seven weeks in Germany, France, Italy, England, Holland, Belgium, Switzerland, Norway, Sweden and Denmark. The first two tracks on

Cowboy Disc 3 were performed by Neil and the Trans Band at Göteborg, Sweden on October 8, 1982.

Track 1, "If You Got Love," is an unreleased song, noteworthy for having been left off *Trans* so suddenly that its name was still listed on that album's back cover. The Neil-quote in the booklet says, *"I omitted it from Trans because it was too wimpy. One of those occasions where I changed my mind at the last minute."* "Wimpy" seems an unkind and inappropriate word for this very likeable, riff-driven song. Perhaps what he was reacting to was the wimpiness of three songs on the same album with similar titles and conceits: "If You Got Love," "Hold on to Your Love," and "Little Thing Called Love."

I think he dropped the wrong "love" song. Of course, I haven't heard the studio performance he omitted, but I regard the song as it comes across in this live take as an overlooked triumph, a rather glorious statement of what Neil Young is about. This is not done in the lyrics particularly, although I like the feeling that comes to me through the lyrics – I like to think it's a celebration of the love he and Pegi feel for each other and for Ben, a celebration of the glory of living in that loving environment. The statement is in the music, the performance, the *feel*. The flip side of *Tonight's the Night*. An expression of joy.

What a groove they get into. Sounds to me like Ben Keith on keyboards is serving as the perfect rhythmic partner for Neil's lead guitar (and vocal), with the rest of the large rhythm section (bass, percussion, drums) supporting him masterfully. Thick, rich music, like a taste of New Orleans here in Göteborg. The more I listen to it the more it says to me. I'm out on a limb here – this song didn't make the top twenty unreleased NY songs list in a *Broken Arrow* poll, and I haven't seen it mentioned anywhere. Oh well, music criticism or appreciation is a strictly subjective matter anyway, in my opinion. So don't take any of my assessments too seriously, yours are sure to differ at times. All I can promise you is that my occasional enthusiasms are an honest and fairly accurate report of what I've felt on repeated listens to these (sometimes newly-discovered) favorite performances/songs.

What is it about "If You Got Love"? It cooks. And that riff, in duet with the vocal, is so meaningful, has so much to communicate to this listener. What a statement! I'll quote the words, but I assure you they have so much more to say when you hear the emphasis the ensemble and the song's rhythmic structure (and that great riff echo) give them (especially when you play the track again and again, like a single). "When you walk in the room/You hold your head up high/You talk to people eye to eye/There's nothing to hide/You're feeling so complete inside/Your heart is open clean inside/'Cause you got love." Sounds good to me, Neil. "When you're standing in the face of scorn/You know your spirit can't be torn." Quite different from the singer-of-sad-songs public image. This man's found something. The hard way, as we know. And (dig that riff!) the deep way.

Track 2, "Transformer Man," introduces the distinctive (and much-disliked, though it does have some appreciators) *Trans* sound. "If You Got Love" does not have the synthesized "computer talk" sound that dominates many of the tracks on the album, and this suggests another theory as to why Neil omitted it as "wimpy." Not weird enough. Anyway, some but not all of the songs performed at the Trans Band shows featured the live vocoder, and "Transformer Man" is one such. Vocoder? An electronic toy that can synthesize and manipulate (distort) the human voice. Young bought one in August '81, and proceeded to write songs for it, some of which, he has reported, he envisioned as songs sung by cartoon character computers, in an animated video.

Two Neil Young comments: 1 (quoted by John Robertson): "The vocoders on *Trans* are me trying to communicate with my younger son, Ben, who is unable to talk. He can understand what people are saying to him but can't reply. The more I am able to communicate with Ben, the less of a heavy thing it is." 2 (quoted in the *Cowboy* booklet, from a 1988 *Rolling Stone* interview conducted by James Henke): "If you listen to *Trans*, if you listen to the words to 'Transformer Man' and 'Computer Age' and 'We R in Control,' you'll hear a lot of references to my son and to people trying to live a life by pressing buttons, trying to control the things around them, and talking with people who can't talk, using computer voices and things like that." He goes on: "It has to do with a part of my life that practically no one can relate to. So my music, which is a reflection of my inner self, became something that nobody could relate to. And then I started hiding in styles, just putting little clues in there as to what was really on my mind. I just didn't want to openly share all this stuff in songs that said exactly what I wanted to say in a voice so loud everyone could hear it."

To understand or identify with Neil Young in his electronic/rockabilly/country/etc. period, read these comments carefully and listen to this live "Transformer Man" from Göteborg '82. What a pretty – even ethereal – piece of music they created together! The vocoder is not just tolerable (often a question on the album), it is mysteriously attractive and marvellously soulful. On the whole, in my opinion, a great performance, an anthem (i.e., rousing statement of purpose) for an artist who has, quite happily, and not without struggle, found the heart of gold he was looking for – both in another, a lover, and in himself. You don't hear it in those bell-like notes of the vocoder (operated on stage by Joel Bernstein) pealing out over the march rhythm of this hauntingly simple and elegant performance? I do. Especially when I take the man's advice and listen to the words – an almost impossible task; but it's worth the trouble to write down the album words, or find a songbook, and then listen to this version with the words in front of you and try to follow along.

The performance fills the words with feeling; the cheat sheet helps the listener's mind follow the poet/singer's intention, which is surprisingly clear in hindsight with the help of his 1988 comments. He's speaking with love to his disabled son and with compassion to the fellow-workers and inhabitants of this world at the dawn of a computer age: "Transformer man/ You run the show/Remote control/Direct the action with the push of a button/Power in your hand/Transformer man." And read this on several levels: "Sooner or later you'll have to see/The cause and effect/So many things still left to do/But we haven't made it yet/Every morning when I look in your eyes/I feel electrified by you. Oh yes."

Another echo of "New Mama." Ridiculously subtle for an anthem, I suppose, but he needed to hide, and he needed to simultaneously express himself. Loudly. And inaudibly. Is it really such a secret that *Trans* is about transformation? Hey, sometimes the best place to hide things is in plain view. And in this case that old trickster Neil has done it quite artfully, slightly demonically (I like the implicit sarcasm – "you run the show") and quite pleasingly. "Your eyes are shining on a beam/Through the galaxy of love/Transformer man/Unlock the secrets/Let us throw off the chains that hold you down."

A good current era literary theme, as in Philip K. Dick's novels *VALIS* and *The Divine Invasion*: "and a child shall lead them."

* * *

So after a song to Ben, *Cowboy* 3 continues, charmingly, with a song to Zeke, track 3, "My Boy." Zeke was recently ten at the time of this January '83 performance, and "My Boy," which shows up in different form on the 1985 album *Old Ways*, is the affectionate musings of a man anticipating becoming the father of an adolescent, a near-adult. The compiler of this bootleg was clever enough, or sensitive enough to the artist/performer's own intentions at this time, to round out the story by including as track 8 of this disc, "Amber Jean," Neil's hymn to his third child, a daughter, born May 1984.

124

"My Boy" is performed here acoustically, on a banjo, in Austin, Texas, at the fifth show of the Solo Trans tour, 36 shows in North America, from Santa Cruz to Louisville by way of Toronto. Nice to hear Neil accompanying himself on banjo, shaping his voice to the pitch and range and tempo of the instrument, evoking great American singers before him who got a lot of feeling across singing with the same instrument. Again, you gotta hear this live version to get closer to what I imagine to be the author's intention, regardless of what happened later in the self-consciousness of the recording studio. I particularly like the way he warbles, "Vacation gone, school is out, summer ends, year in year out." And did I forget to mention the harmonica? "Nearly time to live your dreams, my son."

Track 4 takes us to summer '83 and another song that would later show up on *Old Ways*, the title song of that ill-fated record. Once again, if you wanna understand and connect with the song (and the songwriter, the Neil Young persona), you gotta hear the live version and forget the album track. And do pay attention, because I for one once had the impression that since this song was the title track of a self-consciously "country" album (accompanied by interviews suggesting he'd found the lost side of himself or his truer musical identity), therefore the song must be about how the virtues of the old ways, a good homey "country" theme. But uh uh. "Old ways are like a ball and chain." It's actually another song about the dangers of rusting.

So here's the story of Neil Young's country album and his hassle with Geffen Records (his new record company as of early '82, owned by his former co-manager) – important context for the rest of this CD and particularly for the next track, which is from the same July '83 concert in Sacramento as "Old Ways" except it's with the Shocking Pinks. Who? Where'd they come from? Okay, listen up. March '82, NY signs with Geffen after fourteen years of recording for Reprise/Warner. Immediately after signing he offers them an album he's recently put together called *Island in the Sun*. They reject it.

Motherfuckers. Okay, I believe Neil had to fight for *Time Fades Away* in '73 before Reprise would agree to release it (and definitely they rejected the first *Tonight's the Night* at the start of '73, but in that case I get the impression Neil came to consider it a correct and helpful decision). But this was much worse. And the very arrogance of it was probably also a clear communication of the message: "You're not such a hot commercial property these days, no matter how famous you are, you're half-washed-up and we don't have to coddle you." Indeed, Young's last two albums on Reprise, *Hawks & Doves* and *RE-AC-TOR*, hadn't sold many copies or even gotten much critical praise. And despite the relative success (top ten album) of *Comes a Time* in 1978, Geffen Records probably assessed Young as an artist without a very large loyal following and a guy who's only famous when and if CSNY are on tour. After three years of appropriately (and necessarily) focusing on being a family man, this was presumably a rude awakening to the realities of the music biz. You think you're an artist? You're a fucking slave who's supposed to bring us money! And we know better than you how you should go about doing that.

You might think I'm putting an ugly spin on this. Well, my feelings are genuine, based partly on my own experiences with the publishing biz. Neil reports that his initial response was moderate, but then things got worse. He told James Henke in '88: "There was another record of mine, called *Island in the Sun*, which will probably never be heard. It was the first record I made for Geffen. The three acoustic songs on *Trans* are from it. But they advised me not to put it out. Because it was my first record for Geffen, I thought, 'Well, this is a fresh, new thing. He's got some new ideas.' It didn't really register to me that I was being manipulated, Until the second record. Then I realized this is the way it is all the time. Whatever I do, it's not what they want."

The first Neil Young album on Geffen was *Trans*, 12/82, recorded after they rebuffed *Island*. The second Geffen LP was *Everybody's Rockin'* (by "Neil and the Shocking Pinks"), 8/83. Again, it was Neil's replacement for another album which Geffen Records had rejected (in March '83). Henke: "You'd been trying to get off Geffen for a long time." Young: "They had a very negative viewpoint of anything that I wanted to do, other than straight pop records that were exactly what they wanted to hear. They saw me as a product that was not living up to their expectations. They didn't see me as an artist." Henke: "Geffen actually sued you for not making commercial records around the time of *Old Ways*." Young: "There was a whole other record, the original *Old Ways*, which Geffen rejected. It was like *Harvest II*. It was a combination of the musicians from *Harvest* and *Comes a Time*. It was done in Nashville in only a few days, basically the same way *Harvest* was done, and it was co-produced by Elliott Mazer, who produced *Harvest*."

So the "Old Ways" from July '83 on *Cowboy* was not intended for an in-your-face "country" album but for an unashamed "return of the old Neil Young" album with some country flavoring, which an awkward record company (in the person of president Ed Rosenblatt, although one can hardly absolve David Geffen from responsibility for what happened to his old friend when he dared to enter into a business relationship with him again) responded to ungraciously. Young: "There's *Harvest, Comes a Time,* and *Old Ways I*, which is more of a Neil Young record than *Old Ways II*. *Old Ways II* was more of a country record – which was a direct result of being sued for playing country music. The more they tried to stop me, the more I did it. Just to let them know that no one's gonna tell me what to do." Henke: 'I would have thought that Geffen would have wanted another *Comes a Time* or *Harvest*." Young: "That's what we thought. I was so stoked about that record. I sent them a tape of it that had eight songs on it. I called them up a week later, 'cause I hadn't heard anything, and they said,

'Well, frankly Neil, this record scares us a lot. We don't think this is the right direction for you to be going in.' "

The actual historic event of a large record company suing a much-admired rock singer/guitarist/songwriter, charging him in court with breach of contract for delivering albums containing "unrepresentative" material, happened at the end of summer 1984. John Robertson quotes Young as saying (date of interview unknown): "Eventually they dropped that lawsuit after a year and a half of harassing me, because I told them the longer you sue me for playing country music, the longer I'm going to play country music. Either you back off or I'm going to play country music forever. And then you won't be able to sue me because country music will be what I always do, so it won't be uncharacteristic anymore."

In August 1985 Geffen released *Old Ways* (the version Neil calls *Old Ways II*). But let's go back to spring '83 and the rejection of *Old Ways I*. He had now delivered three albums to Geffen and they'd rejected two of them. He had to give them another record. The *Cowboy* booklet provides this (unattributed) relevant Neil-quote: *"The record company said the original version of the* Old Ways *album scared them. They wanted more rock 'n' roll. Okay, fine. I'll give ya some rock 'n' roll. I almost vindictively gave them* Everybody's Rockin'." He was quick. *Everybody's Rockin'*, Neil's "Fifties rocker" or rockabilly album, was released in August '83. There was a two-year gap before the next Neil Young album, *OW II*.

So in Sacramento, California, on July 26, 1983, Neil Young performed disc 3, track 4, "Old Ways," during the first two-thirds of the concert, the solo acoustic sets . . . and then in the third set Neil and the Shocking Pinks performed track 5, "Kinda Fonda Wanda," and other *Everybody's Rockin'* songs.

I told you already that I enjoy listening to the first six tracks on this CD like a favorite LP-side, so you know I like these two. "Old Ways" live has a lovely "good time" feel, a solo acoustic performance (plus a couple of guys providing harmony voices) that makes it easy to see how the interest in playing a

Gene-Vincent-type rocker, and music to fit, grew out of or alongside the original *Old Ways* cluster of songs. In this performance Neil isn't pretending to be a country guy or a rockabilly guy but is effectively tapping into the rockabilly and country (as in an almost–40 guy in a bar admitting he has something to learn) sides of himself. Good song. Good music. Raises smiles. I particularly like the line, "Economy was getting so bad, I had to lay myself off." And I love the deliberate tempo and the harmonies on "It's hard to teach a dinosaur a new trick."

Okay, it is an anti-rust tune like I said, but along with that it's a clever and no doubt sincere testimony of a substance abuser noticing he's been on automatic pilot: "Lately I've been finding out/I'm set in my ways . . . Oh, I'm gonna stop that grass, and give up all this drinking/Really gonna make my life last/Clean up my whole way of living/Up until the party last night/I was a different man/But old ways got their way again." I'd say he's got a grip here on some of the finer points of the art of writing a country song (not just the clever word-twists and real-life situations but the relationship between words and tune and tone of voice), and is successfully employing them to make a personal statement that also rings true as a statement of musical identity, just as "Cinnamon Girl" does. Not some big concept. Just playful, earnest musical expression. Another side of Neil Young. With a good rhythmic feel – not unrelated to, say, "Dance Dance Dance." Who says rock and c&w are necessarily different genres? Not Carl Perkins.

So after making a personal policy statement about drugs (way back in the early '80s), Neil offers some thoughts on sex in the overtly rockabilly number, "Kinda Fonda Wanda." Same old Neil Young. I like the humorous and honest way he shares himself and talks to us in these songs. Not that this song is as confessional as 1977's "Saddle Up the Palomino" ("it's the neighbor's wife I'm after"). "Kinda" is a successfully playful celebration of '50s rock, including the stomp of "Honey Don't," the references to girls known from other songs *à la* "Splish Splash," and the braggadocio of "Travellin' Man." "Screwed Runaround Sue" is, in context, very funny and clever. But what I put under the heading of "honest" is the self-mocking statement in the hugely clever title. "Kinda Fonda Wanda." That says it all. If I have to explain, he's saying that he (the protagonist of the song, anyway) is prone to infidelity. I'm not suggesting there was a problem in his marriage. I'm saying I like the way he articulates the state of mind of the kind of guy he used to be. More attached to the lifestyle of "wandering" than to any one partner. Why? " 'Cause Wanda always wanna wanna wanna." The fun of playing the field is the enthusiasm of every flower you pick (or, rather, who picks you).

Track 6, "Gonna Rock Forever," also called "Rock, Rock, Rock," is a so-far-unreleased song, performed with Crazy Horse at one of four shows in two nights in Feb. '84 at the Catalyst in Santa Cruz, rehearsals in public for a new album that never did get completed. Since the album didn't come out we can't say for sure what the genre or "style" would have been, but this song suggests that maybe the pastiche this time was of the '70s arena rocker. Instant anthem. And still somehow very likeable. Because it can only be interpreted as making friendly fun of itself. And I also hear it as asserting that the reason we love this big beat music so much is that when we're in a room moving to it all together, we can feel for a moment like we *will* live forever. A heady illusion.

* * *

Disc 3, track 6: "Touch the Night." The author/editor of the *Cowboy* booklet (Erik Lafayette?) editorializes: "Another great song from the Catalyst warm-up show in Santa Cruz. Too much in the same mood as 'Like a Hurricane' to make it to an album like that, 'Touch the Night' ended up two years later on *Landing on Water* suffering a heavy production." Then he quotes Neil: "*Landing on Water was really claustrophobic, really personal, inside – not very happy.*"

Johnny Rogan in his *Complete Guide to the Music of NY* says of *Landing on Water* (NY's 4th Geffen album, released 7/86): "Along with *Everybody's Rockin'* this represented the nadir of Young's recording career." I can't disagree, because the truth is I've never heard *Landing on Water* or *Everybody's Rockin'*. I've been a true fan since I first saw Neil and the Springfield in December '66, but not an absolutely faithful fan. Let's say I liked him too much to want to buy albums that my friends and intuition told me would make me angry at or disappointed in him. I kind of liked *Trans*, was disappointed by *Old Ways*, and never listened to the other Geffen albums. I appreciate that *Rock 'N' Roll Cowboy* is helping me realize that the artist was in fact alive and working during those years – and appreciate how it's bringing me up to date on those years in our relationship when he wasn't telling me his feelings and experiences, or rather, when I wasn't listening. Rediscovery. I trust the great official Archives Box, now rumored for as soon as late '97, will offer us a similar or maybe even better opportunity to meet the man we've known for all these years.

"Touch the Night" (Feb. '84) doesn't sound like "Like a Hurricane" to me, but the booklet guy could be right in suggesting that Neil didn't want to put this sort of Neil Young & Crazy Horse instrumental excursion on record in this period because he didn't want to be pigeonholed as that "Like a Hurricane" guy. Possibly. If so, he certainly changed his mind later. And I have no trouble believing that the version on *Landing on Water* is completely missing the genuine ragged glory that shines through all ten and a half minutes of this Catalyst jam. Thunderous riff. Excellent solos. Great workout. And *very* pleasant listening, as long as you're in the mood, which is probably most of the time.

What I can't wax enthusiastic about is the lyrics. I've been quick, I think, to praise Young's inspired and quite original and communicative craft with words in many of his songs. But inevitably there are uninspired moments, like this, that don't offer any particular word-pleasure and don't seem to have anything particular to say. (As opposed to all those Young lyrics that I don't think I understand but that *seem* to have a lot to say to me. Those I usually like.) But anyway. Let's say it's one example of a Neil Young performance and song that I get great pleasure and satisfaction from even though the words and their story don't reach me or move me. I do enjoy the sound of his speaking voice. And I'm willing to pretend the chorus "and everyone will touch the night" means something to me even if it doesn't, just so I can give in to the pleasure my body and spirit are getting from the music.

Hey, it's an epic. If you're looking for a pre-1991 Young/ Horse long workout to add to your top favorites, this may not be a sure thing but is definitely a serious contender, and therefore one more reason why *Cowboy* is worth having (or why you should complain if the Archives Box somehow doesn't have a Catalyst '84 "Touch the Night"). Let's say it's an epic somehow telling the story, in code or tongues, of Chairman Neil's long march in the Geffen and post-'78-calamity wilderness. It has that glorious resilience that characterizes the man and his work.

*   *   *

Track 8, "Amber Jean," sweet song for a four-month-old, is the first of four *Cowboy* tracks recorded 9/25/84 with the International Harvesters for the Austin City Limits TV show, live at the University of Texas. Yeah, another band. Sort of. Four of the International Harvesters were in the Shocking Pinks, the two others were veterans of the Gone with the Wind Orchestra and *Comes a Time*. The Harvesters were Neil's "country band," featuring banjo, fiddle and pedal steel guitar. The saxophones and trumpet of the Shocking Pinks were gone, as were the Pinkettes, a quartet of dancing girls who accompanied Neil and the Pinks on their 38-city tour in July and September '83. One of the Pinkettes was Pegi Young. The pink suits and heavily greased hair were also gone. Pete Long reports, "Dressed in jeans, plaid shirt and black fedora with his hair tied back in a short ponytail, Young certainly made every effort to look the part of the rural cowboy." Where the Pinks and the vocoder and synclavier of the Trans Band could be considered novelties intended to tease or amuse established Neil Young fans, the International Harvesters tour must also be seen as an effort to reach and cultivate a new audience. The opening acts for this June-October '84 tour included the Judds, Johnny Paycheck, and Waylon Jennings, and at one show Neil sang a duet with Willie Nelson (and two with Waylon).

And in what must be considered a conscious or subconscious effort to blow away his old hippie audience and image, two days after the Austin City Limits taping Young gave a speech on stage in New Orleans praising President Ronald Reagan (during an election year). John Robertson: "Nothing in Young's career damaged his reputation in Europe as much as his partial defence of President Reagan." When *Rolling Stone* asked him in 1988, Young explained, "I was very disillusioned with Jimmy Carter. I don't think we should have ever given back the Panama Canal. I also think it was wrong to have let the armed forces deteriorate . . . I'm not a hawk, but I just don't believe that you can talk from a weakness." Northern man, better keep your head. Dear reader, I (PW) must admit I find this distressing and infuriating. Everybody's entitled to their opinion, and I don't doubt he was sincere. And it is true that when a Bob Dylan or Neil Young or Mick Jagger again and again seems to speak your private or generational truth boldly and accurately in his songs, it's natural to feel a close kinship and attachment . . . and quite a rude awakening when you and he come to an identifiable fork in the road. Abandoned by my revolutionary comrade! Oh hell. The worst part is it makes me (us) look so stupid for having put his opinions on a pedestal in

the first place. Okay, gotta sort out the nature of my relationship with the poet/singer/musician/icon. Hey, if Neil Young
and Stephen Stills have had such a dreadful time getting along
with each other, maybe it's okay for me and Neil to have our
bumpy moments too.

Anyway, can't argue with the man's love for his daughter.
"Amber Jean" (isn't that a marvellous name they came up
with, Amber Jean Young?) is a sleeper. Like "If You Got Love,"
it's a powerful and expressive work of music that seems
likeable but simple (or forgettable) at first, and then after
repeated listens can feel more and more immediate, articulate, profound. Try it. The performance, as opposed to the
song, grows on me and touches me in deeper and deeper
places the more familiar I am with it – like my experience of
certain jazz album tracks. Indeed, the image of Neil Young as a
song composer who learned to write when he was an adolescent in an instrumental band that only added words gradually,
for me illuminates the connection between "Cortez the Killer"
and "Cowgirl in the Sand" and "Love and Only Love" and
"Powderfinger," etc., and "Amber Jean." It's not an obviously
instrumental song. But the more I listen the more I notice how
appealing the instrumental passages are, and how much they
set the mood that draws me deeper and deeper into the
performance on repeated listens. Indeed, I begin to hear the
whole performance as a gentle, good-humored, hugely appealing instrumental with words and singing joining the music
almost two-thirds of the time. Adding to the mood and not
breaking it. Quite an accomplishment. Neil Young has written
a number of songs which are great because the words don't
interfere with or distract from the mood the music creates. Or,
to put it another way, he has a gift for communicating feelings
through the music he brings forth as bandmember and
bandleader, as well as vocalist and songwriter. We're aware of
his significant accomplishments in this realm with Crazy
Horse, mostly in loud rockin' electric guitar songs. But that's
not all there is to Neil Young. The same gift can extend itself

into other combinations of instruments and sounds as long as the music is rhythm-based in some fashion and rhythm and melody and song structure and imagery can all play off each other. "Amber Jean" 's a fine example.

And its simple words become a marvellous and effective part of an intricate and very gratifying musical tapestry. Music creates feelings and words amplify them, or anyway sustain them. "Every morning got sun to shine/Every day got plenty of time/Every night there's a moon so fine/There for you my Amber Jean." Okay, it's a lullaby. So is "Summertime." And both songs are capable of saying a tremendous amount about the relationship between the singer and his or her life in this place and time. Love that bridge, and particularly the instrumental passage that kicks it off: "Amber Jean, oh, Amber Jean/Prettiest eyes I've ever seen." And the reel from there to the return of the first verse. And the other 37-second reel that opens the performance. And the way the whole thing comes to a climax and soft landing and completion. "There for you my Amber Jean." Don't know the lady, but the song says a lot to me. It's good to see a major contemporary songwriter write about love for one's children as an expression of love for life. Please notice also the way some lyrics can be suggestive of autobiographical and universal issues in what I might call the "Heart of Gold" tradition except this song hasn't been a hit, hasn't even been released: "Still some lines that should get crossed/Still some coins that might be tossed/Still some love that hasn't been lost." So what?, you might think, but wait till this music and this vocal get their hooks in you.

On the other hand, track 9, "Let Your Fingers Do the Talking," doesn't go anywhere for me no matter how much I listen. The booklet notes that this unreleased song is also known as "Good Phone," and comments: "A funny humorous song done tongue-in-cheek style akin to Chuck Berry's 'Memphis, Tennessee.' " Well, first, what he sings (three times) in the song is "walking," not "talking." Pete Long calls the song "Fingers." Anyway, the song is certainly intended to be humorous, and

I'd credit it with being extremely clever in a country lyricist fashion a couple of times ("I'm listed under broken hearts" and "I'm your disconnected number now and you're a private line"), but I don't think it succeeds in being funny. And the suggestion that "Memphis" is tongue-in-cheek I consider mistaken. Chuck's song is a sly, poignant classic (and a compact short story), and its only similarity to "Fingers" is that both songs mention telephone calls.

While I'm putting in my two cents worth, I have to report that I find the phrase "when you gave good phone" awkward and inappropriate. Somehow it offends me, even me who loves the more respectful and outrageous references to oral sex in "Bite the Bullet" and "Saddle Up the Palomino" ("I wanna lick the platter/The gravy doesn't matter"). In general, I think "Fingers" an awkward piece of writing, lyrically and musically. I even find the opening lines ("a man had his own way") slightly sexist and dumb, and if it's meant to be a persona, then the problem is the persona isn't sustained and doesn't come through (nor do I notice much evidence of irony). Okay, you can't win 'em all. The song was performed at half of the NY & the International Harvesters shows in '84, and considered for but not included on the '85 *Old Ways* album. I'm not saying it's terrible, just acknowledging the unsurprising fact that not every unreleased Neil Young song and performance is praiseworthy and remarkable. This is a song/performance that doesn't make you believe the narrator/singer's heart is aching, even though he says so. I betcha if his heart had been aching he would have got it across (listen to the '74 "Pardon My Heart" again). And musically, this is – in clear contrast to "Amber Jean" – not a song that says a lot through its music and sound. The instrumental breaks are short and rather routine. Altogether the track strikes me as well-intentioned (maybe he thinks it's naughty to steal a line from phone company advertisements), but mostly further indication that country music singer/songwriter was not Neil's calling in life after all. Tom T. Hall does it better, not to mention Willie.

The third track on *Cowboy* from the Austin City Limits show 9/25/84 is a semi-acoustic performance of "Helpless." The booklet comments, quite aptly and accurately: "Among Neil's most popular songs. Probably the best live version ever is the touching duet performed with Joni Mitchell at The Last Waltz, but listen to this one . . ." Booklet goes on to quote Neil: *"I wrote this in New York, 1970. For Tim Hardin."* This is a misquote of Neil's *Decade* liner notes. He actually said, "Wrote this in New York, 1970. I'd like to send it out to Tim Hardin." So he dedicated it to Hardin in 1976 when he wrote that comment; but of course the person he was thinking of when he wrote the song was himself and his present-day connection to his child-self growing up in north Ontario, and the way our adult feelings of helplessness awaken evocations of deep feelings from childhood. So the song is not about Tim Hardin, but it's understandable that Neil thought to "send it out" to the great singer/songwriter who had long been a junkie but who was more helpless than ever in 1976, still alive but no longer able to record or perform. And it's suggestive that Neil very often, in his solo sets in the middle of the Harvesters shows in '84, sang "Helpless" immediately after "The Needle and the Damage Done." Had it become another heroin lament in his mind? I don't think so, but part of the song's power from the day Neil recorded it with CSNY was its ability to turn around and suddenly seem mysteriously topical, a report on our hidden but collective feelings of helplessness. In any case, I hugely recommend to any appreciator of this song the late John Bauldie's essay on "Helpless" (the best thing ever written on the subject) in the *Broken Arrow* anthology *On a Journey through the Past*. Among other things, Bauldie convincingly demonstrates that Young had been reading, or was otherwise in touch with the spirit of, Russian novelist Maxim Gorky.

And I'm happy to report that the Austin City Limits performance of "Helpless" is another magical and very powerful (and subtly different) rendering of this great song. An intimate moment with a committed performer. Another treasure.

So will you believe me if I say the fourth 9/25/84 *Cowboy* track is another great performance? You don't have to, because I'm going to quote Pete Long, from *Ghosts on the Road*: "In mid-September he made one further addition [to the set list] which seemed rather out of context but perhaps indicated a subtle shift of direction. Towards the end of some sets Young would introduce a song about 'a man who let the dark side get control of him one night' and for the next quarter of an hour or more the band would power through an extended improvised version of 'Down by the River' that invariably brought the house down. Justifiably so. Although substantially different in instrumentation, it generally proved to be the equal of any previous arrangement." Wow. And a pretty fair assessment, I'd say. Not that this could replace the original album track in my affections (mostly for the effect of the ethereal vocal intro and outro on that one), but it is an absolutely astonishing example of Neil Young rock music – hard rock *and* musically and emotionally intelligent (not the lyrics but the feel of the performance, which is primarily instrumental). And *very* hard and not at all a parody of itself. Truly moving.

How is this possible without Crazy Horse? Well, same bandleader and lead guitar player. Anyway, the International Harvesters hereby claim their honors as one of the better bands Neil Young has performed with in his long career. And "Down by the River" demonstrates its extraordinary durability and ever-surprising depths of expressiveness. Wow indeed. Pack a suitcase when you go to visit this nine-minute track. You could get lost for hours.

The *Cowboy* booklet quotes Neil on "Down by the River": *"There's no real murder in it. It's about blowing your thing with a chick. See, now in the beginning it's 'I'll be on your side, you be on mine.' It could be anything. Then the chick thing comes in. Then at the end it's a whole other thing. It's a plea . . . a desperation cry."* Good quote. Johnny Rogan notes this was said around the time of the song's appearance (1969) and adds a quote from fifteen years later where "Young seemed more willing to accept that there was genuine violence at work in the composition." NY: *"Every once in a while you write a song and you do it many times. One night . . . you think, 'What's happening? I'm living this song!' . . . a man let the dark side come through a little too bright . . . he took a little stroll . . . he met this woman . . . he reached down into his pocket and pulled a little revolver out . . ."* (Possibly a 1984 song introduction.)

Which leaves me wondering, what does the song mean to me? Obsessiveness and loss, among other things. Those other things are important to me, but I notice I'm not sure what they are. I do recognize the song as being a young man's literary effort extending the mood of such powerful and mysterious folk songs as "Banks of the Ohio" and "Pretty Polly." In that sense I like his earlier "symbolic" interpretation. But anyway, whatever it means, and however differently it may be understood by each listener, what doesn't seem to vary much is the intensity and the gratification-to-the-point-of joy that it delivers. Scary subject. Ecstatic music. Neil in his *Decade* liner notes reminds us that he wrote it "the same day as 'Cowgirl in the Sand.' Lying in bed sweating with scraps of paper covering the bed. 103° fever in bed in Topanga." Well, with the International Harvesters in fall '84 he certainly does recapture the song's original feverish inspiration. What is it? Um, something that burns very bright. And endures. "This much madness is too much sorrow . . ."

Stunning performance. And there ain't nothing country about it.

* * *

Cowboy 3 track 12, "Interstate," is another marvel, and a good example of why I say Neil Young's body of work is hard to

139

"make sense of," by which I mean, to arrange one's thoughts about. First of all it was unreleased for eleven years, and then officially released in 1996 in a very oblique manner ("bonus track" on the rare American vinyl version of the *Broken Arrow* album and on various singles, not on the CD or cassette). Many dedicated fans had already heard it, of course, on a bootleg album or concert tape, and in fact "Interstate" placed #2 in the listing of best unreleased Neil Young songs as judged by fans who took part in Damon Ogden's 1994 poll. (49 fans sent in lists of their 60 favorite songs and 20 favorite albums, ranked numerically. 283 songs received votes. "Powderfinger" was the clear favorite, followed by "Like a Hurricane," "Pocahontas," "Rockin' in the Free World," "Cortez," "Cowgirl," "Down by the River," "My My, Hey Hey," "Thrasher," and "Cinnamon Girl." And so forth. 38 of the 283 were unreleased songs. Of them, the songs that received the most votes were "Ordinary People" – coming on *Cowboy* disc 4 – and "Interstate.")

Which "Interstate"? The version Young included as a bonus track on his '96 album was recorded in 1990 at the *Ragged Glory* sessions, acoustic, with Crazy Horse. The version on *Cowboy* is a live performance from September 1985 with the slightly revamped '85 International Harvesters, and was originally intended for release in early '86 on a benefit EP Young wanted to put out of five new songs recorded live . . . but Geffen Records refused to allow this, even though Young wanted it to be a fund-raiser for the Farm Aid project he'd been a leader and prime instigator of in fall '85. The two versions have similar arrangements but with very different instrumentation, if that's possible; the same words, but with the second and third verse switched and no repeat of the opening lines at the end of the song in 1990 (very effective in the '85 version). On balance, the *feel* of the two performances is quite different, and I can understand honest disagreements regarding which of the two is preferable. You might like them equally. I greatly prefer the 1985, the *Cowboy* version. Both performances have a kind of beauty, but this one, I think, is by far the prettier. What stands out most of all for me in '85 are the fabulous piano solos (and that fabulous melody/rhythm line he's been given to play) by Hargus "Pig" Robbins, new to the Harvesters and previously known to me for his fine work with Bob Dylan on *Blonde on Blonde*.

So if you manage to get hold of a copy of "Interstate," and focus in on one of these versions, where do you place the song in your mental picture of Neil Young's work? Closer to *Harvest* than to *Ragged Glory*, but that doesn't tell us much – particularly because "Interstate" has another characteristic Neil Young quality, which is one-of-a-kind-ness. You know, like "Pocahontas." Or "Expecting to Fly." Nothing else is exactly like it. So how can we characterize it? Is it from his country period? Yeah, in terms of some of the '85 instrumentation, but it's much more accurate to say it's from his Neil Young period. One of the many. Not particularly weird. Not hugely romantic, although there is a nice romantic quality to the melody and the feel of the music including the singer's voice. Not even a love song, except in the sense that it is about feelings of separation from loved ones (specifically, children, and presumably thus also mate, home, family). And not helpless or very sad feelings. Mature and appropriate feelings. Stuck inside of Mobile with the Memphis blues again, but not making a big fuss about it. Just mentally questioning and reviewing one's priorities.

"Children are laughing in the sun/I count the voices one by one/But I'm not there to share the fun/I'm out on the interstate." Could be a good trucker song, but Neil's not posturing for the market. In the third verse (in 1985) he gets more particular: "I'm happy singing in a crowd/The lights are bright, the music's loud/I like to look at every face/But out here on the interstate/I can hear a soft voice calling/Calling me to bring my guitar home." Exquisite. Not overdone. Just wonderful.

And yet the song is not about the words. Or it is insofar as

141

they define the subject matter, the feeling the listener picks up, the "meaning" we hear in the performance. But again only 40% of the performance is devoted to singing words. The rest of the time the ensemble sing through their instruments, especially the piano, but fiddle and guitars and bass and drums are also very expressive (including a superb banjo solo after the first verse). This is actually American song not unrelated to Gershwin, the classical music side of the popular form. Neil's sonata. Not obviously. Not as a "style." But in fact, what is accomplished here musically is exactly the sort of thing that Neil Young deserves to be remembered for (whether the world notices, or agrees with me, or not). There have been moments when, based on results (as evidenced by tapes of performances), he has been an inspired bandleader/composer/performer not unworthy of comparison to Duke Ellington in his element. I personally argue that the true history of American (and world) music in this century will be a history of music performed live as much as a history of music recorded in recording studios. Both places, stage, studio, something happens amongst the performers as an ensemble (remember what I was saying 30 years ago about popsicle sticks?), often inspired by the singer and/or bandleader, or just by each other and the moment, and out of this a thing is created, a performance, a unit of musical art. On a good night, on a very good night, what is created may be as good as this 1985 performance of Neil Young's "Interstate." In which case it may influence and bring joy and understanding to generations of musicians and listeners yet to come, if we're so fortunate as to have a good recording of the moment, making the unit of art repeatable and durable. I envision a future in which some people will continue to enjoy live recordings of Ellington and Young and their bands, and even learn from them. That vision or faith is one of the reasons I write essays and books like this. So you know how it felt to a listener at the time. Just as I know something, listening to this track, about how it felt to be that performer, that band, out on the interstate that year.

* * *

Rock 'N' Roll Cowboy, Disc 3, ends with three more (colorful and affectionate) postcards from 1985: "Grey Riders," "Nothin' Is Perfect," and "Southern Pacific." All live with the International Harvesters from the summer '85 tour. The first two were new songs, included on the benefit EP Geffen wouldn't let Neil release. The last is a 1981 song, from *RE-AC-TOR*, as if to say: the values expressed and sonics explored in this show are not so new to me as you might imagine. I've always been interested in the sounds of galloping horses ("Grey Riders") and rushing freight trains ("Southern Pacific") and attracted to the simple and earnest everyday values of the honest working person. "I ain't no brakeman, ain't no conductor/But I would be though, if I was younger." I think that's a marvellous couplet. I do find I'm too attached to, fond of, the 1981 album performance to really give my heart to the 1985 "big train sound" live version. So it's not my favorite "Southern Pacific," but it is a chance for me to say it's an underappreciated song. And as a postcard it serves as a cheerful portrait of the kind of fun Dad liked to have with his friends out on that interstate. Band-as-a-toy. Hey, it's an American tradition.

So that's track 15 and last, almost eight minutes of "a train chuggling down the line," in the words of the *Cowboy* booklet annotator. Track 14, "Nothin' Is Perfect," has the distinction of having been premiered (first live performance; it had been attempted in a recording studio two weeks earlier) in front of probably the largest audience Neil Young has ever performed to – the Live Aid benefit concert and broadcast, July 13, 1985. The other songs he chose to play were "Helpless," "Powderfinger" (both with the Harvesters),

"Sugar Mountain," "The Needle and the Damage Done" (both solo) and "Only Love Can Break Your Heart" (with CSNY).

"Nothin' Is Perfect" is, to my ear, the most overtly country song (musically and verbally) Young wrote and performed in this era. But again, it doesn't suggest that he had any particular flair for this kind of songwriting. What he says sounds sincere, even though he's self-consciously speaking in a "country" or "middle America" language – indeed, this is the only Neil Young song I can think of just now in which God is a character. "Nothin' is perfect in God's perfect plan/Look in the shadows to see/He only gave us the good things so we'd understand/What life without them would be." Um, I've heard men I disagreed with philosophically preach much more convincing sermons. The music's not too special either. But as a postcard from Neil, it is good to hear that there's lots of love in his house and "so much to be happy about." A song of gratitude to God and pride in one's community. Not perfect. But sincere.

I'm working backwards to track 13, "Grey Riders," because it's another high point (nice to close a chapter on), full of the quirkiness and contact with the child inside that are characteristic of Neil Young at his best, or anyway that side of him that keeps surprising us and keeps us coming back for more. It's also further evidence that Neil Young and the International Harvesters did indeed have something special to offer. And also, with "Interstate," further evidence that Geffen Records didn't reject Young's work because it was substandard but because the Geffen honchos were morons.

Neil thought enough of "Grey Riders" to use it as his summer '85 show-closer almost every night, not long after full-force performances of "Down by the River" and "Powderfinger." I connect this wondrous ghost story/western rave-up with his ability to contact his child side because the song makes me feel that the songwriter/bandleader must have been thrilled and spooked as a child by Vaughn Monroe's great 1949 hit "(Ghost) Riders in the Sky" (and again as an adult by the Shadows' 1980 version), and therefore determined to capture that mood in a song of his own. So he wrote this sequel, in which his protagonist tells of being awakened on a cold night by mysterious hoofbeats "across my lawn . . . I looked again and they all were gone." This is marvellous writing: "Their hair was long and grey, they heard just one voice calling/Grey Riders on the morning sky/The sun made diamonds of their road-weary eyes." And the music, Neil's guitar, the piano, the rhythm section and the whole ensemble, is as good as the lyrics or even better. Words and music inspire each other, and the listener can feel/see the protagonist's vision. Gorgeous song. Delightful piece of music. I don't know about "country," but the "western" side of Neil Young comes through very powerfully here, like he was born to make this kind of music. At least once.

The composition/arrangement sounds to me likes it's divided into movements. Very skilfully. All strung together by that infernal galloping. The "sound effects" side of Neil is very well served here. I get a lot of pleasure from this track; when I'm in the mood and get on its wavelength, which I can easily do, it seems to me deserving of a place in the canon alongside other very successful sonic sculptures. Indeed, I suggest one can learn a lot about the musical ideas that drive Neil and Crazy Horse on *Ragged Glory* and *Weld* by listening to this International Harvesters performance. First of all, the last 30 seconds precisely foretell the feedback crescendo structures of the *Weld*-era song-endings. Without the feedback, like a barebones demonstration. And then the long instrumental passages in the middle and near the end of "Grey Riders" have that special energy and attack of the *Ragged Glory* epics. Listen to this track just to understand what the artist is after. It's like a good example of, and a blueprint of, his basic strategy. How about the way every time he sings the chorus (four times) "That voice was calling/And it cut through the night/'Come on boys, let her go!' " the word "go" is immediately followed

145

by a glorious instrumental outburst? "That voice" indeed. So evocative. Another unreleased, almost unknown, expressive sonic sculpture by the master.

Worthy to close the show shortly after "Powderfinger." Which is another short story, and in its case I imagine the songwriter inspired by something he remembered reading in a high school Canadian/American history class, that led him eventually to create a very young protagonist who found himself caught up in his family's/era's/nation's deadly conflicts . . . On songs like these, lyricist and guitarist and bandleader and singer/performer work very well together. Not only sonic sculptures but sonic short stories. Neil Young, inventor and proprietor.

A good year, 1985. Never mind *Old Ways*. Just get hold of a tape of an International Harvesters show, and find out what was really going on behind the Geffen curtain.

11

"Rockin' in the Free World"

Written in 1992 for a book entitled Rock and Roll: The 100 Best Singles. *My list, which also included "For What It's Worth," was in chronological order, so this great 1989 single was the next-to-last piece in the book, just before "Smells Like Teen Spirit."*

The death of rock and roll. Well deserved. Leave it to Neil Young to sum it all up in one bitter, uncompromising, off-the-wall, unshakeable image:

> "I see a woman in the night
> With a baby in her hand . . .
> Now she puts the kid away and she's gone to get a hit
> She hates her life and what she's done to it
> There's one more kid that will never go to school
> Never get to fall in love, never get to be cool
> Keep on rockin' in the free world"

I get a physical feeling in my chest and throat and around my eyes every time I hear these words (and the hard-rocking music that accompanies them). It's adrenaline, anger, bitterness, a dangerous sort of righteous emotion (with an edge of violent joy, I admit) that makes me want to smash my fist through a wall. A momentary willingness/desire to burn down everything that's corrupt in my life and my civilization. "Keep on rockin' . . ." Neil's 1989 sarcasm is clearly and appropriately aimed at those in the West who feel self-righteous about the

147

fall of Communism. Three cheers for the free world, indeed. But it's also about the musical movement that has become one of the primary international symbols of the Western/"free enterprise" lifestyle. Rock and roll. Symbol of (as Neil says in the title of the album this single starts and finishes) freedom. And, he seems to be saying, and I heartily agree, freedom without responsibility, without caring, without awareness, is a very ugly thing. Keep on rockin' in the free world . . .

Everything gets old. And anything can be reborn. But not everything will be. There is hope, however, as long as we can look into the heart of our own ugliness and self-dishonesty and see it for what it is (and be moved to make changes). I wish this record had been a #1 hit. But I wonder how many enthusiastic rock fans would still have missed the point.

Rock and roll is not dead. But maybe it should be. Everything turns into its opposite after a while; the noise that breaks open and challenges the façade of our reality becomes in time an important part of the façade, sedating us and reinforcing our imprisonment behind the walls of illusion. I'm not saying the primary purpose of (real) rock and roll is political. I'm saying the primary purpose of all art is personal awakening, and complacency and laziness and self-pity and fear of self-honesty create a death in life, a state of mind that rapidly turns all input to Muzak. I guess I'm saying rock and roll is a set of values. That's obviously a personal opinion, but hey, who sold you on the idea that there is such a thing as an opinion that isn't personal? Let's start from zero here.

Rock and roll is not dead. Neil Young's next album after *Freedom, Ragged Glory* (1990), is the loudest and finest of his career so far. Great music is happening even as I write and you read, around the corner in some club with bad lighting and a minimal cover charge. Check it out. But avoid the museums please, the rock and roll halls of fame and the slick magazines that enshrine them, pretty pictures mixed with sexy ads for booze and tobacco and blue jeans. The stadium tours. The press conferences. Movies about Jimi Hendrix. TV mini-series about Johnny Rotten. Let's make a distinction please. Or choke on our own vomit, like many a rock star and advanced civilization before us.

I like the sound of Neil Young's voice. I like the apocalyptic sloppy dead-eye accuracy of his band's bombastic accompaniment. I like the tension, maybe contradiction, between sound and message. I like the raising of unanswerable questions. I like the beat. I like the explosive guitars. I like to turn up the volume. I like the way some songs tell the truth about what goes on around here sometimes.

12

Harvest Moon

At the end of '92 I decided I wanted to write about new records again, and so I revived Crawdaddy! *as a newsletter, thirteen years after it went out of business and 24 years after I'd resigned as founding editor. For the first new issue I wrote a huge essay discussing* Automatic for the People *by R.E.M. and other recent albums by Bruce Cockburn, Television, Bob Dylan, Sonya Hunter and Neil Young. The essay was called "Six White Horses," and* Crawdaddy! *continues to this day as an idiosyncratic subscription newsletter. So here's the* Harvest Moon *part of "Six White Horses," an atypical piece for this book in which I report on a new Neil Young album that didn't thrill me. It did place #10 in the 1994 poll of fans' favorite albums, so evidently my reaction was not shared by many listeners (*HM *was also NY's biggest-selling album since* Comes a Time*). Well, I don't claim or try to be infallible, just honest.*

Harvest Moon (Neil Young) is strange. It's the nearest thing to a failure among the records discussed here. There isn't a single great song on it, the lyrics throughout are unsuccessful at best, banal and embarrassing at worst, and some of the melodies and arrangements go over the line into real sappiness. And yet there's something about it . . .

It sounds like I'm trying to find something nice to say about a mediocre record because I like the artist. No. Neil Young is a great songwriter/performer/creative force, but he's famously uneven, and if this were another forgettable record like *This Note's for You* or *Long May You Run,* I'd say so. But it's not. It's certainly not a great great great record like *Ragged Glory,* but it doesn't try to be. It's another concept album. No one

151

else has come close to making as many albums, each with its own goofy and/or brilliant (subtle and/or obvious) unifying "concept," as Neil Young – undisputed king of the concept album, yessir. And what an intriguing idea. *Harvest*, Neil's fourth solo album, released in 1972, was his most commercially successful record (if others have sold more units it's because the market as a whole has expanded; but no Neil Young album since *Harvest* has been close to as popular in absolute terms). Ever since then record companies have been pressuring Neil to "make another *Harvest*" . . . and now he's done it, self-consciously, 20th anniversary edition, same all-star band and backup singers, and with a title meant to ensure that you don't miss the point. But how to go about making "another" version of an existing album? Neil's answer hinges, as does the R.E.M. album, on the question of melody. It's a less successful, far less satisfying use of melody than R.E.M.'s triumph, but it is innovative in an odd way, and definitely rewarding if you can scale your expectations down far enough. Why bother? Because it might give you a new perspective on how music communicates. And because you might (I've been taking a survey of Neil fans whose musical tastes I respect, and the odds seem to be about 50/50, much higher than I expected) like it.

I'm not certain if I like it.

I know what most gets in the way of my liking it: the lyrics. Many of Neil's most endearing lyrics have been dumb and/or absurd ("Sugar Mountain," "Cowgirl in the Sand"), but they've *worked,* hit the bell, they still do, they're evocative, attractive, affecting, compelling. That doesn't mean, however, that any sort of nonsense can be okay just because it's dumb (or just because it's Neil). My friend Jonathan said he thinks "Natural Beauty" (the album-closer) may turn out to be a great song on repeated listenings; my response was and is that the central lyrical statement, "Natural beauty should be preserved like a monument," is such bad poetry, such an un-apt and inappropriate image, that it serves as an insurmountable obstacle to the song's achieving what it reaches for. Let's be literal, okay? Natural beauty should *not* be preserved like a monument. That's really the opposite of what Neil presumably wants to say. A monument is, to most of us (language is what we hear, images are what we see when the word is spoken, get away from that dictionary), a dead stone thing, solid unmoving and made by human hand. Natural beauty should be "preserved" (already a bad word) in the wild, as a living thing, un-emasculated, full of its native power. Like a hurricane. Natural beauty is an expression of God, of life, not (as the song's refrain seems to suggest) an abstract concept to be legislated. Truthfully, "should be," "preserved," and "like a monument" are all three inappropriate, clunky, contrary word-phrases to attach to the feeling of "natural beauty" that this song's melody and performance clearly strive to evoke. Is there some value, maybe, in the contradiction? No, not this time. It's too unconscious. There's no grace, not even goofy awkward wacked-out grace (Neil's specialty). It's a simple case of fucking up.

There are redeeming aspects. "Don't judge yourself too harsh my love" is a good line, could be a very moving line if the song weren't built on such a wimpy verbal foundation. I don't care for the "video screen" image but it's the sort of thing that Neil can force on me and make it work (stretch me, surprise me) when he's inspired. Some of the dumb words and images in *Ragged Glory* achieve transcendence (others, including entire songs, remain dumb, but I still flat-out love the album). But "Natural Beauty" is crippled by infelicitous word choices, and perhaps by something deeper: a shallowness or laziness that's in direct contrast to the commitment required by the subject matter. I grant you I like it better than "Mother Earth (Natural Anthem)" on *Ragged Glory*. Oh well. It would be easy to say Neil should stick to love songs (and angry/passionate/sensitive/confused observations on the rock and roll life). But in fact it's probably more true that he's reaching for something here he really cares about, and he

153

should go back and work it even harder, till he captures in sound story what's biting him, till he untangles this truth and makes it bite back with all the ferocity and beauty of "Over and Over" or "Love to Burn" or (soft sentimental melody/sound okay, just as long as it *works*) "After the Gold Rush."

David Geffen sued his former friend Neil to try to force him to deliver an album like this (rather than a computer music album followed by a '50s retro album followed by a mainstream country album) when he was under contract to Geffen Records. Neil resisted. Now he takes up the challenge as though it's an aural experiment, like 1991's *Arc* (a 35-minute CD composition made up entirely of feedback segments from the Neil/Crazy Horse tour earlier that year; a surprisingly likeable piece of music).

Taken purely as sound, *Harvest Moon* works. The weird thing is, it works best at arm's length, CD playing in the background while you go about the everyday business of your life. To call an album "background music" is an insult where I come from, though Brian Eno's Ambient series may have removed some of that stigma; the thing about Neil Young, however, is that he's made so many albums he has a right to narrowcast them, and this one may just retain its dignity by virtue of the fact that it's self-consciously "adult contemporary" (aging ex-rockers seek mellow sounds, identify Neil Young with memories of "Heart of Gold" and his sensitive singer-songwriter days) and that Neil *knows* that them AC fans aren't listening too, er, *closely*. So he gathers up the *Harvest* musicians and backup vocalists (big-name talent used modestly: James Taylor, Linda Ronstadt), goes for similar instrumentation, mix, overall *sound,* and then consciously recasts the memorable melodies and rhythms of the earlier record into slightly new combinations, a little like Holland-Dozier-Holland rewriting the last Motown hit to make the next one, but lovingly, and with a wink (like the wink HDH gave us when they put out a Four Tops hit called "Same Old Song"). A sonic patchwork meant to be heard peripherally. Okay, but . . .

But where's the meat? *Ragged Glory* recreated and updated the sound of "Down by the River" and "Like a Hurricane" so successfully that it actually becomes a new reference point, quite possibly Neil's best album. *Harvest Moon* recreates but doesn't update the sound of *Harvest,* and the identity of its own that it takes on is a very modest one. "Come a little bit closer, hear what I have to say," he sings to his wife on the title track, and if we take him at his word we find that there's very little to hear, neither lyrically ("From Hank to Hendrix" is promising, but the payoff line – "Can we make it last, like a musical ride?" – is almost as bad as the dreadful "American Dream" stuff Neil wrote for the last CSNY album) nor melodically ("Unknown Legend" promises good old musical delights in its intro, and then bops us with every possible steel guitar and backup vocal cliché before the first verse is over).

"I'm still in love with you" is a perfectly valid message, but we've heard much more convincing expressions of it on the last two studio albums, *Freedom* and *Ragged Glory.* Ironically, what's lacking on this journey into sensitive-songwriter land is vulnerability. The original *Harvest* was in fact a very uneven record ("There's a World" is Neil at his emptiest and most overblown, "Alabama" is musically clichéd and horribly condescending lyrically, and "Words (Between the Lines of Age)" is just boring), but the vulnerability of the best songs was totally authentic and I still get my guts twisted listening to both the sound and the words of "Out on the Weekend" or "A Man Needs a Maid." *Harvest Moon* is an experiment to see what happens when you sample yourself, when you bring your famous old sounds and melodies back together for a 20-year reunion to see what's become of them and us, without compromising your self-honesty. And what it proves, I think, is that though melody may be at the heart of the magic, sound and melody alone are not enough. The R.E.M. album achieves what it achieves because each band-member struggles mightily and at considerable personal risk to pursue the uncharted paths that a good melody can point us towards, over and over, song after song. And as a result the ambiguities and obfuscations in both lyrics and performance can take on profound meaningfulness, moment to moment, for both performer and listener. Neil's ambiguities and obfuscations have done the same for us at many's the past moment, and will again, but not on *Harvest Moon.* And yet . . .

"I wanna see you dance again." He knows what we want. And maybe we love him because we identify with his conflicted desire to satisfy us and to withhold himself at the same time. Maybe – in fact I'm sure of it – this album that comes down strongly on the side of withholding is more palatable and reassuring to our everyday selves than albums that scream "You'd better take a chance!!" to cacophonous Crazy Horse accompaniment. And wasn't *Harvest* all about self-conflict in the first place? Yes. But I don't just want to see you dance. I want you to win my heart. Every time. *Harvest Moon* doesn't deliver. But it does add an important new footnote to the saga of how it feels to try to be (both in public and private) "Neil Young."

13

Sleeps with Angels

This was written for Crawdaddy! *in autumn 1994. It might be, along with "Searching for a Heart of Gold," my personal favorite of these review-essays.*

'We have been trying to construct a language and a history." That's what I wrote in my journal a few months ago, in the first flush of excitement, first week of listening to Neil Young's new album *Sleeps with Angels*. Now it occurs to me that what we are (mostly unconsciously) trying to accomplish as we listen to the never-ending flow of new "rock and roll" records is also or more particularly to erase and forget a language and history that aren't true enough any longer, more restrictive than helpful, not close enough to home. Trying to forget and remember. Reprogram the beast.

The beast is me. This is not a boast or confession. It's just a piece of information – I, the creature listening, am a part of, extension of, this undefined larger thing within which I live and with whom I love and struggle. Just a reminder. Safety-pinned to my shirt by my mother in case I wander off.

Books will be written and TV programs filmed about the origins and true significance of the safety pin.

Artefacts. "Jim, I want you to take this entire sector and digitize it." "Yeah and what about all the people who inhabit it?" "So now they'll live forever. Anyway, we need the space."

"Embracing you with this/Must be the one you love/Must be the one whose magic touch/Can change your mind." Neil

Young goes deep. How does he do that?

He does it not by calculation but by intention. The extraordinary power of *Sleeps with Angels* and the very different *Ragged Glory* (the Neil fans I've met who don't yet appreciate *Sleeps* seem to be having trouble with their expectations of what a Neil + Crazy Horse album ought to sound like) versus the mysterious wimpiness of *Harvest Moon* and *Unplugged* can be explained I think by supposing that, consciously or unconsciously, Young didn't intend for the last-mentioned albums to make strong statements. Maybe they're even intended for that part of him and of his audience that doesn't want to kick up the shit. This doesn't have to be cynical. It can be (and, looking at his oeuvre as a whole, is) part of a conscious process of exploration. And Young's success as an artist, I suggest, is partly due to his willingness to explore things and carry them to completion even at the risk of coming up dry. Holding back his own judgmental side may result in albums as empty as *Long May You Run* or most of the Geffen offerings, but I believe it is also what allows an *Everybody Knows This Is Nowhere* or *Tonight's the Night* or *Sleeps with Angels* to come into existence.

Breaking rules. Not just for the sake of breaking them. But because you have this tiny intuition, which you follow in the face of all the inevitable doubts, that this could be the path that will allow you to express or give form to your feelings. Very often it's about what you're not doing more than what you're doing (not requiring yourself to stay within accept-able distortion levels and other universal standards of musical professionalism) (not caring that these two different songs have virtually the same backing track . . . maybe even getting excited about the idea). Freedom. Is not a concept. It's a way of doing the work. And not license either. Because an artist's intention is a cruel taskmaster, and it's on you all the time. Insisting that you do things its way and, unreasonably, even insisting that you learn to love each new assignment. Rejecting hard-fought victories because there's not enough love in them yet, whatever that's supposed to mean. Shit. Back to the drawing board. Back to the salt mines.

Back to the miracle factory. The fucker's done it again.

"Safeway Cart" is a masterpiece. Riding around Germany on the DeutschBahn this past October I'd hear the squeal of metal on metal as the train lurched out of the station and immediately think of the signature guitar sound that opens (and, in a subtle way, recurs throughout) "Safeway Cart." What is that? Not a melody, not a rhythm (the rhythm riff comes in around it), but not just a sound either – it's musical, got a bend in it, two notes so it sort of is a melodic hook of the crudest variety, crude but brilliant in its sophistication, a wail, ancient lament, and then the ticking of that bass line, "like a Safeway cart rolling through the street." I wonder if Neil's overseas listeners know that Safeway is a supermarket (yes we do ... Ed) and that homeless people adopt these carts, but maybe it's as unnecessary as explaining McDonalds (Trans Ams of course are another story) ... The six and a half minutes go by in an ecstatic instant and I want to play it again and again. Music as natural and as powerful as breathing.

Neil Young remembered the assignment. Rock and roll has always (since Elvis) been a topical music. It's about our physical (and emotional, situational) environment and the way it feels to live in it. I went to hear Drive Like Jehu in a local club and I couldn't tell you anything about the words (did they use words?) or the structures of the songs, but they remembered the assignment too. Everything they did spoke eloquently of how it feels to be in this body this year reading this newspaper dealing with the reality or illusion of being exactly this many years old, and just filled with the trembling repressed chaotic uncertainty and power/powerlessness of it all. "Driveby ..." "He sleeps with angels tonight." Kurt Cobain matters not because of himself any more but because we actually are connected through our contemplation of him. "He's always on someone's mind." This is a fact. "The king is gone, but he's not forgotten." It's not about sentimentality. It's

159

about the immortality of our collective need. "It's a random kind of thing." Neil Young has recorded an album about murder and suicide (and the power of love) that is not at all exploitative (almost impossible to achieve in the grunge or rap context, but remember old Neil ain't gonna sell that many albums anyway, western hero though he may unquestionably be). A cry from the heart. An album for 1994.

I'm not done with "Safeway Cart" yet. It's a masterpiece exactly in the sense of being a mature, fully-realized work by a master, as measured by (the only acceptable yardstick) the extent to which it touches the listener. Real as the day is long. What is the nature of this mastery? Not great singing. Not great lyrics. Not even great guitar playing – though that's certainly the element most easily singled out, western hero equals guitar hero, which as with Hendrix is our shorthand for saying master of sonic space. The song's power, its essence, lies in its overall and moment-to-moment sonic picture, the space and feelings (including sense of motion) that its sound creates. In this the sound of the instruments (and their amps and the room etc.) is very important, like Matisse's colors, but just as important (as with Matisse's canvases) is the placement of the colors and forms/images in relation to each other and in relation to their actual or conceptual container, the edges of the canvas, the space and time of the musical performance.

At 00 seconds the train squeal begins, eventually fading at 07. But its primary impact is in the first two seconds, firmly embedding itself in our brains (I realize that in addition to having just railwayed all over Germany, I've been living since early this year in a place where the trains go by, and blow their whistles, several times each hour; the sound is inside me) before bass and drums come in at 02, true start of the song, transition from random loud ambience (you are Here) to motion, order, purpose. Almost simultaneous with the beginning of the rhythmic pulse is the launching of the dominant (contrapuntal) riff, a wonderful groaning sound, bass slide, two continuous descending notes (though sometimes the second is only implied), or, if you will, attack/release.

At about 29 seconds the first bit of guitar punctuation (similar to but sonically and melodically distinct from the bass guitar groan; since both are punctuations we never actually hear them both at once, though the time-space between them is forever changing, a dance) comes in, and then at 36 the start of the vocal. "Like a Safeway cart . . ." and we immediately know, intuitively if not consciously, that the phrase refers to the *sound* we're hearing, that insistent thump thump thump thump of the pulsing rhythm line (bass and/or basslike keyboard plus understated drum), this *feeling* the sound expresses, now it gets a visual image (shopping cart rolling by itself – if there's a homeless man attached he's entirely invisible – through the city at dawn, in the ghetto, darkness on the edge of town, desolation row). Lyrically this is a "Like a" song, like "Like an Inca" or "Just Like Tom Thumb's Blues" or "Like a Hurricane" or "Like a Rolling Stone." Simile. *Something* is like a Safeway cart and/or "a sandal mark on the Savior's feet." What? It. What the song is about. Get the concept? Let it pulse through you –

The lyrics serve purely to locate and evoke. They do not attempt to tell a story, nor should they, although the song itself is so eloquent (particularly the two non-verbal verses of squalling melodic guitar) that a story possibly emerges anyway, the protagonist of which is not the cart at all (maybe it's seen or imagined out a window) but a female named "baby" who's been watching much too much TV. I think she's the whole damn United States of America, but I'm not saying Neil intends that – although of course as a listener (this is what I mean by topicality) I *feel* that he does.

Everything opens out in those marvellous feedback guitar solos, articulate (full of poetry) verses in themselves, the first at 1:42 between vocal verses two and three; the second at 4:18, climax of the song, followed by a long vamp and a final vocal verse (repeat of the first) and still longer vamping (this pulse,

161

not the great punctuation, we're being told, is the real content of the song, feel it, feel it), with a fade starting at 6:08 and a lovely surprise organ part as a kiss and farewell almost at the end of the fade. So atmospheric. What a marvellous series of subtle and deliberate sound effects/melodic fragments this song is! The emotional high points are the guitar solos, screaming, crying, calling out to God, but every part of the song (even or especially the long repetitive vamps) is paradoxically rich in musical and sonic embellishment even as it constantly gives the impression of stark, spare simplicity. Cindy says the driverless cart gives her a feeling of spooky inanimateness, no people here, while Christ's sandal mark is a contrary image of the divine and distant becoming human. I also note the gentleness and poignance of a sandal mark where one is expecting stigmata. The song veers into self-parody (but consciously and effectively, the author breaking his own spell only to impose a greater one) when the two images are combined so that the cart rolls "past the Handi-Mart to the Savior's feet," conjuring an image perhaps of a big plastic Jesus out among the strip malls and fast food joints, hey maybe it's Bob's Big Boy. The main thing anyway is how amazingly graceful the entire sound sculpture is, portrait of the urban moment or whatever you want or feel it to be. Graceful and durable. I always liked "T-Bone" on *RE-AC-TOR*, and this seems to me a huge step further in a similar direction. How great that these musicians are so willing and able to co-operate in the creative process (i.e. the modesty and skilfulness of the drummer; rock and roll's not usually about understatement). I like the "Chopsticks" piano-like bass line following each vocal phrase, reminding me of ? and the Mysterians' "96 Tears" and many other fragments of our collective musical past.

"Trans Am," "Driveby," "Sleeps With Angels," and "Change Your Mind" are almost equally powerful – major works to place alongside "Cowgirl in the Sand" and "Rockin' in the Free World" and "Love to Burn" and "Tonight's the Night" and "Don't Be Denied" and oh, don't get me started. A really good

Neil Young album always sends me back into his catalog, an astonishing place I could wander around in for months. *Sleeps with Angels* as an album stands up gorgeously when confronted with all this brilliant history – its five potential classics are bolstered by seven other very likeable and intriguing tracks, and the entire 63 minutes goes by like a one-hour reunion with a close friend who has all these stories to share about what's going on in his life right now.

The un-self-conscious musicality of this album is stunning. It creates an environment in which it is possible to imagine ourselves as living within a greater human community linked by shared values, even as so much external evidence (the elections, the "news") seems to say otherwise. What music communicates above all else is immediacy of feeling. Barriers and defences dissolve. When this happens we feel our commonality. Every emotion is actually a constellation of feelings, and so it's not so easy to put what we feel into words. But words and music, in the motion-structure of a song, a performance, do the job very well. They allow for ambiguity. And they also speak eloquently the specifics of the emotional moment the music arises from.

Listen to "My Heart," the opening track. It has a childlike innocence about it, a sound and a deliberateness that for some reason make me think of the Nutcracker Suite or a Shirley Temple film. It's an unusual sound, lilting and magically still both at once, created by the harpsichord (if that's what it is) and the way it's played, and also by the vocal phrasing and the delicate, deliberate stops and starts of the melody, the arrangement. It works very consciously as an introduction, an invocation, announcement that we are departing on a journey together. The final track of the album, "A Dream That Can Last," brings back the instrumentation and the mood of "My Heart." It's a twin performance, a benediction and completion, this time punctuated by a slow, powerful drumbeat that somehow incorporates much of the musical territory that has been covered since the record began. Now the lead instrument sounds like hammer dulcimer. Whatever. The resonances between the two tracks, and the more subtle resonances within the album as a whole, are wonderfully effective. The album hangs together as mysteriously and memorably (all one distinct flavor, even with all this splendid variety) as *After the Gold Rush*. In addition to the strong sonic links between these bookend songs, notice the thematic bridgings. "When dreams come crashing down like trees" becomes "I know I won't awaken, it's a dream that can last," spooky image and a spooky sound but still in context somehow affirmative. "A young girl who didn't die" and the angels on the corner provide echoes of the defining songs of the album, "Driveby" and the title track. A story has been told. And continues to unfold, as we listen and listen again.

And again. Crazy Horse is a fabulous band. Songs that seemed unremarkable at first, like "Prime of Life," just grow on me and grow on me, and the groove has everything to do with it. Wow. That rhythm section. The rumor I heard was that this album was recorded as a kind of continuous rehearsal or jam, just get together day after day and play and play, no takes, just live recording, and maybe listen to the tapes later to see if you got anything. Long stretches in the studio, interrupted because of Kurt Cobain's death, finally back in the mood and then another interruption when someone close to the band was killed in a driveby shooting. Anyway, if you go through Neil Young's catalog, you'll find how much of it is really Crazy Horse's catalog as well. What freedom they've attained together! The band formed 25 years ago during the sessions for *Everybody Knows This Is Nowhere*, also produced by David Briggs and Neil Young. Go find another set of co-workers in rock as consistent or as loyal to each other. Ralph Molina on drums; Billy Talbot on bass; and Frank Sampedro joined in 1975, rhythm guitar, replacing Danny Whitten, whose death along with Bruce Berry's was exorcised on *Tonight's the Night* (not listed as a Crazy Horse album, but in fact it's Young, Talbot and Molina with Nils Lofgren and Ben Keith sitting in).

Going back to "Prime of Life," the lyrics are nothing special but the performance just shimmers, driving the vocals so they say more than these words seem capable of. Love that "Cinnamon Girl" taste on the borrowed chorus. And the whistling sound. *All* these sounds. Hats off to the horse. And faithful rider.

And in the midst of life comes "Driveby." A simple, beautiful, heartbreaking song. Listen to that fuzzed guitar tone, after the last "shooting star" in the bridge, after and coexistent with all those noble piano chords, music that will live inside every one of us at least as long as "Helpless" has, if we survive that long. A 22-year-old friend of mine vanished suddenly this month, accidental drowning not driveby but just as random and senseless. What can be said? The drums again are the very heart of the track. And the mood, the buzz of the bass, the colors in the vocals, the whole sad perfect fierce *mood* of the thing. "You feel invincible." And then you don't. "Driveby . . ."

"Driveby" 's an elegy. "Sleeps With Angels" is just as powerful and totally different. Single of the year on my personal radio station. A song like this can't be invented. It has the kick of pure inspiration. The freshness of this riff is exactly what rock and roll at its best has always been about. The boldness of the sound sculpture is breathtaking, and the risk pays off beyond any possible expectations. For those of us who thought the digital age might mean the end of such perfect imperfections, wrong again. How about the tone of that guitar after "town to town"? This is the whole movie in less than three minutes. A different sort of heartbreaker. Sympathy for our own devils. The song also captures the intensity of the news. With compassion for "she" who is the survivor, who is the other confused one, who is us, living at this tempo, who is everyman.

It was pointed out to me, after I'd been listening to this album for a little while, that "Western Hero" (fifth song) has exactly the same backing track (different vocals, of course, and different guitar overdubs in spots) as "Train of Love" (song nine). As soon as it's pointed to it's obvious, but I don't know how long it might have taken me to notice on my own. Despite all the similarities, the songs don't sound the same, and even now I can't easily impose "Train" lyrics on "Hero," or vice versa. This is fascinating. It's like a little essay on what gives a song its identity. The low vibrating guitar in "Western Hero" does give it a different mood than the lyrical, slightly generic "Train of Love," but I think what really keeps the songs from sounding alike is the difference in where the title phrase falls in the melodic line – "western hero" at the end of the line ("sure enough, he was a western hero") and "train of love" at the beginning ("train of love, racing from heart to heart"), so that when we think of or hear each tune, the notes/beat that we first think of are different, unrelated. Another song pairing within the album, and a delightful mindfuck. This many years into the rock and roll era, how can there still be dumb little ballsy tricks like this that no one (in my admittedly limited memory) has ever played on us before? Two songs same album same music different words. And where does Neil find the nerve to be so simplistically outrageous? It's his power, his nature, and he's never lost it. "Western Hero" comes closer to being a Neil Young cliché than anything else on the album ("Train of Love" 's not far behind), but it's saved I think by its lack of irony. The message is refreshingly unclear. The Marlboro Man image (and self-image) of America has changed, the "black and white" clarity (or seeming clarity) of the frontier or World War II is gone and how should we feel about this? The singer's not sure. The listener's not sure. The hero himself is unsure, which is what keeps him from being a hero still, perhaps. Shall we open fire on him? Wouldn't that be cowardly on our part, now that his six-gun and iron hand are gone . . .?

More pairings reveal themselves. "This time we're never going back"/"This train is never going back." (The one moment where the two songs merge together.) And the re-examination of absurdly familiar language – "he fought for you, he fought for me" "to love and honor, till death do us part" – to see what truth might be hidden inside its mind-numbing ordinariness. "To love and honor" actually becomes the emotional high point of "Train of Love," full of pain and risk and commitment, whereas the most haunting moment in "Western Hero" is "He's different now . . ." One possible message in the pairing of the songs is that the clichés that apply to personal life can be more easily redeemed, redis-covered, made new, than the clichés of public life. Putting it another way, to be heroes to ourselves and our loved ones is still possible and indeed necessary, however difficult, as we grow older and wiser; but public heroism and the values that underlie it are a much more tangled and less available realm.

This resonates with the obviously personal (but somehow public as well, if only because it comes at the start of the album) assertion in "My Heart": "This time I will take the lead somehow." *Sleeps with Angels,* like so many of Young's albums, is about marriage – his marriage to his wife and family, and his marriage to the world, through his work. When "shadows climb up the garden wall" and "the first leaf falls" in "Prime of Life," these signs of autumn can be felt as cultural (what's going on out there in the world that he releases albums into) as well as personal (he and his wife are getting older). And the message of the song (the mirror shows both ways) seems to me to have to do with the *I Ching*'s advice on how to lead in such a circumstance (even though "a sage might feel sad in view of the decline that must follow"): "Be not sad. Be like the sun at midday." Not surprisingly, the theme of nostalgia (personal *and* cultural) that runs throughout Young's oeuvre ("Sugar Mountain," "Mansion on the Hill") shows up here as well: "When I first saw your face, it took my breath away." But the way Young locates this statement within the song (he speaks of the past but specifically as a gift in the present, from the king to his queen – and to his people too, perhaps), makes it too an act of conscious leadership (do as I do) (tell her you love her) and generosity, an act of non-sadness, of renewal. (You have to be careful of your gestures these days, since Kurt presumably died partly of guilt at only pretending to be a hero. Neil, indirectly, offers us a different model.)

When I say the album is about marriage, I'm thinking of course of "Change Your Mind." When you take this 14-minute, 40-second song, and add to it its 6-minute, 20-second coda, "Blue Eden," you get a 21-minute epic pretty much smack in the middle of this (surprisingly listenable) 63-minute extravaganza, and it certainly asserts its presence by sheer size (well-balanced however by the other major songs, which assert their presence through their beauty or their subject matter or both) (and then at least four of the lesser songs gain strength by their location within the record and the way they make pairs with each other – an extraordinarily well-structured album). So the unambiguous message of "Change Your Mind" – one of Neil Young's earnest, exhortative works, like "Don't Be Denied" or "Don't Let It Bring You Down" or "Last Dance" ("you could live your own life") or "Tired Eyes" ("please take my advice") or "Love to Burn" – is powerfully felt throughout this CD, and necessarily colors how we listen and respond to every song. In "Sleeps with Angels" the impact of the suicide is described not in terms of a generation or the music biz but in the context of a marriage, a relationship. This is disturbing, surprising. It makes these people more real. "Train of Love" is overtly a song about marriage, while the line "I know in time we'll meet again," and the repetition of "lonely" and "lonesome," set up a contrary tension. The two songs that start the album ("my love I will give to you it's true/although I'm not sure what love can do") ("when I first saw your face . . .") also support a hearing of the album up through "Train of Love" as a story of courtship and renewal of vows (a recurring story on post-Geffen Young albums, methinks). The last three songs, however, offer no suggestion that the first-person narrator is or is not in relationship with someone. They're about other aspects of the individual's adventures in the universe.

The "unambiguous" message of the epic is, you need love. It

is the only thing that will protect you from the world (verses two and three) and from your restless ego (verse one). You need to make love. You need the "magic touch" of your partner, the person you make love with. *Don't let another day go by!* Tonight's the night. Or this morning. You need to be touched. And what that touch does (this is the interesting, the slightly-unexpected, the hypnotic part) is change your mind.

I'm telling you (he's telling me), change your mind.

A song with a message. He tells us what to do. And he is also very specific about *how* to do it (by regular lovemaking). Okay. I'll give that some serious thought.

Meanwhile, the musical spell the song creates, during the singing of these words and during the long musical passages between words, is mesmerizing. There are several ten-minute songs on *Ragged Glory*, and they're wonderful, and they're also obviously, invigoratingly, long, but "Change Your Mind," unless I'm listening very closely, goes by so quickly that often I find myself wanting to hear it again. Some kind of latter-day evolution of "Cowgirl in the Sand," it doesn't have the same extraordinary climaxes and yet in its own way it's almost as satisfying, another masterful piece of sound sculpture. Driven by a bandleader who needs to say something. And by three other musicians and a co-producer, David Briggs – and a faithful manager, Elliot Roberts, somewhere off in the wings – who want only to support and empower him in getting that something said, who let it become their something, as he also lets it become their something, so that finally it's this fabulous creation with endless twists and turns and musical subtleties to please us indefinitely that they have built together.

And perhaps to emphasize the point, which is that "Change Your Mind" is not precisely a jam (it's more like a jazz composition), "Blue Eden," which I regard as the dark side of relationship heaven, a little blues in the night, *is* credited as a joint composition among the four musicians, while every other song here is "words and music by Neil Young." What is particularly unsettling about "Blue Eden," which I like a heck of a lot better than I would ever expect to like a Young & Crazy blues jam stuck in the middle of an album, is the way the lyrics snatch bits of other songs – "Change Your Mind" in particular, but also vital chunks of "Train of Love" and "Driveby." What does it all mean? I don't know, but it's very successful at making us *feel* it means something, and that really is all we need to make it so.

"Change Your Mind" 's music is so compelling and pleasurable I don't even flinch at the phrase "magic touch." When you're truly cool, uncoolness just rolls right off you. I laughed when I saw an ad for the album "featuring the single 'Change Your Mind' " (a fifteen-minute single!), but then I realized they must have put out an edited version. It wouldn't be the same. Some tunes just need space to spread out in.

"Safeway Cart" next, and then "Train of Love" and "Trans Am." Vehicles. "I've got to get somewhere." ("My Heart," again.) This is an album about motion.

Motion and stillness. "Trans Am" is a great visionary shaggy dog story, in one sense a spoof on every dramatic Neil Young narrative that's gone before (including "Driveby," though this in no way detracts from the earlier song's power), but also a sincere and thoroughly charming salute to the modern cowboy's best friend, his car. It's modelled on mock-heroic '60s pop songs like "Ringo" and "Big Bad John," except this time the hero is an automobile, a distinctively American mass market sports car beloved by young males in the 1970s. The car gets to be the hero of this disjointed narrative mostly through messages contained in the structure of the song (not the lyrics). Song starts with this great guitar figure, a readymade that transports us instantly (how does he get that gloriously low, resonant guitar tone?) into an emotionally very familiar setting, something from the movies, very mythical in a modern sort of way, reinforced perfectly by a ghostly chorus (might be only one voice, but it still sounds like a chorus) superimposing words on the musical picture: "Trans Am." Whew. Narrative starts up immediately, resolving this

170

temporarily into a wagon train western, but then it takes some funny bounces. Meanwhile each of the four verses ends with that trademark chorus, "Trans Am," and after the fourth verse and chorus the guitar figure returns (a simplified version has been playing throughout the entire performance) and we get a very expressive instrumental last verse, wordless until the final exquisite pronunciation of the title phrase. The Trans Am's role in the lyrics themselves is more suggestive than specific: in the first verse it's an old Trans Am (always old) that the narrator heard the massacre story from (yes, the TA is not just the subject of a yarn, but a spinner of yarns). Second verse is the car's big scene: "It crawled along the boulevard with two wheels on the grass/That old Trans Am was dying hard but still had lots of gas." Western hero. Third verse it shows up in the last line, as though we now realize we've been seeing the scene from the car's point of view: "The old Trans Am just bounced around and took another road." Cool and wise. The fourth verse swerves, de-anthropomorphizing the car but you can be sure we still perceive it as having a personality, maybe dreaming about its past adventures, even though here it's just an actual car that broke down and "needs a headlight fixed."

"Trans Am." What is achieved here is primarily, as in almost all of these songs, a sound, a mood, a musical experience. The words are part of the assemblage – even though they are the container for the surface narrative (the deeper narrative, I'd say, is communicated by the guitar figure and the chorus) and the source of all specific visual images, they are still in fact just well-chosen elements of the overall (musical) effect. Neil's great, great gift is this ability to ride a feeling. He is phenomenally good at finding the right guitar sound(s) and chord sequences to bring home the mood. He is also very very good at working with other musicians, especially if they happen to be Crazy Horse. With his guitar, and the other instruments, and his voice, and the sound of the band at this moment (that groove, that looseness), he creates a sonic experience in which the role of the words is to point in the

171

direction the feelings are going, without overly getting in the way. A sonic master is a master of space (space *in* time, if you will), and the role of words in a rock and roll song is to deepen and focus the space without crowding it or violating its essence. Goofy words (check out the great songs of the Beatles or the Rolling Stones) will often do fine as long as the chorus phrase is right and the other lyrics don't break the mood or cross over some line of insipidness or absurdity.

Anyway, even if they're not the primary reason I love the song, I think the words to "Trans Am" are delightful. In the first verse there's a strange (neilyoungian) transition which can be explained if we accept the suddenly-arrived cowboy as the narrator of the first four lines, and which anyway leads into an image that perfectly suits the fantasy (talking cars) mood of the whole piece: "He used to ride the Santa Fe before the tracks were laid." Oh. Astral cowboy. Okay. Second verse doesn't totally gel for me but the imagery works well with the music. Third verse takes us into a timely, political/economic, satire (I'll get into the politics of *Sleeps with Angels* in a moment): "Global manufacturing, hands across the sea . . ." The earthquake that upsets the trade convention reminds me of Vonnegut's *Cat's Cradle* and Dylan's "Black Diamond Bay." The last verse is magnificent, very visual (we keep switching movies but it doesn't matter, because we are so immediately and successfully projected into each new scene), with two great moments. In the opening lines, "An old friend showed up at the door/The mileposts flying by." This is inexplicable, I think. But it feels right. Like we saw them fly by as we drove up with him, before he got to the door. Or as Cindy suggests, the mileposts are a cinematic image of the time that's passed since you saw him last. Whatever. Very funny. And then the climax of the big build-up, off to rescue the girl . . . from a broken headlight? Hmm. I like it a lot. Twists and turns. Makes me smile every time.

And "Piece of Crap" is funny in a less subtle but extremely likeable way, yes I know this particular temper tantrum all too well. The spoken parts, the drum sound, the guitar sounds are just more evidence of a guy who knows exactly what he wants when he hears it, each song a different vignette with its own brilliantly intuitive sonic specifications. Sometimes maybe the singer songwriter bandleader arranger isn't motivated to re-invent his art form for every little song that asks to be recorded – but when motivation and intention and inspiration (and intuition) do get into alignment, and apply themselves not just to a song but to that collective entity called an album (this year's model), look out. "The guy told me at the door . . ." Yahoo! We needed a little catharsis right about now. The transition from "Trans Am" is excellent.

"A Dream That Can Last" turns around the familiar "and then I woke up" in startling fashion – in effect, "and then I didn't wake up . . . thank God!" Why must the album end? Why must the dream always be interrupted by the so-called "real" world? The other side of this fascinating last-song-on-the-album is that it is not an evasion of reality but a demand (as in "Crime in the City" and "Rockin' in the Free World") that we stop ignoring and denying the reality all around us. "I feel like I died and went to heaven" (this on an album whose title song has the chorus, "He sleeps with angels tonight"). "The cupboards are bare but the streets are paved with gold." Here in my neighborhood of San Diego some of the richest and poorest people in the United States live side by side, and the rich and comfortable are working themselves up into a rage of hatred at the poor for raining on their parade. Oh Lord. But Neil's song is about optimism. I think. I wouldn't swear to it. He talks about seeing a glimmer in a young per-son's eye, and hears the angels say there's a better life for him someday. You can interpret this in all kinds of different ways, or not at all (except that how you feel about the album or the song is itself a kind of interpretation, maybe the only import-ant one). Do I wake or dream? I think he's saying the compas-sionate and necessary response to what we see is to go on dreaming, meaning, I think, with eyes open. Not TV eyes,

173

either. "Somewhere someone has a dream come true." Why do I feel so strongly that this album is not about the dream of a better life for one slowly aging rock *auteur*? Or rather, why do I feel so certain that his vision of a better life is one in which the poor people of the earth share more equally, more bounteously, in its gifts? He never says that. Not in words, anyway. Maybe it's in his feelings as he's singing and playing and recording, and those feelings speak to me directly from the music. Or maybe when you really do remember the assignment and make topical music, an album for all of us its listeners at this moment, autumn 1994, right now, maybe you thereby contribute to our effort to construct a language and a history (read: dream) by the sheer force and joyousness and freshness and honesty of your communication.

The politics of *Sleeps with Angels*? You'll have to determine that for yourself. But I hear a lot of compassion for Everyman. And a demand that you, I, all of us change our minds. "It's not too late," says the first song. "(Too late)", says the title track. The message seems to be, it's up to us to choose whether it's too late or not. Are you feeling alright, my friend?

Another paper boat floated out onto the waters of the collective consciousness (and subconscious; I love the way music reaches both at once). I, the creature listening, playing the CD, watching the trajectory of the boat, am a part of the beast that needs reprogramming. And I (not the guy who made the CD) am also the reprogrammer. "Change your mind." "It's not too late, it's not too late. I've got to keep my heart." Yeah, well, you've done it again. Thanks, friend, for the encouragement, the music, and yes, the excellent role model.

Don't. That's one way to describe the message I hear. Don't sleep with angels tonight.

14

Neil Young's – and Rock and Roll's – Finest Moment

This is the last essay I wrote about a new Neil Young album (in this case, video and audio album, not just audio) before it occurred to me that I might assemble this book. I assigned it to myself during my brief unhappy reign as "pop music editor" of a "high end audio" magazine called Fi, *winter 1996. The title is a succinct (and, I hoped, attention-getting) summation and expression of my excitement when I stumbled upon this little-known film. Wow.*

At my local record store, I recently came across a video-cassette which apparently has been available for a year, but which I'd never heard about, called *Neil Young and Crazy Horse: The Complex Sessions*. Bought it, brought it home, watched and listened and was absolutely astonished. Don't fall into the trap of believing that the great moments in rock and roll history are all in the past. This 27-minute performance by one of rock's greatest and most enduring artists and bands is head-line news. Is what rock and roll has always tried to achieve, and never come any closer to than this, or Chuck Berry's "Johnny B. Goode," or Janis and Big Brother live in 1967, or Springsteen and E Street live in 1975. You shoulda been there. And in this case, thanks to the miracle of recording technol-ogy, you can be. This videotape will wear out no faster than your all-time favorite 45, it is just as deserving of repeated plays, just as possibly able to continue to deepen its resonance through the rest of your lifetime. Hot stuff. The best argument

I've ever heard for owning a "home theater" set-up with superior audio capabilities. The mix on this tape is so brilliant it even sounds good on a damn TV, but I keep wanting to turn it up louder than the TV will go.

Quietly, without fanfare that I'm aware of, rock and roll has reached a significant new aesthetic plateau, lead by an indefatigable explorer of the medium's possibilities, as a songwriter, as a live performer, as a recording artist, and even as a filmmaker. Leaving behind him an oeuvre, or a pile of "product," songs, albums, shows, and in this case a (wonderfully short) audio/video album. Four songs. A live recording by Neil and the three band members in the same studio where they had recently completed their fine album *Sleeps with Angels.* New, completely live performances, filmed by Jonathan Demme, who directed one of the absolute greatest rock and roll films ever made: *Stop Making Sense.* If you own that and *Sign O' The Times* and *The Complex Sessions,* you have the cornerstone works in this contemporary art form. Demme and Young and the Horse have now proved, like Phil Spector and Brian Wilson and Billie Holiday before them, that there is such a thing as perfection.

The Complex Sessions seems to me to represent a pivotal moment in rock history (as, say, "Smells Like Teen Spirit" did), not only because it's so good but also because it is a breakthrough in the creative use of a medium (the long-form rock video as a work of art) that has defeated most supplicants, including Neil as often as not. On the other hand, it isn't selling many copies, and in our increasingly corrupt pop culture, that and inches of press coverage are the only measurements of "significance." Oh well. Great music is still great music. If a tree falls in the forest but nobody writes a review, did it make a sound?

This footage from the Complex Recording Studios in Los Angeles was shot Oct. 3, 1994, six weeks before Neil's 49th birthday. By way of quick recapitulation, the Canadian singer-songwriter and guitar hero first came to the attention of the rock world (I wrote the first nationally published review of his group's first album, and was fortunate enough to see them live at the Whisky in '66 and L.A.'s Shrine and NYC's Ondine in 1967) as a member of Buffalo Springfield, with whom he recorded three albums. He also recorded three albums as a member of Crosby Stills Nash & Young, and, between 1968 and 1996, has recorded some 32 albums under his own name. More than a third of those albums also feature Crazy Horse, who were called The Rockets when Neil met them in 1969 and renamed them and enticed them to perform on his (brilliant) second "solo" album, *Everybody Knows This Is Nowhere*. One original member of the Rockets, Danny Whitten, died in 1972, and was later replaced by Frank Sampedro. Neil Young has recorded with other musicians, including, in 1995, Pearl Jam, and his greatest commercial success came with the non-Crazy-Horse album *Harvest* (1972), but a lot of critics and Neil fans believe he has done most of his best work in collaboration (performing live on stage or live in the studio) with Crazy Horse.

Neil's finest moment? Listen, I told you I saw Buffalo Springfield at the start of 1967 when "Mr. Soul" was much better live than it ever would be on record (just trying to establish my credentials for making such a bold claim). And I saw/heard Neil sing "Don't Be Denied" live with CSNY in the summer of '74 (and it was great) the day Nixon was pardoned, and I was present at the very show in San Francisco in '78 that was filmed for the *Rust Never Sleeps* movie. And have fallen absolutely and helplessly in love with his music again and again from "Nowadays Clancy" to "Cowgirl in the Sand" to every note of the *After the Gold Rush* album, to much of *Harvest* and later all of *Zuma* and *Tonight's the Night* and also way back with "Helpless" and "Ohio" and onward through "My My, Hey Hey" and "Rockin' in the Free World" and *Ragged Glory* and *Sleeps with Angels*, so goddamn many masterpieces and unforgettable moments, music that truly touched and released my soul, and many more I haven't mentioned, even things as obscure and un-obvious and as utterly indispensable to me as

"Winterlong" and "Star of Bethlehem" and "Journey through the Past" (live '71) and "Ride My Llama" and oh, I could go on and on. So yes, I'm a very serious Neil Young fan, even if I haven't yet written long books about him as I have about Bob Dylan. Very serious indeed, even though I am able to pull my attention away from some phases, and I do occasionally take a while before I really check out a new album (like, I still reserve judgement on *Mirror Ball*, but the enthusiasm of other folks means I'll at least give it another try). And so. When I say this could be or, more simply, *is*, Neil Young's finest moment, that's a strong statement indeed. And, I insist, an informed one. And deeply felt.

Rock and roll's finest moment? Yes, damn it, why do we listen to the stuff, what do we get out of it or hope to get out of it? Why is it so important in so many lives? Answer the questions as best you can, and I propose that what you talked about in your answer is what I find (and, I hope, perhaps you also will find) in this sight-and-sound recording *The Complex Sessions*. At last! "I've been waiting for you, and you've been coming to me, for such a long time now . . ." Yeah, "here we are in the years." The good old days – if we want to open our hearts and ears and actually listen to this "Young" geezer already past his 30th rock 'n' roll year – are here right now. And if my lyric quotes from his first album are too obscure for you, that's okay, it's quite possible to start as a Neil Young fan right now, with the songs and performances on this videotape. And if you're mostly into current, contemporary music, that's okay, most of the musicians you're listening to are already Neil Young fans. Start listening to Neil's opus and you'll quickly notice how pervasive his influence is on so many different kinds of rock band in the 1990s. But the best news is, that doesn't stop him from continuing to follow his own muse, wherever it takes him right now. What more do you want from a courageous and talented artist who's alive while you're alive? Still spitting. Though there were years when we had our doubts, this present-day Neil's not rusting at all.

What have we here? Turn on the video. When the unpleasant "intro music" Warner-Reprise sticks on the front of all its v-tapes is over, the movie starts, and almost immediately and very handsomely focuses on the singer's hands, beautiful hands, so rich in character, and caught in action, dancing, playing a keyboard, something like a harpsichord, so deliberately, those wonderful opening notes of "My Heart" that also open *Sleeps with Angels,* and we hear his voice while we see his fingers, and it is that extraordinary voice so full of feeling that has already given you gooseflesh on other favorite Neil Young performances. The intensity of *feelings* in this performance connects for me immediately. That's his gift, much of what makes this artist so special.

This *feeling*ness is so unforgettably powerful, so moving, when it happens, and it doesn't always happen (just often enough to make it worthwhile to hang around). It's interesting for me to contrast, as I did today, this performance on *The Complex Sessions* with the Neil Young videotape you're most likely to come home with if you don't know better, *Unplugged.* Yes, Neil solo accompanying himself on acoustic guitar or piano can be absolutely transcendental, but not, to my taste, on this particular "MTV Unplugged" performance. He's got a nice voice, but who cares when he's giving such an emotionally flat performance? The contrast is fascinating, though, because looking at one tape and then the other you have the opportunity to see more clearly what the difference is between a great performer on a great night and the same guy making a sincere effort in a situation or at a moment that doesn't really inspire him. OK, he fakes it perfectly okay. But there's no real pleasure for the listener in it. And such inescapable visceral pleasure (gooseflesh) as I watch/hear this other video! If I watch and experience these two tapes in sequence, can I perhaps learn a little more about what it is the performing artist does that touches me so deeply and arouses my spirit so completely? Wow, here it is absent and here it is present. As simple as that. And still so mysterious! See how the look in a man's eyes changes when he's truly present and (for whatever reason) inspired, and filled with conviction?

Anyway, it just happens that's also what the song's about. "My heart, my heart, I've got to keep my heart. It's not too late, it's not too late. My love, I will give to you. Although I'm not sure what love can do." If he knew, maybe it would scare him so much he wouldn't dare sing in public or with the tape and cameras rolling . . . Such power. If I remember right, that's also what "Mr. Soul" was about. The singer's fear of his voice, his power. But this song, anyway, is about the power of dreams ("in the night sky a star is falling down from someone's hand"), and is a brilliant, and gorgeously naked and authentic, re-statement of faith. And on this video, you can see it in his face (and hands) while you hear it in his voice. What? Well, many things, but sincerity more than anything else.

Let's say it's a powerful and rewarding (and very pleasingly musical) emotional experience. The kind that people are hoping to find again as they browse in the record store. What an amazing performer he is! As we will see again in quite different ways on each of the other three tracks. And what a gift he has for melody, and for chord-patterns, especially minor chords I guess, and for matching words to melodies, so that fairly simple phrases can take on extraordinary ambiguity and grace and attractiveness. "When dreams come crashing down like trees/I don't know what love can do/When life is hanging in the breeze/I don't know what love can do." What a quatrain! So simple. But once you let yourself fall under its spell, will you ever be able to shake it?

Anyway, the movie (OK, 27-minute videotape) starts with a solo performance, just like Young's best previous film, *Rust Never Sleeps,* and then after three quick minutes the singer gains a band. This is an astonishingly gratifying concert film visually, and combined with *Stop Making Sense* leaves me convinced Jonathan Demme must be a genius (without even talking about that scary movie that won him an Oscar), how many zillion directors have shot rock bands in action and almost never this intelligently or gracefully or pleasingly? He makes authenticity look easy, while almost every other director involved with rock films and videos make it seem impossible, else why would they fail so consistently? Let them study Demme's two masterpieces. *This* is rock and roll! Notice for example how wonderful Neil looks, and how terrific each Crazy Horse member and all four musicians together look all the time, as though they were cast for this film so perfectly that again you wonder why almost no other rock filmmaker ever got it so right before. A lovely cinematic touch, for example, is the way drummer Ralph Molina's face opens (as he counts off) and closes (as he seems to perform the very silence with his non-drumming presence) "Prime of Life." Wow. And the way the singers (Poncho and Billy, or Billy and Neil) stand and sing together, or the way the guitar players combine visually on stage as we hear them combining musically, yes indeed, this is the visual and musical equivalent of that extraordinary interaction between musicians that Buffalo Springfield represented from the very beginning in their music. When I wrote about it 29 years ago I called it tightness. The way the pieces of the music fit together. The groove. The voices. The personalities. The guitars bouncing off each other. To make a whole somehow greater than the sum of the parts. Yes, much greater, even though Neil the writer singer leader is only one of those parts. Neil Young and Crazy Horse are more than he is, or as much as he is alone at his utterly transcendent moments (1971 solo concert bootleg or the opening song of *Complex*). "Prime of Life" is a soft-rock rave-up, in the best possible sense, so pleasing, and so ecstatic when its ecstasy moment is reached (very well-represented visually, as we see and hear the guitars and guitar-holders all at once, at natural but odd angles to each other). This is it. I been waiting since I was in knee pants for them, someone, to make records or movies like this. More please. I like this art form.

And so we come to the center of the video. One song makes up more than half its length. The jam. "Change Your Mind."

The perfect jam, visually and musically. The piece is consciously related to "Cowgirl in the Sand," and less obviously but very directly related to three decades of Young and Crazy jams, from "Down by the River" to "Like a Hurricane" to "Love to Burn" and so many others, including such peculiar and non-Crazy Young excursions as "Natural Beauty" and "Like an Inca." And as wonderful as the performance on the *Sleeps with Angels* album is, this take benefits from the group's familiarity with the studio they're playing in and the opportunities they've had to do this jam together over and over, notably in public the day before this session, at Neil's 1994 Bridge benefit concert extravaganza. Like "Cowgirl in the Sand" it's a song that likes to be played, and its texture just gets richer the more chance the musicians have to explore it. Anyway, a superb performance, and what an incredible opportunity the intimacy of the seeing-eye camera turns out to be for us the viewers/listeners. Again we see as well as hear the personalities bouncing off each other. The development of the rhythmic and melodic and emotional themes. All orchestrated by God. Not a show-offy spontaneity. Something better. The real thing. We can feel it. And feel our own minds and hearts changing.

Fifteen minutes of rock and roll trance. A journey. An experience filled with pleasure and feeling and beauty. And in addition, an opportunity to see into the process of a rock and roll band creating and playing together (all the more visible because of the simplicity of the rhythm and chords and words and structure), really a very rare opportunity to see so far into the mechanism, and so clearly. A rock and roll education. And, appropriately, an education that's fun to experience. Rockin'. And isn't Neil's voice beautiful on that final ("the morning comes") verse? Return of the vocal, with those words, strongly suggesting awakening or anyway getting up and stretching after a long night (fairly explicitly, a long night of love).

And somehow this incredible centerpiece, "Change Your Mind," manages not to dwarf the rest of the film, each song is so pleasing in its own way, and the four flow into each other and go together so well, that no single track is my favorite or even the one I notice the most. A good trick, when a super-long rock track sits so well with the rest of the album. Anyway, a bit of Falstaffian comic relief, the most muscular rock music of the whole tape, closes the album, invigorating, hilarious, and again and in still another way so very very pleasing. "Piece of Crap." You gotta love these guys. And so alive that Neil even sings lyrics that aren't on the *SWA* album: "Went to buy an LP, the guy only had CDs, so digitally clean, it was a piece of crap!"

Makes me shout along, every time, every chorus. This videotape is great rock and roll, a superb work of art like "Satisfaction" or "Hey Jude" or any single creation, production, performance, work of rock art. Also available on laser disc. A milestone. Not a heavy one. Lighter than air. Rock on. "Rock and roll will never die . . ." Not as long as it leaves recordings like this (auditory or visual-*and*-auditory) where future listeners/viewers can find them. Hey, even if some huge disaster wipes out our civilization, if this and a few other high points survive and our descendants find some way to retrieve 'em and play 'em back, they'll be starting their own rock bands, and breeding their own singer-songwriters, before long. "There's more to the picture than meets the eye." Usually that's true. But Neil Young and Crazy Horse and Jonathan Demme have here created a masterpiece in which *everything* they put into it does meet the eye and ear, again and again as you watch and listen some more. My my, hey hey. A namecheck for the Horse, please: Billy Talbot on bass, Ralph Molina on drums, Frank "Poncho" Sampedro on guitar, and all three on back-up vocals so wonderful to hear and see that we are reminded in timely fashion how such harmonies are as central and vital to rock as the beat. And the words. And the tunes. And the passion. And the look. *The Complex Sessions* is a work of art. And a thing of beauty. And proof that rock and roll not only isn't dead, it's just hitting its stride. Where can we go from here?

183

15

Rock 'N' Roll Cowboy, Disc 4

Today is Sunday, January 5, 1997, thirty years since I saw Buffalo Springfield play "Mr. Soul" in a dance club in New York City . . . and the day I'm going to start writing about the selections on the last disc of the *Rock 'N' Roll Cowboy* set.

But first I want to recapitulate. As you can see, I've been interested in Neil Young and powerfully affected by his performances and songs since 1966. What have I learned, as I've tried to figure out what his work means to me and why I like it so much? Well, the chapters of this book, old and new, are all reports from the front. So let's see what conclusions I arrived at in these notes from the various stages of our Listener/Artist relationship:

Chapter 1 (1976): "A great artist is someone who says 'I am' more honestly, more powerfully, more beautifully, more straightforwardly, more inclusively than anyone else except other great artists. I've been wondering why certain people can do it again and again, without really repeating themselves. Why are they great? What are they doing that's different? They are being themselves more completely."

Chapter 2 (1967): "Honesty, warmth – these are key words in describing a Buffalo Springfield performance. There's love in their music . . . It's the extraordinary amount of honest emotion conveyed in this LP that makes it exceptional."

Chapter 3 (1996): "We fall in love with the *sound*. And all the things it says (which can't be found anywhere else) about who we are and how it feels and why it fucking matters."

185

Chapter 4 (1972): "If we all are to become mere myths, and subjects for each other's essays and songs, I hope we can keep our sense of humor and walk through myths like butter."

And so forth. He keeps discovering himself and I keep discovering him. And jumping to new conclusions.

Chapter 5 (1974): "Emotionally, the blues on this album are the expression of an introverted person who has to sing to earn his supper, who *needs* to sing to feel like a person, but who can only sing about his feelings, and who fears that what he feels has become too personal to share."

Chapter 13 (1994): "Young's success as an artist is partly due to his willingness to explore things and carry them to completion even at the risk of coming up dry. Holding back his own judgmental side is what allows an *Everybody Knows This Is Nowhere* or *Tonight's the Night* or *Sleeps with Angels* to come into existence . . . *Sleeps with Angels*, like so many of Young's albums, is about marriage – his marriage to his wife and family, and his marriage to the world, through his work."

Chapter 14 (1996): "The intensity of *feelings* in this performance connects for me immediately. That's his gift, much of what makes this artist so special. See how the look in a man's eyes changes when he's truly present and inspired and filled with conviction?"

Chapter 8 (1975): "Neil Young, by staying true to himself, has not pleased his various audiences every time; but he has kept himself alive, which is a lot more than you can say for many great rock performers, including quite a few who are still breathing."

Chapter 12 (1992): "Maybe we love him because we identify with his conflicted desire to satisfy us and to withhold himself at the same time."

Obviously, the title of this book is my way of acknowledging that the story of this artist is that he *has* had love to burn and has taken a lot of chances and for more than thirty years has lived by the credo that it's better to burn out than it is to rust. Has listened to what the spirit said to him. And "speaking out" is what he's done by continuing to write and record and perform. On that note, the repeated verse in "Speakin' Out" (1973, included on *Tonight's the Night*) can be heard as being addressed to us, the audience, at the same time that it's addressed to Carrie Snodgrass (to hear it this way, consider that the works of art he gives us are also his baby): "I've been a searcher, I've been a fool/But I've been a long time coming to you/I'm hoping for your love to carry me through/You're holding my baby, and I'm holding you. Yes I am. Speakin' out . . ."

* * *

Thank you, Neil, again, for holding me in your songs. And what about *Cowboy* disc 4? It covers 1986–1994, but not really, because it completely skips over the *Ragged Glory* and *Sleeps with Angels* songs – understandably, because those are well-documented on officially-released live albums, *Weld* and *The Complex Sessions*. And of course some of these disc 4 performances fall somewhat short of the Olympic standards of *Weld* and *Complex*. But that's okay. The two previously-unreleased (and -unheard-by-me) performances at the heart of the disc, "Bad News" and "Ordinary People," are so *great* and groundbreaking and unexpected they easily justify whatever time, energy and money you have to spend to get to hear them. Sit tight. Rumors continue to fly that the Neil Young Archives CDs will be officially available simultaneous with or soon after the publication of this book. The iceberg heaves up out of the water.

Track 1, "Mideast Vacation," is a song from Young's 1987 album *Life*, also included on *Lucky 13* – which suggests that Neil, like Johnny Rogan and others, regards this as one of his better songs from the Geffen era. I however must admit it does nothing for me. Nice to have this solo acoustic version from August 1986 (the *Life* version was with Crazy Horse, recorded live in fall '86 and then "digitally assembled"). But I still have to say I don't much enjoy listening to it, though if you do you're probably not alone. There's not necessarily any accounting for the differing tastes of Neil Young fans. Things strike us differently. For me, the song is a good set-up for a humorous bit of yarn-spinning (like "Bob Dylan's 115th Dream" or Richard Fariña's "House Un-American Blues Activity Dream") but it never quite manages to be funny, and I don't find myself empathizing with the comic protagonist as one should in a good "fool" saga. The singer doesn't sound like he's connecting with the character, either. Indeed, it's a listless performance (one of four songs he sang at a "Tough on Toxics" benefit with other artists, to help get an environmental initiative on the California ballot).

The *Cowboy* booklet offers a good quote: *"There's a lot I get out of doing this acoustic thing that I don't get any other way. It opens up the music and the songs and what they're about. Being able to pick things out and change them around."* Yes indeed. But for me this "Mideast Vacation" is not an example of what Neil's talking about in the quote. In my (audio) observation of Neil Young and Bob Dylan, those moments when a song is really opened up and changed around in live performance happen when the singer is feeling something at that moment that this song becomes a vehicle for. You can hear and feel that the singer is unusually *present* in the song and performance, and able to convey a lot of feeling. Go back to "On the Beach" on disc 2 for an example. Or almost anything from the 1971 *Young Man's Fancy* bootleg.

Track 2, "Road of Plenty," also doesn't do a lot for me, though I feel I *should* like it more. It's an early version of "Eldorado," live with Crazy Horse in October 1986, longer and with different lyrics. "Eldorado" was the title track of a 4/89 EP (released only in Asia) that served as a kind of breakthrough, winning critics and other influential fans back for Neil, preparing the ground for the enthusiastic reception of *Freedom* (10/89), which also included "Eldorado." The *Cowboy* booklet provides a very informative quote:

"I put Eldorado [the EP] *out so people would know I was still here. There's something about the way things have gone for me that made me want to put it out and make sure my handwriting was on it. Pick the artwork, do everything with my friends, and put out this little record. But then, I'm sick. I only made 5000. I said, 'that's all, that's it.' That's the way I did it – it emerged, just like I'm re-emerging from myself. It's a funny thing. I feel my feelings coming back."*

John Robertson in *Neil Young, The Visual Documentary,* comes up with another relevant quote (also uncredited): *"Just as it* [*Times Square,* the album the *Eldorado* tracks were recorded for, late '88] *was being made ready for release, I changed my mind, because I really wanted to have an album that would make an effect. I felt that* Eldorado *by itself was a really fine album. But if you don't have a song they can play on the radio . . . So I took the songs that really created the feeling of* Eldorado *and put them out as an EP, 5000 copies, thereby eliminating any of the crap that I have to go through with the radio stations and promotion and record companies. I eliminated all that completely by not even entering the arena. But I still put out a work that was distinctly mine, that I really believed in."*

These quotes indicate clearly that what Neil Young's 1980s were about was losing control of the process by which he as a recording artist made contact with or felt in contact with his listeners. Symbolically and practically, the obstacle appeared in the form of record companies and radio stations and "the crap" of promotion. Yes. But it seems reasonable to assume that the obstacle between the artist and his "feelings" (meaning his ability to be public with intimate feelings and trust the faceless listeners he was sharing them with) also had its origins 1) in the very fact of his fame and his ambivalence about it, as anticipated in "Mr. Soul" and "Broken Arrow" but multiplied by the success of "Heart of Gold" and the celebrity of CSNY . . . and 2) in the fact that like Kerouac he reached a place where he wasn't so sure he wanted to go on documenting his own life story in public. Remember his 1988 comments looking back at *Trans*: *"It has to do with a part of my life that practically no one can relate to. I started hiding in styles, just putting little clues in there as to what was really on my mind. I just didn't want to openly share all this stuff in songs that said exactly what I wanted to say in a voice so loud everyone could hear it.*" The artist finding himself resisting playing his strongest suit, for good and understandable reasons. And the record company clumsily joining in the game, playing the "heavy." Well, Neil, you know . . . "they give you this, but you pay for that." You were so wise in that song for Johnny Rotten and yourself, and small wonder Kurt Cobain thought of it at the end. "Out of the blue and into the black." Amen, brother. Anyway, the obvious end for this long paragraph is a footnote to the next line, "And once you're gone, you can never come back": But you did come back, man! That's why we admire you so much.

So in the history of this artist-audience romance, "The Road of Plenty"/"Eldorado" is an important song. *Eldorado*, the album, was the comeback. And it got its name from the song, and the song evolved out on the road, the road of plenty so to speak, as Neil rewrote it from show to show in fall 1986 touring North America with Crazy Horse, then rewrote it more for the 1988 *Times Square* sessions that became *Eldorado* and then became *Freedom*. Too bad (in my opinion) the song never really got anywhere, the story never did emerge successfully, in the song or the performance, but I can imagine the artist replying that it didn't need to. It was a horse to ride, and indeed it did its job (carried its rider) very well.

So since, in my opinion, "Eldorado" never did reach a point where it succeeds in saying what it probably desired to say/express from the beginning . . . and thus it's more moving as a relic of the artist's process than as a song to listen to for itself . . . then a Neil Young fan must appreciate having this eight-minute recording of "The Road of Plenty" from Minneapolis, October 17, 1986. And it can be pleasant to listen to. But (sez me) not very satisfying. The words and storytelling definitely don't come together, and neither does the music, for me, although it certainly sounds promising. Well, if you like unfinished works (and if like me you hear the *Freedom* centerpiece "Eldorado" as also unfinished), "Road of Plenty" will intrigue you. And maybe, like me, you'll get to a point where you suspect that the lines "And when the gates go up/ The crowd gets so excited/Then he comes dancin' out/ Dressed in gold lamé" are somehow related to his own experience of being a performer, even if that thread isn't followed even obliquely elsewhere in any of the versions of the song . . . Hey, just a page back didn't he say he eliminated "all that" "by not even entering the arena"?? Interesting choice of words. He was talking about the music business and the *Eldorado* mini-album. The arena! Yeah, I think he did identify with that bullfighter. And I also think he eventually *did* finish the song . . . by writing and recording, creating, *Ragged Glory* and *Sleeps with Angels*. Great art is certainly the artist's best revenge.

* * *

Track 3 is "Computer Age." And first of all, it's cool that he would be doing songs from *Trans* in a 1987 concert with Crazy Horse. And this time, I find the track not just interesting but musically and emotionally satisfying. Makes me reach out to turn up the volume. A simple song, a straightforward performance. And it's got the *feel.* The pieces of the puzzle are definitely coming together again.

Yeah, even though we're back in '87, I'd say Neil's handwriting is all over this one. *Great* Neil Young/Crazy Horse sound, and not at all formulaic. Superb rhythmic drive, and of course the "story" of the song comes alive in the middle of all this noisiness in a way it probably never did before. It's not just the "acoustic thing" that can "open up the music and the songs and what they're about." The Young-and-Crazy thing can do it too. The performers create by performing. Oh, and let me point out that it's not all noise, there's a gorgeous neo-classical melodic bridge –

191

"Days and nights, week and months and seasons, running through me, so microscopically." Quite beautiful, actually. The lost years were not so "lost" when you have the concert tapes and a good guide. Thanks, Great Dane Records of Milano (the town where Young and Crazy performed this particularly invigorating and pleasing "Computer Age," 5/5/87). The *Cowboy* booklet simply says, "This is an interesting one. Neil sings it without the vocoder he used for the studio version and during the Trans tour in 1982."

Funny how it can all start sounding like love songs to the listener/audience after a while. Last verse of this one: "I need you/To let me know that there's a heartbeat/And you need me/Like ugly needs a mirror/And day by day/The horizon's getting clearer/Computer Age."

*   *   *

So the good news is that then this quite non-ordinary man created "Bad News" and "Ordinary People." First he had to create (evolve) a whole different kind of band. Here's how *that* happened:

After the spring '87 European tour with Crazy Horse that produced *Cowboy*'s "Computer Age," Neil went to Winnipeg (Manitoba, Canada) for a high school reunion that turned into a regrouping of his 1963–65 band the Squires. Two decades on, three of the original band-members plus friends played an impromptu performance very early in the morning 6/28/87 at the Blue Note Cafe in Winnipeg.

Back in the U.S.A., Young and Crazy played eighteen shows in three weeks beginning August 13. Like the European shows, they opened with an acoustic set and closed with an electric, full band set. But somewhere between June and August, Young decided to add a mini "blues" set between the other segments – two or three slow blues (or rhythm & blues) numbers, with the Crazy Horse rhythm section, and CH guitarist Frank

Sampedro playing organ, plus roadie/spare musician Larry Cragg on baritone sax.

That was fun, apparently, so lo and behold in November 1987 Neil Young played ten shows in California with a new outfit called the Bluenotes, composed of the three Crazy Horse guys plus six horn-players, including Cragg and the redoubtable Ben Keith. Of course, for a change of "style" Neil needed a new name and new clothes. He was introduced at these shows as "Shakey Deal," and Pete Long reports, "Young made every effort to dress for the part, sporting long sideburns, dark glasses, a black fedora with an Indian design band, a shabby sports jacket and a shirt and tie, but retaining his characteristic patched jeans."

Neil: *"Every night I'd listen to the tapes, and the acoustic set didn't move me very much and the Crazy Horse set I'd just skim through, because it seemed a little obvious. But that little blues set I did with Crazy Horse and our roadie on the baritone sax, well, I liked listening to that. The crowd seemed to like it too, 'cause they were going fucking nuts and no one was shouting for 'Southern Man' like they've done throughout my whole fucking career."*

The song "Bad News" was first heard at the first Bluenotes show, Nov. 2, 1987 in Santa Cruz. But it wasn't included on the album *Neil and the Bluenotes* (with a different rhythm section) recorded in February '88, *This Note's for You*. (The title song was first heard at one of the August '87 Crazy Horse shows.) "Bad News" did return, however, when the slightly altered Bluenotes began performing again in April 1988. They played ten shows, again, east and west coasts this time, and followed that with their farewell tour, mid-August to late October 1988. *Rock 'N' Roll Cowboy* disc 4, track 4, "Bad News," was performed by Neil & the Bluenotes August 16th, 1988, in Chicago. Track 5, "Ordinary People," is from August 27th. Both songs were performed at almost every one of their twenty-seven fall '88 shows.

"Bad News" is quickly becoming one of my new all-time-favorite Neil Young tracks (so many on this bootleg . . . isn't that what makes a great album?). Alan Jenkins, secretary of the Neil Young Appreciation Society, had this to say about "Bad News" in his 1994 *Mojo* Magazine survey of 25 unreleased NY songs (cleverly titled "These Notes Aren't for You"): "A marvellous deep-soul 'n' blues epic complete with a shivery minor shift in the bridge and plaintive sax and trombone interludes. Performed regularly by the Bluenotes during 1987 and 1988, and intended to appear on the second Bluenotes album, *This Note's for You Too*. The closing sax solo is heart-stopping."

I have to agree, and also have to marvel that I love this performance so much and yet I find extremely little pleasure in any of the tracks on *This Note's for You*, the Neil and the Bluenotes album (the intended follow-up, recorded live, has never been released). There are people who like that album, I know. But insofar as this is one listener's diary, I have to ask myself, what's the huge difference (as reported by my feelings, my music pleasure meters) between this and that? Same band, same sound sorta, but . . .

But a different song, first of all. And a whole different kind of performance. It is absolutely remarkable to me as a listener that Neil could arrive at such a brilliantly successful new musical form – new kind of song! – as he does on "Bad News," and then not pursue this direction in any of the songs he recorded with the same band for their 1988 album. Well, one of the pleasures of listening to recordings of live performances by committed artists like Young or Dylan is that you get to visit the artist's workspace and see the mysteries and wonders of the creative process unfold un-self-consciously before you. Listening to this live recording of "Bad News," it occurs to me again – the simplest explanation for the difference between triumphs like this and forgettable stuff like all the *This Note's for You* songs – that Neil Young is primarily an inspired artist. Where do you get ideas (lyrical, musical) like "Like a Hurricane" or "Powderfinger" or "See the Sky About to Rain"? You don't arrive at them by thinking. You're just sitting there at the guitar or piano or notebook and suddenly this thing just starts coming through you, and you capture it and learn from it (it shows you how it wants to be done). Inspiration. "Bad News" seems to me an absolutely inspired creation. Almost nothing like it before or since (although "Ordinary People" and "Crime in the City" do belong to a related category of composition/performance/arrangement)! And it's wonderful. One more great stop for young bands studying at the Neil Young School of Rock Sound and Performance and Songmaking. Of course, they'll have to have horns in their band to learn very directly from this one. (Although the extraordinary balancing of narrative vocal verses and jazz-like exploratory/expressive instrumental passages does have structural implications for any kind of songwriting for an electric band.) Have I said "Wow!" already? I want to say it again.

What is "Bad News"? Well, Alan Jenkins is certainly right to call it an epic, and to place it in the realm of "soul" and "blues" (the jazzier side of the blues, I would say). And it's still not precisely like anything you've ever heard before. It's even arguable that few other singers/bandleaders could have come up with this, and certainly Neil couldn't have done it with any other band. This performance is eight minutes long, and before I attempt to describe its structure and content I need to vent my irritation at those damn guys standing near the guy who taped this show, and chattering loudly right over the performance. I've had lots of praise for the assemblers of this bootleg set, but I do think it a grave error that they stuck this distractingly noisy taping of "Bad News" on when there must be many other tapes (he sang it every night) of performances of comparable quality. (On the other hand this is such a sublime performance of the song I have to be sympathetic if they found it too transcendent to be passed by for technical reasons . . .) So be warned that if, like me, you fall in love with this *Cowboy* track, you'll find yourself wincing in discomfort every time the sacred spell cast by horns and vocals is fouled by the sounds of disinterested, disrespectful voices.

Lyrically, this is two quatrains (four-line verses) repeated once, plus the opening line repeated at the end as a perfect resolution. No chorus. Each quatrain is one declarative sentence, for a total of two, very dramatic, descriptive statements. The instrumental passages flesh out the descriptions and sustain and heighten the drama. The interplay of instrumental and vocal passages runs like this: instruments for the first 54 seconds, voices for 96 seconds (except a seven-second flourish between verses), instruments (particularly horn solos) for an absolutely defining two and a half minutes, then the verses come back for another 99 seconds, followed by 72 seconds of triumphal instrumental resolution, with the five-second vocal coda ("Bad News is come to town") enclosed inside. Got that? Slightly less than half the eight minutes are vocal, but somehow it sounds like a song the whole time, not like an instrumental with vocal attachments. In other words, the instrumental passages reach us as very informative and satisfying non-verbal verses; they not only sustain but hugely deepen the narrative. Got something to say. Of course we look to the words for a clue as to the subject matter of all this saying (signifying) that so impacts on us.

Well, this is not an evidently autobiographical song. "Bad News" is not just an emotional condition but a person, a protagonist, fictional character. Excellent song-poetry: "Bad News is come to town/He's walking three feet off the ground/He's ordering another round/Bound by his own ideal love/Doesn't know where she is found." It comes across as a genuinely spiritual statement, in the Neil Young "searching for love" song sequence or tradition. Verse two says BN's fighting mad, 'cause he "lost the biggest prize he ever had," presumably an ideal lover who got away, but the verse extends this thought by observing that "a prizefighter can't be sad, when he smiles under golden lights . . ." That arena image again. This time Neil doesn't sound like he's talking about himself but about a third party he finds it easy to empathize with. Somehow all the songs of love troubles on *This Note's for You* added together don't add up to a tiny fraction of the feeling

196

expressed in the short verses of this song for someone who isn't necessarily the singer but is another human for whom the singer has strong and genuine feelings of compassion. Whatever. Anything that makes a listener feel this much has just got to be the real thing. Arguably, straight from the source of whatever it is we like so much in Neil Young's body of work.

So I was trying to figure out how this mostly instrumental performance casts such a spell on me and brings me so much pleasure, without even any of the familiar Neil Young guitar ecstatics (some good guitar work, yes, but not in that identifiable genre) or catchy choruses. Certainly no duelling guitars. Something different, something one-of-a-kind that is still surely full of that characteristic Neil Young-ness that to my taste is completely missing from *This Note's for You* (except for the likeable attitude in the anthemic title song's words). And here's what I found, not the whole answer probably but certainly an interesting device. I think the song is dominated by a simple hook/riff that is mostly unheard but just about always *felt*.

The riff: first three notes of the song, blared by the horns from 02 to 05, repeated at 10 seconds and again at 18. Simple descending pattern. Absolutely addictive. This addictiveness is exploited right away, as we wait eight seconds to hear the riff again and instead get a fake at 29. We get the first note but not the riff; instead the melodic theme is toyed with very cleverly, charming us even as the tension of need-that-hook builds in the listener. This tension is built up and played with very knowingly by the band, so when the vocal starts and then the riff returns right after the first words ("Bad news is come to town") it is a big fat hook-release worthy of Phil Spector or a Beatles single. Groovy. The riff returns after the second line, and this turns out to be a brilliant sucker game when we get to the end of the third line and the familiar town/ground rhyme isn't followed by the expected riff but instead repeats itself and leaves us quite dazzled, especially as this is one of the key phrases in the song ("bound by his own ideal love"). Yeah. And

I assure you we'll hear that riff again, and mostly feel the tension of its promise and absence, throughout the rest of the song. No wonder the music sustains so powerfully. There are also fine moments where the expected riff is replaced by a drum riff, eloquent and perverse stand-in. Who wrote these charts? I dunno, but the whole performance is more evidence of Neil Young's unique gift, even, at times, his genius. Genius at letting inspiration guide him home.

And then there's the sound. Except for the people talking on this tape, the sound is absolute perfection, unique sonic pleasure, to be treasured and re-experienced again and again. All telling us more and more, every time, about the story of Mr. Bad News, a story that presumably takes on different and very powerful personal meanings and resonances for each listener. For me it somehow echoes "Love in Mind" ("I've seen love make a fool of a man, he tried to make a loser win") and then mysteriously (because I know Neil wasn't suffering any failed love-search at this time in his life) echoes the "bullfighter before the crowd" scene in "Road of Plenty": "taking klieg-light fights again and again." Neil bruised but unbowed, back on tour. What can it all mean? Sure sounds fine.

* * *

And then we come to the one unreleased Neil Young song that can *never* be overlooked, #1 vote-getter among unreleased songs in the fan poll, that more-obvious epic (so many words, such an outburst): "Ordinary People."

Before I start raving about this astonishing nine-verse, twelve-minute song (over fifteen minutes some nights), let's go back to a night in early April 1988 that must stand beside that fevered day when "Cinnamon," "Cowgirl," and "River" came forth. Neil is quoted: *"I was on my sailboat sailing to Hawaii, and I'd just received word that the video for 'This Note's for You' was not going to be played* [banned by MTV]. *I hadn't seen anybody for about eight days, so I was pretty spacey out there. In one night I wrote three songs: 'Ordinary People,' 'Sixty to Zero' and 'Days that Used to Be.' "* The latter turned up on *Ragged Glory.* 'Sixty to Zero' is an epic even longer than "OP," performed at the Aug.-Oct. '88 shows, unreleased except that five of its eleven verses became the great *Freedom* track "Crime in the City (Sixty to Zero Part I)." "Ordinary People" and "Sixty to Zero" are as unique in Neil's history as a songwriter as the Topanga fever songs. When your gift is to be an inspired artist, you never know what might come through when the channels get opened . . .

What is "Ordinary People"? Still a song with the Bluenotes, but not so much emphasis on the instrumental passages this time. The verses are mostly broken by short (ten-second) breaks, except for two breaks that are 30 seconds and one that's 65, plus a 44-second intro and 78-second outro. That still leaves a lot of singing in a twelve-minute song. At one show Young introduced "Ordinary People" as *"too long to be a video, too long to be on the radio, and too long to be on an album."* In an interview with *Rolling Stone* probably conducted shortly after he wrote "OP" and "Sixty to Zero," he said, *"Right now I love the Bluenotes . . . I think it's the best support I've had for the kind of music I was into. That makes me write a new song every morning when I wake up, instead of thinking, 'Well, if I write this, are the guys gonna be able to play it, or have I got the right band, or do I know anybody who really understands who I am who I can actually play music with?' "* Okay, that's the songwriter speaking about the relationship between performing and writing. The *Cowboy* booklet offers a brief comment by the performer about the same relationship: *"It's fun to play new songs. They're easy. It gets to be work playing the old ones."*

So what have we got here? One of Neil Young's greatest songs ever, or one of his greatest performances ever? Take your pick. Or take both at once.

Footnote on who the Bluenotes were to Neil: a regular song at the Bluenotes shows both years, later included as a live track on the compilation *Lucky 13*, was "Ain't It the Truth," a song he wrote and performed and recorded with the Squires in 1964. He isn't known to have performed it publicly again until 1987. Oh, and a second footnote. It doesn't seem too widely noticed that "Crime in the City," which along with "Rockin' in the Free World" is the heart and soul of *Freedom,* is performed on that album by Neil Young and the Bluenotes – the 1988 line-up, precisely. Small wonder it is the only recording in the NY catalog that bears any resemblance to "Bad News" or "Ordinary People." Product of the same extraordinary (aural?) vision.

"Ordinary People" is overwhelming. It staggers the mind. On first listen or first several, it's all feeling, the feeling of these many words coming at you and of the strange and very confident intelligence that seems to hold all of them, and all this music, together. A hot shower. A just-out-of-reach visionary panorama. You probably don't hear much of what he's saying most of the time – just phrases, vivid images, that jump out here and there. My friend the novelist Jonathan Lethem describes the song's impact in cinematic terms (appropriate, the song's opening scene is from a movie), and finds something (Raymond) Chandleresque in Young's bitten-off language and hardboiled persona here. Jumping to a third medium, the word Jonathan said that most struck me when we talked briefly about "Ordinary People" was that there seems to be something "pointillist" about Neil's verbal technique here. Yeah, sounds right to me, and in fact I had written down the word "impressionistic" in my own notes on the song. So I looked up the dictionary definition of "pointillism": "the method of painting of certain French impressionists, in which a white ground is systematically covered with tiny points of pure color that blend together when seen from a distance, producing a luminous effect." Yes! Precisely how "Ordinary People" works. And my God is it luminous . . .

Johnny Rogan says "Ordinary People" and "Sixty to Zero" "were heavily influenced by mid-period Dylan." Which is a good call, particularly if they were written the same night as "Days That Used to Be," which can fairly confidently be read as being addressed to Dylan. And Neil is outspoken about being a big Dylan fan, and so of course as a songwriter he must have occasionally dreamed of writing his own "Desolation Row" or "Gates of Eden" or "A Hard Rain's A-Gonna Fall." "Ordinary People" and "Sixty to Zero/Crime in the City" fit the bill better than almost any other epics that have been written in the spirit of mid-sixties Dylan (unless you count "Sister Ray" or "Land"). And yet these Neil songs are not at all Dylanesque in language or concept. But I'm sure Rogan's right to point out that Dylan's the inspiration.

But don't expect "Ordinary People" to be "Desolation Row." Its intentions, and its strengths, are very different. Except insofar as the artist's intention in both cases is to let out a big glop of feeling or thoughts, with the hope of impressing a listener with his cleverness and with the scope of his artistic feeling and ambition. Unconscious intention, maybe. But you succeeded, Neil. I'm impressed, and so are almost all of your other listeners who've heard this song.

Almost anyone's impression of the message of "Ordinary People" (including mine) is likely to be as unreliable or subjective as the impression/message one receives from "Down by the River" or "Pocahontas." "He's saying . . . Well, I don't know what he's saying, but I know how it *feels* to me . . ." Since not many people have commented in print yet about this song, I'll pick on Alan Jenkins again, who calls it a "superb, fiercely emotional song that can surely lay claim to being the best unreleased Young tune. Its ten verses can take over a quarter of an hour to unfold while Young conjures images of the evil done by, for and in the name of 'the people.' In between he delivers some of his most blistering guitar solos ever."

Except that after writing out the nine verses (to the *Cowboy* version; now I wanna hear the tenth!) and studying them by reading along while listening over and over for hours and days, I think I could make a good case that although there are a few activities discussed that could be called evil (certainly, "selling guns to the underground"), by and large evil is not a central or important element in the stories told and pictures painted in "Ordinary People" 's text. "Crime in the City," yeah, but that's a different song. "Ordinary People" really is primarily about people, a certain feeling about "people" (the human race as a buncha individuals and as an environment we individuals are aware of living next to or in), and more than anything else that feeling is love. Neil loves (feels affection for) us, them, in all their humanness. And he expresses it not by conscious plan but by spilling out his own impressions, conveying to us how it *feels* to take this all in at once, as Dylan does (in more orderly, even more linear, fashion) in "A Hard Rain's A-Gonna Fall."

Yeah, so can you believe Neil Young has found a (successful) way to be less linear than Bob Dylan was when he made his non-linear breakthroughs?! Neil is surprisingly unconcerned with getting a good grade for his composition. He lets it flow and go where spirit guides him. And (sez me, and I'm not alone) it works. Brilliantly. *Neil's* non-linear breakthrough – this wasn't his first use of the method but is one of the strongest examples thereof – is giving himself permission in a song not to tie things together or make them seem to make sense upon close examination. It's not about close examination (though that can be fun). It's about the *gestalt*, the way the points of color blend together, the sound, the impact of the whole performance.

So why does the song start (lyrically; it's already started instrumentally) with a scene from the great 1952 western *High Noon*? Because it wants to. And because, in my opinion, Neil is thinking about the sweep of historical change, and cleverly saying that the gunslinger showdown of two hundred years ago (oops – how about 100?) can now be seen in a similar or the same small town in two hot rods drag racing down Main Street. (Different movie.) Then in the same verse he describes the

202

urbanization of small-town Texas or Arizona in empathetic, human terms as "a half a million people moved in to pick up the pace, a factory full of people, making parts to go to outer space . . ." Nice poetry, especially that last touch. Along with Dylan, the English-speaking writers Young reminds me of in this song are Allen Ginsberg and Walt Whitman. Not that he (or Dylan) can compete as a page poet with the better page poets. And not that he needs to. Neil Young should be Neil Young. And a songwriter/performer must finally be judged or appreciated as a songwriter/performer. I like Allen's occasional rock and roll, and there are no recordings of Walt's guitar playing, but Neil with this song, meaning the singing and the rhythm and the ensemble performance and the words as dramatic/musical experience, here lays proud claim to his place in their bardic tradition. Spit the words at the people. Get a good rhythm into it.

The tradition of the Old Testament prophet, okay? And what is also remarkable about Neil Young is that he manages, in this song and others, to be so unpretentious and – given the subject matter – so unsentimental. No awkward Dylan imitation here. No self-conscious attempt to make a great statement. Just no censorship of a wacky great statement when it presents itself and starts pouring out of him. Un-self-conscious. Inspired. Outrageous. Astonishing.

And therefore courageous. Neil Young in his many good moments has been a very courageous artist, not overly concerned about public or critical or marketplace censure. "To thine own self be true." Yeah. He writes and records like he plays guitar. Like self-expression is the basic human right. And is synonymous with love.

Let me point to a few of the very unusual and admirable literary devices employed (probably intuitively but maybe also consciously) in the writing of "Ordinary People." (I could say, in the writing of the words of "Ordinary People," but when you realize the words contain and direct the rhythm, in the author's mind, you realize words and music are not separable

203

in a case like this. Each defines the other. And who can say which came first? I'm sure Neil would tell you they arrived together.)

The essence of the song, and its most Ginsbergian element, is the use of the word "people" as the last word of each of the three and a half chorus lines in all nine of the verses. The entire poem and song and performance are strung on this word, this riff, this beat, this "rhyme." The lines of each chorus are completely different except for that one repeated word and its placement, which is what makes them choruses. Great device. Repetition opens the soul. And is the heart of music. Listen to those chorus lines (the last three and a half lines of each six-and-a-half-line verse) and the way the words build up every time to the stirring climax "*people.*" Gives me lots of feelings. And is in absolutely no danger of being confused with any other ideas or feelings I associate with the word "people." In this case, for as long as I'm listening to the song, Neil makes the word his own. So the feelings conjured by the music of the song, and by the singing and guitar playing and sax playing and drumming, all become one great articulate description of "people" as seen (perceived) by Neil Young. The plural of us. The multitude. Without sentimental Marxist crap, or anything from any other ism. Just this poet's report on how he feels when he's off on his sailboat reading the newsmagazines and newspapers and contemplating the world he's been born in.

Other devices. Well, internal rhyme is a big one. Let's divide the song into verses and (attached) choruses. Four of the nine verses have regular internal rhymes in addition to the normal line-ending rhymes. Each of these verses is three lines that rhyme with each other at their endings ("for sale" "jail" "bail") and that also rhyme in their middles (in this case "cigar" "car" – only two rhymes, but the other three verses like this have internal rhymes in all three lines). This is a very effective device, a lot of fun for the listener regardless of whether you notice it consciously or not. It sounds great. And then guess what? The last three chorus lines (which of course "rhyme" with each other and with the bridging half line by all ending in "people") *always* have internal rhymes – seven of the choruses have rhymes in the middle of all three lines, and the other two choruses rhyme in the middle twice and then lay off the rhyming in the third line. For example, after the second verse with its jail, bail and cigar, the second chorus is "Sellin' guns to the underground, livin' off the people/Skimmin' the top when there's no one around, tryin' to help the people/Lose their ass for a piece of ground, patch-of-ground people."

Great rhyme scheme. Nine stanzas: three lines that rhyme with each other at the ends and sometimes in the middles, four lines that "rhyme" by ending on the same word, and three of those four usually rhyming with each other via their middle words. Gets a great rhythm going. Scratches your mind and feelings in places that haven't been touched for years.

Of course, there are other devices I could mention (a little bit of restrained alliteration: "company car," "sellin' safety"), but I think my English prof must be satisfied already. "But hey," some of you who've already heard the song are asking me, "what else can you say about the subject matter?" Well, it's going to vary for each listener. The opening verse/chorus we discussed ("In a dusty town a clock struck high noon . . ."). The second and third verse/choruses are about the gun-runner and aren't preachy so much as humorous and sly, dealing with the humanness of the protagonist (and his customers and victims, us, "the people"). "He was dealing antiques in a hardware store, but he sure had a lot to hide." "Get the drugs to the street all right, tryin' to help the people."

Fourth verse/chorus continues the same thought but it turns into an image of "vigilante people" conscientiously or perhaps hysterically "takin' the law into their own hands." If I make it sound like it could be linear, that's not the way it's experienced when you're listening to it, even if you're trying to hear all the words. It keeps changing frames on you. Verse/chorus five is a marvellous portrait of homeless people living in an abandoned factory they once worked in and might someday work in again. Could be a metaphor for the whole nation! And it ends with what could be a message to our leaders: "They've been livin' in a nightmare, ordinary people/And you don't know how they got there, hard-workin' people/And they don't think that you care, patch-of-ground people."

I could go on, but remember the truth is what you think you hear, what you feel when you hear the song. What he actually says is only a vehicle for that, like the notes he may happen to be playing on his guitar. If we like the way it sounds, again and again, we rightly praise the notes, whether we know their names or not. And hey, how about those breaks where the guitar and sax dance with each other?

Most of all, the information in the song is conveyed in the sound (including, particularly, the sound of the man's voice) and the rhythm. This performance is so much about the rhythm and sound of language it could be said to be Neil's excursion into rap music. Nah, no hip-hop beats. But man, that dude sure lays it down. In addition to "Leaves of Grass" and "Desolation Row" and "Wichita Vortex Sutra," I can hear this performance as related to John Coltrane's "Meditations" or Grandmaster Flash's "The Message." Not that it specifically resembles any of those works. But it is in their league. It shares their ambitions and inspirations and successes.

"Things'll be different soon, we're gonna bring her back on line." Consider it an optimistic ending. But you already know from that last sax and guitar segment that this vision is ultimately a positive one. Stirring. Reassuring. Stimulating. Mind-boggling.

* * *

Track 6: "Rockin' in the Free World," live on the "Saturday Night Live" television show, Sept. 30, 1989. A month before the release of *Freedom*, month after the release of the single, not with Crazy Horse nor with The Restless (the band that backs Neil on the official release) but with two guys who as far as I know never played with Neil before, Charlie Drayton on bass and Steve Jordan on drums, plus a third guy on rhythm guitar who plays with both Crazy Horse and The Restless, Frank ("Poncho") Sampedro.

The *Rock 'N' Roll Cowboy* booklet annotator says: "*This is one of the very few non-tour songs featured in this 4-CD set. It is simply the song's best version ever.*"

Wait a minute, Erik. I totally understand and relate to your enthusiasm for this particular performance – indeed, the reliable Pete Long calls it a *tour de force*. Yeah. And when I'm under its spell I might start babbling that it's the best something-or-other I ever heard in my life. It is intoxicating. But comparisons are odious, and ranking the different Neil Young or Bob Dylan performances of a beloved song is intrinsically misleading and risky. Some days I've listened to this version (in the context of your high praise) and felt it couldn't touch the official release (band version or the impact of the solo and the band versions remembered together). Other days I've also played the fabulous *Weld* version and again thought you were off the mark. Other days I've fully shared your enthusiasm for this one. Neil Young fans not only disagree with each other, we have disagreements inside ourselves. In any case, the brilliance of this performance does not take anything away from the familiar *Freedom* (The Restless) and *Weld* (Crazy Horse) versions. For that matter, the *Freedom* Videocassette version (solo, like the first track on the CD, but from a different show) is very likeable too. How marvellous to have so many different and outstanding live recordings of the same song! A song which happens to place #4 (among all songs) in that 1995 poll of Young fans.

Comparisons aside, the "Saturday Night Live" performance is quite spectacular, and good to have a recording of in your bag of tricks when you're trying to persuade a friend what a *great* guitar player and bandleader Neil Young is. And I haven't even seen it (yet), though I can easily imagine that seeing it is a wonderful opportunity to observe Neil Young in full joyous passion and abandon of performance (as in the footage of his moments in the 1992 Bob Dylan Anniversary Concert). There are some very interesting quotes from Neil about how he worked himself up to deliver this performance; we'll get to them in a moment. First let me say I have some further thoughts on what this song "means" and some surprising information on its historical timing, since my 1992 essay (chapter 11), and will get to them before the end of this section. Um, and how about this tidbit? At the rehearsal for the TV show, on the afternoon before this performance, Neil up and wrote the exquisite *Ragged Glory* song "Fuckin' Up."

And let me also say that if you, like me, find yourself sceptical about Erik's (and my) over-the-top enthusiasm the first time you hear this performance, wait for the right night and then listen to it ten times in a row. Loud. You'll be slapping fives with both of us.

The quotes. Well, one is in the *Cowboy* booklet, and the other is quoted in Pete Long's *Ghosts on the Road*. Both (I think) are from a *Musician* Magazine interview conducted by Fred Schruers (hi Fred – I remember we had some great conversations about Neil 22 years ago), but I don't have a copy of the interview itself (or time to track it down), so I have to guess at how the two fragments go together. Marvellous stuff, in any case, and here 'tis:

[The first part, Long tells us, is about how Young worked out with his trainer moments before showtime. The, ahem, Keith Moon part of the story is from the *Cowboy* booklet and no, I don't think it was made up in Milano . . .] *"Pushups, situps, I worked up a real sweat to be where you should be at the end of a stage show. No wonder everybody looks like old farts playing 'Saturday Night,' everybody's being cool, but that don't have shit to do with rock 'n' roll . . .*

". . . I removed myself from the whole fucking scene, went to a room in the other end of the building, never hung out, never watched the

show, completely ignored the skits. Steve Jordan and Charlie Drayton were playing with us on the gig and Poncho and I went up and trashed their dressing room, fucking graffiti, broke everything in it and painted it with spray-cans. In my mind you gotta be jacked into it, man. It's fucking life and death and you're only as good as your last note. So I had to ignore what was going on there. I never do live r'n'r on TV – that was a huge exception to the rule – and I probably never will again. I was very, very lucky that I played well and everything came off good."

Amen. Man, does it come off good. That lead guitar. That rhythm section. That groove!! You gotta love it. Enough said. But when an anthem is this gloriously rousing – okay, in a sense what it really is is a great instrumental with words (voice is an instrument too), plus a catchy and indeed rousing seven-word chorus – you gotta wonder if anyone's hearing or thinking about the lyrics other than the tag-line. In which case, the heart of my argument for that other performance as being one of the 100 best rock 'n' roll singles of all time is kinda lost here. Oh well. Just proves there's more than one way to skin a cat (get *greatness* out of a good song).

And then I do have to ask myself, am I so sure the tag-line ("Keep on rockin' in the free world!") is meant sarcastically? Yes, I am, even though Neil's vocal inflection, on all versions, is not sarcastic. How else to account for the juxtaposition of the miserable suffering girl and infant and the tag-line? Funny thing is, I just noticed that Nick Kent in his book *The Dark Side* interprets those lines I love so much in 1973's "Last Dance" ("You can live your own life . . . oh no!" – see chapter 1) as being sarcastic: "Young seemed to have suddenly become openly cynical in his lyrics about the freewheeling hippie doctrines he'd once been associated with." I completely disagree. And I think I'm right in both cases. But you know what, readers/listeners? You have to make the call. We're just commentators. Each of us hears and interprets his or her own song, according to my, um, experiential theories of art appreciation and evaluation.

209

So though I try to keep an open mind, I'm not gonna recant my theory that "Rockin' in the Free World" is actually the great rock and roll anthem that says (at last): "Great rockin' anthems and anthemic feelings are cool but they tend to put us to sleep. Wake up!!!" (Or else we'll all be as pretty vacant as we ironically say we are.) Come to think of it, that's what I think "Last Dance" says, too. Neil's message.

But I did make one reasonable assumption in my 1992 piece which is upset by Pete Long's careful dating of performances and first appearances of songs. Seems like Neil was a genuine prophet, as I always thought rock songwriter/performers (Jim Morrison, Mick Jagger) could be at their best and in their moments of grace. *Freedom* came out in November 1989, so it was natural for me and many other attentive listeners to consider the album's theme and particularly the lyrics of "Rockin' in the Free World" as a very timely commentary on the fall of European Communism (the "free world" is a mid–20th-Century term that only has meaning in relation to the "Iron Curtain" or some other characterization of the Communist nations). Yeah. But that historic collapse basically happened (quite unexpectedly) in autumn of 1989. And Neil Young first sang "Rockin' in the Free World" at a concert in Seattle February 21, 1989!

Going back to the subjective interpretation of rock song messages, I must admit I am made quite uneasy (given my own peacenik background) by the American flags that can be seen being waved by audience members during this song on the *Weld* videocassette. (Filmed – and performed ambiguously, but gloriously – during the Gulf War.)

Anyway, finally, if you think I'm over the top in saying Neil Young was a genuine prophet when he wrote this song in (or before) February 1989, I cite in support of my case comments by the songwriter that you can hear yourself in two very moving live performances from September 6, 1989 that are included in the *Freedom* Videocassette. The first of the performances (everything on the tape is solo acoustic) is "Ohio," which he very appropriately (and if you don't get the connection, you'd better fucking well wake up) dedicates: *"This is a song for the students killed in China this summer."* (The Tiananmen Square massacre happened three months before the show, and three months after he first sang the song publicly.) After finishing "Ohio," he continues his thought (his stream of consciousness thought/feeling; the man thinks with his feelings, God bless him) by saying to the audience: *"So many pictures of the Statue of Liberty made out of paper falling over, and the kid with the tulips standing in front of the tank and later on they picked him out of the crowd on TV, and then I think they put him to sleep. And then a kid standing there singing why they want democracy, and they talk about how it's like this dream and everything, and they're . . . they want to have it so bad."*

And then he strums and sings "Rockin' in the Free World."

* * *

This is a book about the experience of listening to Neil Young. Listening is not a science. It is a kind of personal art, in the sense that lovemaking is a personal art. We express ourselves in our listening, and, unless you carry your boom box on the subway, we do so fairly privately. Okay, I don't. I write about it. But I insist that I write not to be the artist's judge, some kind of "critic" who presumes to determine what's good and what's not, but to report on private experiences that have had considerable impact on me. And to call my readers' attention to marvels they may have missed or not yet know about (I haven't changed since I was trying to turn my friends and handful of readers on to this new *Buffalo Springfield* album).

And I write to argue the case for the artist's work. That's what I was up to with Neil Young in 1967 and 1972 and 1974 and so forth. And what I'm still up to in 1996 and 1997. Burning (expressing) my love for the man's music. Songs. Performances. Work. And, in the case of this book, trying to

211

share with fellow-appreciators tidbits of information, quotes from the artist, chronological, circumstantial, even biographical details, that help to clarify, or in some cases even deepen our relationships with, the works of art themselves.

This is meant as a prelude to describing a tiny personal mystery in connection with listening to *Rock 'N' Roll Cowboy*, disc 4, track 7, "Winterlong," a live performance from Holland (but not in Dutch), December 1989. If I were, let's say, teaching a class on appreciating the art of the late–20th-Century master Neil Young, in addition to seminars on *Tonight's the Night* and *Ragged Glory* and *The Complex Sessions* and various rockin' high points like "Cowgirl in the Sand" and "Ordinary People" (two very eccentric examples of rockers, but then one thing we like about Neil Young's work is its eccentricity or heterogeneity), I imagine I would also hand out a short tape of songs including "Winterlong," "See the Sky about to Rain," "Journey through the Past," and "Here We Are in the Years." "Here," I'd say to my students, "these kill me. Please listen to them and then let's discuss what we heard and experienced."

There'd be a lot to talk about, I believe. And I know I'd be very particular about which performances of these songs I'd present. And that's where the mystery of track 7 comes in. It's a very good solo performance, Neil on vocals and piano and harmonica, and I can find no fault in it but I do find, after weeks of experimenting on myself, that for some reason the 1973 recording of the song (song written in 1969, and released only on the *Decade* album) has an impact on me that this quite pretty 1989 solo version can't seem to replicate. And I can't put my finger on the difference between the two (apart from the obvious presence of other musicians and backing voices on the 1973 version), apart from how they make me feel. One makes me smile most of the time, the other almost invariably thrills me. Why?

Well, I guess a big part of it is a little melodic hook on which the bass is the lead instrument, and the backing harmonies as well as the subtle second voice that augments Neil's lead.

212

These elements work so extraordinarily well, and cast such a reliable spell on me. I would expect to be equally delighted by a solo piano-and-harmonica version (indeed, the versions of "Journey" and "See the Sky" that I'd require my students to listen to are solo piano versions from 1971). And there's nothing wrong with the playing or singing on the '89 track. But that 1973 session *has it*. And, I ask, as a serious commentator on the art of late–20th-Century rock and roll: what's *it*?

I can't claim to know with any certainty. But I do look forward to hearing from you in the seminar.

* * *

I'm gonna rush through the last seven tracks of *Rock 'N' Roll Cowboy*, which are all worth hearing even if they're not extraordinary masterworks (though "Separate Ways" with Booker T. & the MGs in '93 comes close). Three unreleased songs, two oldies reinvented, and two rarities: more presidents added to "Campaigner" and a 1994 Oscar-nominated song live at the Awards ceremony. That Neil Young keeps giving us more reasons to wonder what else he might have up his sleeve (or stashed in his cupboards). A few quick annotations before the NY Archives CDs come out and presumably give us even more reasons to scratch our heads and ask, "Who was that masked man?" Musta been the strange loner . . .

Track 8, "Silver and Gold," is performed (almost solo, on acoustic guitar and harmonica, plus attractive backing vocals) with CSNY at a March 1990 benefit for their former drummer Dallas Taylor, who needed a liver transplant. The show also raised funds for a non-profit drug abuse research and education organization. The *Cowboy* booklet sez: "Recorded for the original version of the album *Old Ways*, and then re-recorded in 1985 along with a great number of country-oriented songs. Later recorded with Crosby, Stills and Nash but still unreleased." John Robertson agrees it was recorded in

1/83 for the rejected *Old Ways,* and an article by Jerry Fuentes in *Broken Arrow* 61 further notes that "Silver and Gold" was copyrighted on September 7, 1982 along with other songs recorded for the *first* rejected Geffen album, *Island in the Sun.* Always a bridesmaid but never a bride. Not a great song, but a striking performance.

Track 9, "Campaigner," is from the winter 1991 tour (though it certainly doesn't get the full Crazy Horse/*Weld* crashing feedback treatment). Michael Piehler's *Broken Arrow* article "The Reprise Years," supposedly "a complete listing of all the songs Neil Young finished and handed in to Reprise Records between 1969 and 1981," dates "Campaigner" as recorded in 1974, which if true would contradict Neil's comment in the *Decade* notes that "Campaigner" was *"written during the Stills/Young Band tour on the bus. Sort of a modern day Cortez, you know."* Johnny Rogan adds that the song's original title was "Requiem for a President," and that "Young had watched news footage of Nixon visiting his wife in hospital after she suffered a stroke. He was sufficiently moved to compose the sympathetic refrain 'even Richard Nixon has got soul.' " Elsewhere I read that what struck Neil was Nixon's "dejected" look as he left the hospital. This 1991 version adds "even Ronald Reagan has got it" and "even George Bush has got soul." Neil also improvises a closing sequence in which Muhammed Ali, John F. Kennedy, Marilyn Monroe, Godzilla, jet fighter pilots, and Linda Lovelace also turn out to have "it." He closes, "Stand up if you've got –" (and the choir sings) "soul . . ." The performance, and the proximity to track 12, "Mr. Soul," naturally make me wonder what "soul" means to Neil Young. That's okay, I think one purpose of the song is to make us reconsider what it means to us (definitely coming from the perspective that it's a virtue, a highly positive quality).

Track 10, "Homefires," is a fairly soulful 1992 solo perform-ance of this 1974 gem. First, you gotta (as a fan or curious onlooker) love a guy who'll drag out a song he wrote eighteen years ago (and never released, because it was too personal) and hasn't played live since . . . and suddenly offer it to his audience (some of whom are fans who've surely heard it on a bootleg tape) at a solo acoustic concert in New York City. Those of us who make the effort to go to as many concerts as possible by a beloved performer really appreciate being surprised one night by a seldom- (or never-) played song. And how much better when it's an autobiographical song per-formed with genuine feeling almost two decades after the fact (well, one's separation from a past lover does tend to keep its poignance when she happens to be your second committed relationship and the mom of your first kid)! A touching song, and this time (Boston, March 19, 1992) it truly communicates the protagonist's feelings regarding his situation, particularly in the harmonica playing, and when he sings, "I'll walk these borders in search of a line/Between young lovers who lead separate lives." Could be the story of almost any young-movie-star romance, though in this case it's movie-star-and-rock-star. And I'm impressed too that when Young reintroduced the song (Beacon Theater, NYC, Feb. 17, '92, on a tour mainly focused on songs from his forthcoming *Harvest Moon* album), he played it on piano, but a month later when he chose to try the song again (Orpheum Theater, Boston) he played it on guitar. I'd like to have been at both shows. And I appreciate the opportunity offered by the *Cowboy* album to hear even one "Homefires" (first time for me – one reason this *Cowboy* set comes as such a revelation is I haven't listened to many other Neil Young bootlegs). I also like the couplet (not so much on the page, but the way he sings it): "So for me the wheels are turning/Got to keep the homefires burning."

Track 11, "Only Love Can Break Your Heart," is mainly notable for the backing vocals by Paul Simon and Art Gar-funkel (at a benefit concert for the Children's Health Fund, March '93). And for being the only song that appears on *Rock 'N' Roll Cowboy* twice. The benefit was at the Dorothy Chandler Pavilion in Los Angeles, where twenty-two years earlier Neil played the show recorded on the *Young Man's Fancy* bootleg.

Track 12 is "Mr. Soul," performed with Booker T. & the MGs (including the great Steve Cropper on guitar, the almost equally legendary "Duck" Dunn on bass, the brilliant and durable Jim Keltner on drums, and of course Booker T Jones on organ and backing vocals) at the Ahoy in Rotterdam, July 5, 1993. Quite good, indeed, though it can't compete with my cherished memories of the absolutely spectacular versions I saw and heard at the Whisky in Hollywood in December '66 and at Ondine in New York in early January '67, just before Buffalo Springfield recorded it (kinda unsuccessfully). Their best live song in those days. And the beginning of my connection with Neil Young as a live performer. Wish this '93 "Mr. Soul" were as Dionysian, but that wasn't how Neil chose to approach it that year. Instead it's a genial, groovin' show-opener. One important historical footnote about the song's lyrics is that this was written just before (not after) Buffalo Springfield got some national fame and attention via "For What It's Worth." They were just another local band in L.A. with a record contract and big dreams. And, as "Mr. Soul" documents, nightmares too. Fear of attention along with desire for it. "In a while will the smile on my face turn to plaster?" It could have, man, happened to many of your friends and contemporaries, but I think one thing Neil Young fans can agree on is that it never happened to you. You've managed to keep your independence even from your own public image. And from your fans' expectations, the key issue in the song. Nice going, buddy. When you know from the start that rust never sleeps, it's easier to stay a jump ahead of it. "Is it strange I should change? I don't know . . ."

* * *

Now, for dramatic effect, I have to reverse the last two tracks. "Separate Ways," a centerpiece at every one of the Booker

T/Neil shows in summer '93, is so bloody marvellous I want to end this story with it. No disrespect to the real closing track, "Philadelphia," but "Separate Ways" in this case is a hard act to follow. "Powderfinger" could do it, and usually did in '93, but it's not on *Cowboy*. ("It might surprise you the absence of such classics as 'Cortez the Killer,' 'Cinnamon Girl,' 'After the Gold Rush' and 'Powderfinger,' " Erik tells us in his introduction to the *Rock 'N' Roll Cowboy* booklet, "but they are already available on Neil's official live albums. So we preferred to save some room for unusual material.")

Track 14, "Philadelphia," is the 1994 track to justify *Cowboy*'s subtitle, "A Life on the Road, 1966/1994." The end of the road in this case, believe it or not, is again the Dorothy Chandler Pavilion. Now the scene of the 66th annual Academy Awards ceremony, live on TV and live in front of a well-dressed audience in this theater. Neil like Bruce Springsteen was nominated for an Oscar for the title song he wrote for a 1993 film by Jonathan Demme, *Philadelphia*, a drama about AIDS. Bruce's song won. Both men performed at the ceremony. Neil accompanied himself on piano, and was joined (on backing vocals) by his wife Pegi Young and by his half-sister Astrid. The song was released on a single and a soundtrack album. But it has never been on a Neil Young album, unless you count this live version on *Rock 'N' Roll Cowboy*.

Disc 4, track 13, finally, is "Separate Ways," with Booker T & the MGs, at a festival in Belgium, July 3, 1993. Another song from 1974, written for the ultimately unreleased *Homegrown* album recorded at the end of that year after Neil's separation from Carrie Snodgrass. And performed live for the first time nineteen years later at the first Booker T show in June. Such a good song. Bob Dylan once said: "A lot of artists say, 'I can't sing those old songs any more,' and I can understand it because you're no longer the same person who wrote those songs. However, you really are still that person some place deep down. So you can still sing them if you can get in touch with the person you were when you wrote the songs."

217

Bob knows. And on "Separate Ways" and "Homefires" Neil Young demonstrates an impressive ability to be, become, be in touch with the part of himself who wrote these heartfelt affirmation-of-love-in-the-face-of-its-loss songs. Very impressive singing, not for technical reasons but emotional ones. Mr. Soul, indeed.

And it occurs to me, under the spell of the clarity and expressiveness of "Separate Ways," that hidden in this *Rock 'N' Roll Cowboy* set is a kind of perfect EP version of that legendary lost *Homegrown* album. "Separate Ways." "Love Art Blues." "Pardon My Heart" in that revelatory solo version. "Homefires." "Hawaiian Sunrise." A song cycle. I certainly don't regret that Neil decided to release *Tonight's the Night* in 1975, even if it was in place of *Homegrown*. I just appreciate that his reasons for holding back the latter were exactly the reasons he gave in that Cameron Crowe interview at the time. Again: *"I've never released any of those. And I probably never will. I think I'd be a little too embarrassed to put them out. They're a little too real."* And that's what's so lovely about "Separate Ways" (along with the arrangement and the guitar playing, either Cropper channelling Young or Young channelling Cropper but either way it's exquisite) – it's so *real.*

Nick Kent in his book *The Dark Stuff* quotes and describes a conversation he had with Neil in autumn 1989: "Later he would talk about this dream he'd just had in which he'd encountered these miraculous songs he'd never heard before and how he was currently obsessed with getting those songs out of his dreams and down on tape, whatever the consequences:" [Talk about being an inspired artist! But read on for what Young told Kent]

"I feel I'm moving in the flow of something that is easier for me now. My music has taken me to a place now where I'm not fighting things any more. Through most of the eighties I didn't want my innermost feelings about life and everything to come out. Back then I had a lot of dark thoughts weighing on my mind, tied into experiences that happened in my immediate family. Things happened to me over those years

I had no possible reason or way or capacity to expect to explain. At the same time, this inner voice has always dictated exactly what I have to do, but sometimes I'd wake up in the morning and I'd be given my orders, 'OK, Neil, today you're going to make this kind of music.' And I'd think, 'Oh my God . . . OK, I want to do this, I have to do this, but not too many people are going to like it!' But I'd still go ahead 'cause I'd want to hear it anyway."

Yeah, artist and audience can go their separate ways too. But that doesn't mean they have to hate each other. After all, "It's all because of that love we knew, that makes the world go round." I love it. And I love the way he starts, "I won't apologize," defiant but (as it turns out) actually loving. You're still the beautiful creature I fell in love with, he asserts. We didn't destroy each other. Just learned a lot. And created something together . . .

16

Ragged Glory and *Weld*
("when fans are fools")

We fans are fools, in my opinion, when we get stuck in conventional (like, you know, *square*) ideas when evaluating the body of work of an artist whom we admire for his or her stubborn and articulate unconventionality.

What is conventional? Well, for one thing, to suppose that the body of work of a performer-songwriter like Neil Young or Bob Dylan or Patti Smith consists of the sum of the studio albums she or he has released. And thus to overlook very significant parts of the body of work just because they're live recordings, not "new" albums, even when officially released. Okay, true, *Live Rust* received high praise from quite a few reviewers (the album, at least; I don't know what was said about the film). But I have evidence that a (possibly significant) cross-section of Neil Young "fans" did not think of Young's live albums when asked (in the poll Damon Ogden and friends conducted in late 1994) to list his best albums. But stop press! To show that I can be as foolish as the next fan, I took this to be evidence of many fans' disinterest in "live" albums, until I finally read more carefully the introduction to the poll listings in *Broken Arrow* issue 58, and realized I was wrong. The three friends (all actuaries) who put together the poll decided to "compare only released albums and not include any live recordings. We wanted to judge albums based on the writing and innovation as well as performance and feel. Thus we decided not to include

Journey Through the Past, Decade, Live Rust, Weld, or *Unplugged* because the material was virtually entirely conceived on previous albums." So it wasn't the 49 participants who left *Weld* and *Live Rust* off their list of the top 25 Neil Young albums; it was the ground rules set by the poll-takers. A reasonable approach, even though I don't agree with it. What I was (over)reacting to was the idea that people might not think of these excellent (officially released) albums when making long lists of the artist's best work. And my conversations with other Neil Young fans over the years do leave me suspicious that many of us sadly underrate the live recordings of Neil Young that *have* been legally made available to us via our local record or video store. Heck, I even have to confess my own foolishness when I tell you that I liked *Weld* when I first heard it and loved two of those early '91 (during the Gulf War) concerts when I attended them, but have barely ever listened to *Weld* since. And now at last I'm discovering or rediscovering it (or them – most versions come in two separate cases, *Weld* Disc One and *Weld* Disc Two) with great joy. And, I must say, with moments of revelation. Wow. The artist speaks. Loudly and confidently and with extraordinary grace. Don't leave this off *your* best-of list. This is near the heart of the matter.

The 49 fans who responded to the poll did rank *Ragged Glory* #5 in terms of total votes when they awarded 20 points for each #1 choice, 19 for #2, and so forth. Good. It's certainly in *my* top five, most days. So for my sacrificial fool (fan-type fool, since he's a true NY fan, not just a critic/author) in this paragraph I'll have to pick on Johnny Rogan, a fine writer and researcher and good fellow, who made himself an easy target by daring to write a book called *The Complete Guide to the Music of Neil Young.* Since I believe people (young people, particularly) will be discovering the recorded music of Neil Young a hundred or more years from now, and some of them may look in the book part of the library to see what people said about these record-ings in the artist's era, I have to go on record as being quite certain that my friend Johnny's evaluation of *Ragged Glory* on page 137 of his book is quite mistaken. Hey, future kids and ladies and gents, listen to this album.

And don't listen to Rogan when he asserts that critical enthusiasm for *Ragged Glory* was simply because "With Crazy Horse's grunge-style now the height of fashion, the album was perfectly timed. It was the classic example of raw excitement overcoming substance. Critical hyperbole conveniently ignored the fact that the songs weren't that strong by Young's best standards, while the extended guitar forays failed to match the power and passion of Crazy Horse's finest work." Wrong, sir. This *is* Neil Young and Crazy Horse's finest work. Alongside several other comparable examples. Oh dear reader/listener, don't be a fool. If Young were a North American novelist, *Ragged Glory* would be a *Huck Finn* or a *Moby Dick* or a *Tropic of Cancer* or . . .

When fans or other listeners, whatever century they might be from, get stuck in conventional ideas of what strength and power and passion sound like, they run the risk of somehow not hearing it when it's right in front of them. "Love to Burn," "Over and Over," and "Love and Only Love" not "strong" by Young's best standards?? You must be deaf, sir. These are precisely as strong as his work gets. And perfectly good examples of how and why this artist's body of work deserves and rewards as much attention as we can give it.

Another way fans are fools, and I do include myself in this at weak moments, is when we fail to make the simple investments of time and attention that might repay our efforts with such rich rewards. So okay, even though these albums have been out for a few years, let me wrap up my ragged volume by saying something about the rewards I find, and believe are readily findable, in these two 1990 and 1991 artworks.

* * *

Which album shall I talk about first? Well, to demonstrate how lovingly interwoven these two masterworks are (similar to *Live Rust* and *Rust Never Sleeps*, but with a different panache because this is a different moment, or era, in the artist's work), I'm gonna start with my current favorite track from all these wonderful ones. Snuck up on me and hit me hard. Check it out. "Love and Only Love" from *Weld*. Yeah, same song's on *Ragged Glory* a few months earlier. And I've always adored that version. But this one is something else (so near and yet so far). Even better, if that's possible. Anyway, an alternate take that is in my opinion as significant in his *oeuvre* as the original take. The differences between the two are subtle. But if you try to take either one from me, I'll scream. I love both. Passionately. And to contemplate the subtle difference between these two very pleasant experiences can lead directly to a deeper understanding and appreciation of Neil Young's purpose in his art and the nature and character of his particular mastery.

He's a fucking jazz musician, okay? Like nobody else in rock and roll except the Grateful Dead. No two solos or melody-rhythm interactions alike. He and his band are improvising. Neither are those solos and melody-rhythm interactions self-consciously "different" from each other. He and Crazy Horse are not into gimmicks here, no matter what you think of those feedback endings. This is fiery, alive, very intelligent and passionate music.

How do they improvise, you ask? Not by changing the arrangement or the patterns. Just by varying the *sound* and *feel* in a big way by altering subtle aspects of each musician's approach (including, of course, the tone of the singer's voice). Remember, the "original album version" is also live, live in Neil's home studio, summer 1990. Raunchier than the early '91 on-stage version. Which in turn, surprisingly, is sweeter than the "studio" version. But don't be misled. Both versions are wonderfully raunchy, wonderfully sweet, unique and exhilarating, and fucking triumphs. What happened to the Rolling Stones rule that rock musicians can't select the right tracks for their live albums? Neil plays by his own rules, and *Weld*, like *Ragged Glory*, is a masterpiece.

In fact, if there's any single album (okay, two discs, but one album) that sums up Neil Young as an artist, it's *Weld*. *Sleeps with Angels* also does the job rather well. But *Weld* is extraordinary in its ability to be a retrospective *and* a portrait of the artist at this particular living moment both at once. Breadth and depth. Sincerity and presence. And very, very good music. Wow. Okay, *Live Rust*'s a fine concert album with the same virtues. But few fans are such fools as to stop at one favorite live tape. Thank God we've got two such excellent "official" live albums to choose from. All I'm really saying is, don't make my (temporary) mistake. Don't over-look *Weld*. It's *Ragged Glory* part two and also something else, something more. (Ya could also say it's *Live Rust* part two, proving that a dozen years going by hasn't rusted *this* machinery.) *Weld* is the legacy. That shaggy clown with the peace symbol on his sleeve on the back covers herein makes his statement. And not by himself, nor his alone. Billy Talbot, Ralph Molina, Frank Sampedro and David Briggs. The three other members of Neil Young & Crazy Horse (Neil has always rightly insisted he's a member of the band) and the producer who nailed the sucker with them, the late great David Briggs, co-producer of *Weld*, *Ragged Glory*, *Everybody Knows This Is Nowhere*, *After the Gold Rush*, *Live Rust*, and *Sleeps with Angels* . . .

And "Love and Only Love" is the ten-minute (or nine-minute) concise summation of that statement. As is "Love to Burn." "Love and only love will endure." "You've got love to burn; you'd better take a chance on love!" Amen, brother. And with the aid of all five partners you can hear it burning. I'd like to thank Nick Kent, again in his book *The Dark Stuff*, for reassuring me that I'm not alone in hearing *Ragged Glory* and *Weld* as the glorious rock equivalent of *A Love Supreme*. Kent wrote: "There was something else to the feel of

Ragged Glory, something truly remarkable. For no longer was Young's most physical electric music powered by a spirit of taut anger. It had been replaced by a force somehow guided by a mixture of joy and exhilaration. 'You've got love to burn/You've got to take a chance on love,' Young would admonish on one track, before joining the Horse to lose himself in a throbbing jam every bit as ecstatic and spiritual as one of John Coltrane's classic extrapolations with his own mighty quartet."

Amen, Nick. And, dear reader/listener, if you want to go to the very heart of *Ragged Glory* and *Weld* (and of Neil Young's public opus), then after you've bathed yourself thoroughly in *both* ecstatic performances of "Love to Burn" and listened pleasurably to the rest of all three discs, advance your *Weld* Disc Two CD to the 3:45 location on track 3, "Love and Only Love":

"Spirit, come back to me/Give me strength and set me free/Let me feel the magic in my heart . . ."

Yeah, his heart, our hearts. The very heart of both albums, of all this gold. And I challenge me to explain myself before the soon-coming end of this essay and this book.

* * *

If I really said something, as I kinda promised a while back, about *all* the rewards I find and believe are readily findable on these two albums, we'd be here for weeks. Uh, for example, it would be difficult to convince me that *Weld*'s is not the best "Hey Hey, My My" or "My My, Hey Hey" to be found anywhere. And did you know that "Farmer John" (on both *Ragged Glory* and *Weld*) is almost the earliest song in Neil Young's repertoire? He used to play it with The Squires in late '64. It was a cover of a summer 1964 hit by a Latin-rock band from southern California. Wind me up and I'd have plenty to say about almost every one of the 26 tracks on these three discs. But I already did that for *Rock 'N' Roll Cowboy*. So, though I would love to go into more detail about the glories of these performances, let's take a more focused approach here, and just look at the *message* these albums communicate, singly and collectively.

Actually, the inclusion of "Farmer John" on both is a good place to start. John Einarson, in his book *Neil Young, The Canadian Years*, quotes Young (probably from a conversation with Einarson in 1986) on the subject of a two-week stand by The Squires in Fort William, Ontario in November 1964, during which bandleader Neil turned nineteen and wrote "Sugar Mountain":

"We did 'Farmer John' really good back then in Fort William. We used to break loose in it. That was one of the first times I ever started transcending on guitar. Things just got to another plane, it was gone. And the people would say, 'What the hell was that?' We didn't even know what we were doing. People knew they had been watching a normal band playing these cool songs, then all of a sudden we went berserk and they didn't know what was happening . . . We just got way out there and we were really playing. We just went nuts, Kenny, Bill, and I. That's when I started to realize I had the capacity to lose my mind playing music, not just playing the song and being cool." Ragged glory – get it?

Young looks back to a different side of his formative years as an artist in a song first released on *Ragged Glory* but written in spring 1988, that extraordinary night on his sailboat on the Pacific when he wrote "Ordinary People" and "Sixty to Zero/Crime in the City" and this song, "Days That Used to Be." The song is clearly addressed to Bob Dylan (the tip-off is the "borrowed tune," the melody of Dylan's "lookin' back" song "My Back Pages"), speaking partly as a listener/fan who was set free by Dylan's songs in the mid-'60s, and also as one singer-songwriter and financially successful "rock star" from those days to another, a fellow-traveller. And as old friend to "long lost friend": "I wish that I could talk to you and you could talk to me. 'Cause there's very few of us left, my friend, from the days that used to be." This theme of coming to terms with and staying in touch with the past is certainly one of the anchors of *Ragged Glory* . . . and, not surprisingly, also of *Weld*.

So "Farmer John" is from 1964 and "Days that Used to Be" from 1988. The first two songs on *Ragged Glory*, "Country Home" (originally called "Spud Blues," which calls attention to the adultery theme, *à la* "Saddle Up the Palomino") and "White Line" (a drug song and a road song, another relic of the bad old days) date from December 1975, when they were debuted at Neil's first shows with Crazy Horse after the long post–1970 hiatus. "Like a Hurricane" was also introduced at those shows, a series of unannounced, guerrilla performances at California saloons, called "The Rolling Zuma Tour" in reference to Dylan's Rolling Thunder Tour a few months earlier, which was in fact intended to introduce and promote a new (or reintroduce a very old) way of being a travelling artist. You roll into town and play. One more moment where Neil Young heard Bob Dylan speaking directly to him.

"Fuckin' Up" (or, as it is "properly" known, "F*!#in' Up") was written in September 1989 at that "Saturday Night Live" rehearsal. "Mother Earth (Natural Anthem)" was premiered at (and the album track was recorded live at) the fourth annual Farm Aid concert, April 7, 1990, a musical benefit Neil had helped launch, again inspired by something Bob Dylan said (at the Live Aid concert in 1985).

That leaves four *Ragged Glory* songs written for or first performed at the recording sessions for that album, June-July 1990: "Over and Over," "Love to Burn," "Mansion on the Hill," and "Love and Only Love." As I've already said, three of these are, in my view, as good and as close to perfect as Young's work gets, "Over and Over" and the two "Love" songs. Then there's "Mansion on the Hill," attractive but insubstantial on *Ragged Glory*. It gets a lot closer to perfect on *Weld*, a new version of the song which sounds more like a hit single than the original version (released in edited form as a single) ever did. And therefore one of several reasons you don't have the complete *Ragged Glory* unless you also have *Weld*.

My experience of *Ragged Glory* and my fierce attachment to the album have, from the beginning, centered on those three somehow interrelated "guitar epics," profound and irresistible love songs, not songs about a loved one but songs about the value and power of love in one's life and in all our lives. Powerful theme. And well-expressed lyrically as well as musically:

"I love the way you open up and let me in/So I go running back to you/Over and over again my love/Over and over with you." Very sexual, and very devotional.

"Love and only love will endure./Hate is everything you think it is./Love and only love will break it down." This is well said, and strongly felt, and well worth contemplating. Not the usual truisms. A hard-won and heartfelt message that really says something. And matters. And sounds great.

"You've got to let your guard down./You've got to take a chance/A chance on love." An album with a message. One that has gone on speaking powerfully to me every time I've come back to it ("my heart goes running back to you") in these six years. Sonically, and in terms of strength of feeling, very much the equivalent of those earlier NY/CH statements, excursions, triumphs, *Everybody Knows This Is Nowhere* and *Tonight's the Night*.

Art this good is innately mysterious. I'm not gonna try to sum it up. But I could point to some threads: Between "You've got love to burn" and "somewhere in the fire of love, our dreams went up in smoke" ("Over and over"). Between "The spirit came to me and said" ("Love to Burn") and "Spirit, come back to me" ("Love and Only Love"). And even "I got a load to love" ("Mansion on the Hill") and "They drag you down and load you down in the guise of security" ("Days That Used to Be") and "Feel like a railroad, I pull the whole load behind" ("White Line") and "Carry such an easy load" ("Fuckin' Up").

229

Don't start me talkin' . . . Interesting how *Ragged Glory* manages at times to be unashamedly nostalgic: "There's a mansion on the hill/Psychedelic music fills the air/Peace and love live there still." "There's very few of us left my friend/From the days that used to be."And even frankly political: "Mother earth . . . how long can you give and not receive/And feed this world ruled by greed?"

And then there's *Weld*, whose two discs are so filled with juice one can receive all kinds of interwoven messages from them. For politics, there's the magnificent trilogy of "Crime in the City" (first electric/full-band version), "Blowin' in the Wind," and "Welfare Mothers." The tour and, according to Young, his and the band's performances every night were colored by the Gulf War, which started during the tour. Neil challenged his audiences to think about his and their positions regarding the War by displaying a large peace-symbol banner at the start of the concerts and at the same time playing a recording of "The Star-Spangled Banner" (by Jimi Hendrix). For nostalgia (not unrelated) – or integration of past and present – there's a glorious revival of "Roll Another Number" ("I'm not goin' back to Woodstock for a while") and of course the inclusion of "Farmer John" (not surprisingly, much more convincing and more fun in the concert version), and the revamped and searing "Mansion on the Hill." And then there's the extraordinary beauty of these performances of "Cortez the Killer" and "Powder-finger" and "Like a Hurricane" and "Cinnamon Girl," and the pure power and joy of these performances of "Hey Hey, My My" and "Rockin' in the Free World" and "Love to Burn" (anthem after anthem) and "Fuckin' Up." And all those graceful, sweet, expressive feedback crescendos (so I finally listened to *Arc*, and I am surprised to find I really like it) (a 35-minute "feedback compilation composition" made from song endings recorded live plus a few unaccompanied vocal fragments, released as a partner album to *Weld*). Think about the statement of calling a pair of recordings *Arc* and

Weld. The junkyard artist describes his process.

And it sounds great. Come on, what else is there to say? "Welcome to Miami Beach"?

And "spirit, come back to me" is a description of what happened to the artist when he re-found his inspiration (and his willingness to go public with his feelings) in the late 1980s. "Give me strength, and set me free." What an autobiography he has written!

I love the man because he sings the song.

Appendix One

Checklist of Neil Young albums

This list includes all albums released by Neil Young in the United States (and one released only in Japan) between 1967 and 1996, plus albums by Buffalo Springfield and Crosby, Stills, Nash & Young (on these albums, songs written or co-written by Neil Young are marked with *).

1. *Buffalo Springfield*, released 1/67. Baby Don't Scold Me (replaced by For What It's Worth on later pressings)/ Go and Say Goodbye/Sit Down, I Think I Love You/ *Nowadays Clancy Can't Even Sing/Hot Dusty Roads/ Everybody's Wrong/*Flying on the Ground Is Wrong/ *Burned/*Do I Have to Come Right Out and Say It?/ Leave/*Out of My Mind/Pay the Price.

2. *Buffalo Springfield Again*, released 12/67. Mr. Soul/A Child's Claim to Fame/Everydays/*Expecting to Fly/ Bluebird/Hung Upside Down/Sad Memory/Good Time Boy/Rock 'N' Roll Woman/*Broken Arrow.

3. *Last Time Around* (by Buffalo Springfield), released 8/68. *On the Way Home/*It's So Hard to Wait/Pretty Girl Why/Four Days Gone/Carefree Country Day/Special Care/The Hour of Not Quite Rain/Questions/*I Am a Child/Merry-Go-Round/Uno Mundo/Kind Woman.

4. *Neil Young*, released 11/68. The Emperor of Wyoming/ The Loner/If I Could Have Her Tonight/I've Been Waiting for You/The Old Laughing Lady/String Quartet from Whiskey Boot Hill/Here We Are in the Years/What Did You Do to My Life?/I've Loved Her So Long/The Last Trip to Tulsa.

5. *Everybody Knows This Is Nowhere* (with Crazy Horse), released 5/69. Cinnamon Girl/Everybody Knows This Is Nowhere/Round and Round (It Won't Be Long)/Down by the River/The Losing End (When You're on)/ Running Dry (Requiem for the Rockets)/Cowgirl in the Sand.

6. *Déjà Vu* (by Crosby, Stills, Nash & Young), released 3/70. Carry On/Teach Your Children/Almost Cut My Hair/*Helpless/Woodstock/Déjà Vu/Our House/4+20/ *Country Girl/*Everybody I Love You.

7. *After the Gold Rush*, released 9/70. Tell Me Why/After the Gold Rush/Only Love Can Break Your Heart/Southern Man/Till the Morning Comes/Oh, Lonesome Me/Don't Let It Bring You Down/Birds/When You Dance I Can Really Love/I Believe in You/Cripple Creek Ferry.

8. *Four Way Street* (live album by Crosby, Stills, Nash & Young), released 2/71. Suite: Judy Blue Eyes/*On the Way Home/Teach Your Children/Triad/The Lee Shore/ Chicago/Right between the Eyes/*Cowgirl in the Sand/ *Don't Let It Bring You Down/49 Bye Byes/America's Children/Love the One You're With/Pre-Road Downs/ Long Time Gone/*Southern Man/*Ohio/Carry On/ Find the Cost of Freedom. (Later CD release included a Neil Young medley: *The Loner/*Cinnamon Girl/ *Down by the River.)

9. *Harvest*, released 2/72. Out on the Weekend/Harvest/A Man Needs a Maid/Heart of Gold/Are You Ready for the Country?/Old Man/There's a World/Alabama/The Needle and the Damage Done/Words (Between the Lines of Age).

10. *Journey through the Past* (album cover says "original soundtrack recordings" "a film by Neil Young" above and below title). For What It's Worth/Mr. Soul (Buffalo Springfield; live recordings from 2/17/67 and 4/8/67)/Rock & Roll Woman (BS live 11/6/67)/Find the Cost of Freedom/Ohio (CSNY live 6/5/70)/Southern Man (CSNY live 6/5/70)/Are You Ready for the Country? (rehearsal during *Harvest* sessions)/Let Me Call You Sweetheart (unknown girls' chorus)/Alabama(rehearsal)/Words(extended rehearsal version)/Relativity Invitation/Handel's Messiah/King of Kings (the Tony & Susan Alamo Christian Foundation Orchestra & Chorus)/Soldier (same recording as on *Decade*)/Let's Go Away for Awhile (the Beach Boys).

11. *Time Fades Away* (live), released 9/73. Time Fades Away/Journey thru the Past/Yonder Stands the Sinner/L.A./Love in Mind/Don't Be Denied/The Bridge/Last Dance.

12. *On the Beach*, released 7/74. Walk On/See the Sky About to Rain/Revolution Blues/For the Turnstiles/Vampire Blues/On the Beach/Motion Pictures/Ambulance Blues.

13. *So Far* ("greatest hits" album by CSNY), released 7/74. Déjà Vu/Helplessly Hoping/Wooden Ships/Teach Your Children/*Ohio/Find the Cost of Freedom/Woodstock/Our House/*Helpless/Guinnevere/Suite: Judy Blue Eyes.

14. ***Tonight's the Night***, released 6/75. Tonight's the Night/Speakin' Out/World on a String/Borrowed Tune/Come On Baby Let's Go Downtown/Mellow My Mind/Roll Another Number (for the Road)/Albuquerque/New Mama/Lookout Joe/Tired Eyes/Tonight's the Night (Part II).

15. ***Zuma*** (with Crazy Horse), released 11/75. Don't Cry No Tears/Danger Bird/Pardon My Heart/Lookin' for a Love/Barstool Blues/Stupid Girl/Drive Back/Cortez the Killer/Through My Sails.

16. ***Long May You Run*** (by the Stills/Young Band), released 10/76. *Long May You Run/*Midnight on the Bay/Make Love to You/Black Coral/*Ocean Girl/*Let It Shine/12/8 Blues (All the Same)/*Fontainebleau/Guardian Angel.

17. ***American Stars 'N Bars***, released 6/77. The Old Country Waltz/Saddle Up the Palomino/Hey Babe/Hold Back the Tears/Bite the Bullet/Star of Bethlehem/Will to Love/Like a Hurricane/Homegrown.

18. ***Decade*** (3 LP compilation), released 11/77. Down to the Wire (by Buffalo Springfield; previously unreleased)/Burned (BS)/Mr. Soul (BS)/Broken Arrow (BS)/Expecting to Fly (BS)/Sugar Mountain/I Am a Child (BS)/The Loner/The Old Laughing Lady/Cinnamon Girl/Down by the River/Cowgirl in the Sand/I Believe in You/After the Gold Rush/Southern Man/Helpless (CSNY)/Ohio (CSNY)/Soldier/Old Man/A Man Needs a Maid/Harvest/Heart of Gold/Star of Bethlehem/The Needle and the Damage Done/Tonight's the Night (Part I)/Tired Eyes/Walk On/For the Turnstiles/Winterlong (prev. unreleased)/Deep Forbidden Lake (prev unrl'd)/Like a Hurricane/Love Is a Rose (prev. unrl'd)/Cortez the Killer/

Campaigner (prev. unrl'd)/Long May You Run (Stills/ Young Band).

19. *Comes a Time*, released 11/78. Goin' Back/Comes a Time/ Look Out for My Love/Lotta Love/Peace of Mind/Human Highway/Already One/Field of Opportunity/Motorcyle Mama/Four Strong Winds.

20. *Rust Never Sleeps* (with Crazy Horse), released 6/79. My My, Hey Hey (Out of the Blue)/Thrasher/Ride My Llama/Pocahontas/Sail Away/Powderfinger/Welfare Mothers/Sedan Delivery/Hey Hey, My My (Into the Black).

21. *Live Rust* (live album with Crazy Horse), released 11/79. Sugar Mountain/I Am a Child/Comes a Time/After the Gold Rush/My My, Hey Hey (Out of the Blue)/When You Dance I Can Really Love/The Loner/The Needle and the Damage Done/Lotta Love/Sedan Delivery/ Powderfinger/Cortez the Killer/Cinnamon Girl/Like a Hurricane/Hey Hey, My My (Into the Black)/Tonight's the Night.

22. *Hawks & Doves*, released 10/80. Little Wing/The Old Homestead/Lost in Space/Captin Kennedy/Stayin' Power/Coastline/Union Man/Comin' Apart at Every Nail/ Hawks & Doves.

23. *RE-AC-TOR* (with Crazy Horse), released 10/81. Opera Star/Surfer Joe and Moe the Sleaze/T-Bone/Get Back on It/Southern Pacific/Motor City/Rapid Transit/Shots.

24. *Trans*, released 12/82. Little Thing Called Love/ Computer Age/We R in Control/Transformer Man/ Computer Cowboy/Hold on to Your Love/Sample and Hold/Mr. Soul/Like an Inca.

25. ***Everybody's Rockin'*** (with the Shocking Pinks), released 7/83. Betty Lou's Got a New Pair of Shoes/Rainin' in My Heart/Payola Blues/Wonderin'/Kinda Fonda Wanda/Jellyroll Man/Bright Lights, Big City/Mystery Train/Cry, Cry, Cry/Everybody's Rockin'.

26. ***Old Ways***, released 8/85. The Wayward Wind/Get Back to the Country/Are There Any More Real Cowboys?/Once an Angel/Misfits/California Sunset/Old Ways/My Boy/Bound for Glory/Where Is the Highway Tonight?

27. ***Landing on Water***, released 7/86. Weight of the World/ Violent Side/Hippie Dream/Bad News Beat/Touch the Night/People on the Street/Hard Luck Stories/I Got a Problem/Pressure/Drifter.

28. ***Life*** (with Crazy Horse), released 6/87. Mideast Vacation/ Long Walk Home/Around the World/Inca Queen/Too Lonely/Prisoners of Rock 'n' Roll/Crying Eyes/When Your Lonely Heart Breaks/We Never Danced.

29. ***This Note's for You*** (with the Bluenotes), released 4/88. Ten Men Workin'/This Note's for You/Coupe de Ville/ Life in the City/Twilight/Married Man/Sunny Inside/ Can't Believe You're Lyin'/Hey Hey/One Thing.

30. ***American Dream*** (by Crosby, Stills, Nash & Young), released 11/88. *American Dream/Got It Made/*Name of Love/Don't Say Goodbye/*This Old House/Nighttime for the Generals/Shadowland/*Drivin' Thunder/Clear Blue Skies/That Girl/Compass/Soldiers of Peace/*Feel Your Love/*Night Song.

238

31. ***Eldorado***, released in Japan only, 3/89. Cocaine Eyes/Don't Cry/Heavy Love/On Broadway/Eldorado.

32. ***Freedom***, released 10/89. Rockin' in the Free World/ Crime in the City (Sixty to Zero Part I)/Don't Cry/Hangin' on a Limb/Eldorado/The Ways of Love/ Someday/On Broadway/Wrecking Ball/No More/Too Far Gone/Rockin' in the Free World.

33. ***Ragged Glory*** (with Crazy Horse), released 9/90. Country Home/White Line/F*!#in' Up/Over and Over/Love to Burn/Farmer John/Mansion on the Hill/Days That Used to Be/Love and Only Love/Mother Earth (Natural Anthem).

34. ***Weld*** (2-CD live album with Crazy Horse), released 10/91. Hey Hey, My My (Into the Black)/Crime in the City/Blowin' in the Wind/Welfare Mothers/Love to Burn/Cinnamon Girl/Mansion on the Hill/F*!#in' Up/ Cortez the Killer/Powderfinger/Love and Only Love/ Rockin' in the Free World/Like a Hurricane/Farmer John/Tonight's the Night//Roll Another Number.

35. ***Arc*** (with Crazy Horse), released 11/91. One 37-minute track, a "compilation composition" constructed from snippets of NY&CH making feedback noises in and at the ends of songs performed on a '91 tour.

36. ***Harvest Moon***, released 11/92. Unknown Legend/From Hank to Hendrix/You and Me/Harvest Moon/War of Man/One of these Days/Such a Woman/Old King/ Dreamin' Man/Natural Beauty.

37. ***Lucky Thirteen*** (compilation selected by Neil from the Geffen albums plus some unreleased tracks – marked # – from that period, 1982–88), released 1/93. Sample

239

and Hold/Transformer Man/#Depression Blues/#Get Gone/#Don't Take Your Love Away from Me/Once an Angel/Where Is the Highway Tonight?/Hippie Dream/Pressure/Around the World/Mideast Vacation/ #Ain't It the Truth/#This Note's for You.

38. *Unplugged* ("live" in a TV recording studio), released 6/93. The Old Laughing Lady/Mr. Soul/World on a String/Pocahontas/Stringman/Like a Hurricane/The Needle and the Damage Done/Helpless/Harvest Moon/ Transformer Man/Unknown Legend/Look Out for My Love/Long May You Run/From Hank to Hendrix.

39. *Sleeps with Angels* (with Crazy Horse), released 9/94. My Heart/Prime of Life/Driveby/Sleeps with Angels/ Western Hero/Change Your Mind/Blue Eden/Safeway Cart/Train of Love/Trans Am/Piece of Crap/A Dream That Can Last.

40. *Mirror Ball* (with Pearl Jam), released 6/95. Song X/Act of Love/I'm the Ocean/Big Green Country/Truth Be Known/Downtown/What happened Yesterday/Peace and Love/Throw Your Hatred Down/Scenery/Fallen Angel.

41. *Dead Man* (soundtrack composed and performed by NY), released 2/96.

42. *Broken Arrow* (with Crazy Horse), released 7/96. Big Time/Loose Change/Slip Away/Changing Highways/ Scattered [Let's Think About Livin']/This Town/Music Arcade/Baby What You Want Me to Do? LP bonus track: Interstate.

Appendix Two

Checklist of selected Neil Young films and videotapes

1. *Swing In with Neil Young*, Dutch TV documentary, 1971, including footage of a 1/71 solo performance in Connecticut.

2. BBC Broadcast, twelve songs recorded at BBC Television Theatre in London, Feb. 1971.

3. *Journey Through the Past*, "a film by Neil Young," first shown theatrically at the U.S. Film Festival, 4/73.

4. *Rust Never Sleeps*, concert film directed by Neil (under the name Bernard Shakey), first shown theatrically 7/79. Later released on videocassette and laser disc 10/93 by Warner Reprise Video. Songs performed (solo and with Crazy Horse in San Francisco, 10/78): Sugar Mountain/I Am a Child/Comes a Time/After the Gold Rush/Thrasher/My My, Hey Hey/When You Dance I Can Really Love/The Loner/Welfare Mothers/The Needle and the Damage Done/Lotta Love/Sedan Delivery/ Powderfinger/Cortez the Killer/Cinnamon Girl/Like a Hurricane/Hey Hey, My My/Tonight's the Night.

5. *Human Highway*, "a film by Neil Young," completed 1982, released on videocassette circa 1993 by Warner Reprise Video.

6. ***Neil Young Live in Berlin,*** concert film of 10/82 concert with the Trans Band, directed by Neil Young and Michael Lindsay-Hogg, broadcast on HBO TV 9/83 and later released on videocassette and laser disc. Songs performed: Cinnamon Girl/Computer Age/A Little Thing Called Love/Old Man/The Needle and the Damage Done/After the Gold Rush/Transformer Man/Sample and Hold/Hey Hey, My My/Like a Hurricane/Berlin.

7. ***SoloTrans,*** 90-minute documentary of a 9/83 performance in Ohio by Neil and the Shocking Pinks, filmed by Hal Ashby, apparently partially broadcast on U.S. TV and later released on laser disc. Songs performed: Old Man/Helpless/Heart of Gold/Don't Be Denied/Ohio/I Got a Problem/Mr. Soul/Payola Blues/Get Gone/Don't Take Your Love Away from Me/Do You Wanna Dance?

8. Austin City Limits segment, performance with International Harvesters, taped 9/84, broadcast on US TV 1/85 and 3/92. Songs performed: Are You Ready for the Country?/Comes a Time/Fingers/Are There Any More Real Cowboys?/Heart of Gold/Amber Jean/Roll Another Number/The Needle and the Damage Done/ Helpless/California Sunset/Field of Opportunity/Old Man/Powderfinger/Get Back to the Country/Down by the River.

9. ***Muddy Track,*** unreleased full-length video by Neil about a 1987 tour with Crazy Horse. In spring 1988 he had "just finished" this. He told *Rolling Stone,* "I had two little video-8 cameras, which I left running all the time ... People start talking to the camera ... There's a lot of guts in it, a lot of feeling."

10. ***Freedom,*** "a live acoustic concert," directed by Tim Hutton, filmed 6 and 9/89, broadcast on MTV, and

released on videocassette and laser disc 1990 by Warner Reprise Video. Songs performed: Crime in the City/This Note's for You/No More/Too Far Gone/After the Gold Rush/Ohio/Rockin' in the Free World.

11. ***Ragged Glory***, collection of music videos of songs from the album, directed by Rusty Cundieff and Julien Temple, released on videocassette 1991 by Warner Reprise Video. Songs included: F*!#in' Up/Farmer John/Over and Over/Fuckin' Up/Mansion on the Hill.

12. ***Weld***, concert film directed by "Bernard Shakey," of NY & CH on the "Ragged Glory Tour" at various locations in the U.S. 2/91 and 4/91, released on videocassette and laser disc 11/91 by Warner Reprise Video. Songs performed: Star Spangled Banner (by Jimi Hendrix at Woodstock)/Hey Hey, My My/Crime in the City/Blowin' in the Wind/Love to Burn/Cinnamon Girl/Mansion on the Hill/F*!#in' Up/Cortez the Killer/Powderfinger/Love and Only Love/Rockin' in the Free World/Welfare Mothers/Tonight's the Night/Roll Another Number.

13. Center Stage segment, solo performance taped in Chicago 11/92, broadcast on U.S. TV 12/92, 2/93 and 6/93. Songs performed: Long May You Run/From Hank to Hendrix/Love Is a Rose/Like a Hurricane/War of Man/Tonight's the Night/Harvest Moon/Dreamin' Man/Mr. Soul/You and Me.

14. ***Neil Young Unplugged***, taped with acoustic band and backup singers at Universal Studios in Los Angeles 2/93. Broadcast on MTV 3/93 and released on videocassette and laser disc 1993 by Warner Reprise Video. Songs performed: The Old Laughing Lady/Mr. Soul/World on a String/Pocahontas/Stringman/Like a Hurricane/The Needle and the Damage Done/Helpless/Harvest Moon/

Transformer Man/Unknown Legend/Look Out for My Love/Long May You Run/From Hank to Hendrix.

15. ***Sleeps with Angels***, unreleased Shakey Pictures film directed by L. A. Johnson; includes six songs from the album apparently filmed as the actual album track was being recorded: My Heart/Prime of Life/Sleeps with Angels/Trans Am/Safeway Cart/Piece of Crap.

16. ***The Complex Sessions***, directed by Jonathan Demme, NY and Crazy Horse performing songs from *Sleeps with Angels* live in the studio 10/94 (after finishing the album). Released on videocassette and laser disc 1993 by Warner Reprise Video. Songs performed: My Heart/Prime of Life/Change Your Mind/Piece of Crap.

Appendix Three

Checklist of Neil Young tours

EARLY BANDS:

The Jades (1/62), The Stardusters (2/62), The Classics (11–12/62), The Squires (2/63–6/65), Four to Go (10/65), The Mynah Birds (1/66), Buffalo Springfield (4/66–5/68).

KNOWN PERFORMANCES, '68–'72:

solo: 10/68–2/69, 6/69, 10/69, 6/70, 11/70–2/71, 7/72
with Crazy Horse: 2/69–6/69, 1/70–3/70
with CSN&Y: 8/69–9/69, 11/69–1/70, 5/70–7/70, 10/71, 3/72

TOURS:

'73:
The Stray Gators (Time Fades Away tour):
    North America, 1/73–4/73, 8/73, 9/73
The Santa Monica Flyers (Tonight's the Night tour):
    North America and UK, 10/73–11/73

'74:
CSN&Y ("the doom tour"):
    North America, 7/74–9/74
    UK, 9/74

'75–'76:
The return of Crazy Horse:
  No. Calif, 12/75
  Japan, 3/76
  Europe, 3–4/76
  US, 10/76–11/76
The Stills/Young Band:
  US, 6/76–7/76

'77:
The Ducks:
  Santa Cruz CA, 7/77–9/77
The Gone with the Wind Orchestra:
  Miami FL, 11/12/77

'78:
Solo (One-Stop World Tour):
  San Francisco, 5/78
Rust Never Sleeps Tour (Crazy Horse):
  North America, 9/78–10/78

'80:
The Hawks & Doves Band:
  Berkeley CA, 10/3/80

'82:
The Trans Band:
  No. Calif, 7/82–8/82
  Europe, 8/82–10/82

'83:
Solo Trans:
  North America, 1/83–3/83
The Shocking Pinks:
  North America, 7/83–10/83

'84:
Crazy Horse:
  Santa Cruz, 2/84
The International Harvesters:
  North America, 6/84, 8/84–10/84

'85:
The International Harvesters & Crazy Horse:
  New Zealand & Australia, 2/85–3/85
The International Harvesters:
  North America, 7/85–9/85

'86:
Crazy Horse ("In a Rusted-Out Garage" Tour):
  North America, 9/86–11/86

'87:
CSN&Y (Greenpeace Benefit):
  Santa Barbara CA, 2/6/87
Crazy Horse:
  Europe, 4/87–6/87
  North America, 8/87–9/87

'87–'88:
The Bluenotes:
  Calif, 10/87–11/87
  US, 4/88
  North America, 8/88–9/88
Ten Men Workin' (renamed Bluenotes):
  US, 10/88

'89:
The Restless:
　North America, 1/89–2/89
The Lost Dogs (same as The Restless, new name):
　Australia, Asia, Japan, 4/89–5/89
Solo Acoustic:
　North America, 6/89–11/89
　Europe, 12/89

'90:
Crazy Horse (the Ragged Glory Tour,
or the "Smell the Horse" Tour):
　North America, 11/90–4/91

'92:
Solo Acoustic:
　US, 1/92–6/92, 9/92–4/93

'93:
Booker T & the MGs:
　No. Calif, 6/93
　Europe: 6/93–7/93
　North America: 8/93–9/93

'94–'95:
Crazy Horse:
　six shows in US, 9/94, 10/94, 1/95, 10/95
Pearl Jam:
　US, 6/95 Europe, 8/95

'96:
Crazy Horse (Broken Arrow Tour):
　Europe, 6/96–7/96
　North America, 8/96–11/96

Appendices

MAJOR BANDS, 1969–1996:

Crazy Horse through '70: Ralph Molina drums, Billy Talbot bass, Danny Whitten rhythm guitar. And Jack Nitzsche keyboards at some '70 shows. Crazy Horse from '75 to present: Ralph Molina drums, Billy Talbot bass, Frank Sampedro rhythm guitar. And Jack Nitzsche keys at '76 shows.

The Stray Gators ('73): Ben Keith steel guitar, Jack Nitzsche keyboards, Tim Drummond bass, Kenny Buttrey or Johnny Barbata drums.

The Santa Monica Flyers: Talbot bass, Molina drums, Keith pedal steel and piano, Nils Lofgren guitar, piano and accordion.

The Trans Band: Lofgren, Molina, Keith as above, and Bruce Palmer or Bob Moseley bass, Larry Cragg banjo, Joe Lala percussion, Joel Bernstein vocoder and synclavier.

The Shocking Pinks: Keith guitar and alto sax, Drummond acoustic bass, Cragg banjo and drums and pedal steel, Bernstein vocoder and synclavier, Karl T. Himmel drums, Larry Byron piano and trumpet, Anthony Crawford guitar, Craig Hayes baritone sax. And extra vocalists; and as in all the bands, some of the musicians occasionally sing backing vocals.

The International Harvesters '84: Keith steel guitars, Himmell drums, Crawford banjo fiddle guitar, Cragg banjo, autoharp, Drummond bass, Bernstein acoustic guitar, Rufus Thibodeaux fiddle, Spooner Oldham piano.

The International Harvesters summer '85: as above, but replace Drummond with Joe Allen on bass, Oldham with Hargus "Pig" Robbins on piano, and add Matraca Berg and Tracy Nelson on back vocals.

249

The Bluenotes '88: Frank Sampedro keyboards, Ben Keith alto sax, Larry Cragg baritone sax, Chad Cromwell drums, Rick Rosas bass, Steve Lawrence tenor sax, Claude Cailliet trombone, John Fumo and Tom Bray trumpets.

The Restless (aka **The Lost Dogs**) '89: Cromwell, Rosas as above, Sampedro guitar and keyboards, Keith steel guitars

Booker T & The MGs '93: Steve Cropper guitar, Donald "Duck" Dunn bass, Jim Keltner drums, Booker T. Jones organ, synthesizer.

Pearl Jam '95: Stone Gossard and Mike McCready guitars, Jack Irons drums, Jeff Ament bass, with Brendan O'Brien on keyboards.

Appendix Four

Other Sources

These are books and other valuable resources (besides listening to his albums, watching his films, and attending his performances) I used in the writing of this book.

NEIL YOUNG, *Rock 'N' Roll Cowboy, A Life on the Road, 1966/1994.* 4-CD bootleg album, including a 44-page color booklet with photos and annotation and quotes and listings of Neil Young tours. Released in May 1994 by Great Dane Records, Milano, Italy. Not authorized by the artist. The credits in the booklet say, "Concept and executive production: Erik Lafayette. Research by Maurice Colt, Ernie Lawler, Frank Lunders, Stephen Fripp. Artwork and design by Rattus Norvegicus IV and Alec Sold." GDR CD 9407/ABCD

Ghosts on the Road, Neil Young in Concert by Pete Long, The Old Homestead Press, London 1996. Published in a hardback and paperback edition (ISBN 0–9526517–0-X). This is a first-rate reference book that has been enormously helpful to me while writing the new sections of *Love to Burn.* Long has gathered all available information about Neil Young's live performances from 1961 to 1995: date, location, songs performed, accompanying musicians, and circumstances of the performance. The book is well-organized, easy to use, and seemingly very careful and reliable. The only limitation is that because it is about Neil Young "on the road," information is not provided about studio recording sessions. Perhaps future editions will attempt to be more comprehensive, or someone will produce a companion volume. Meanwhile, I recommend *Ghosts on the Road* very highly to students of Young's work. In general it is organized in sections corresponding to years or portions of years, opening with well-written and detailed essays about the circumstances of the tours and other performances covered. This is followed by a listing of performance dates, and then listings of the songs played at each performance insofar as the information is available. There are also helpful footnotes to indicate the names of bootlegs (and offically released albums) that a particular performance is included on. To order or get information about availability, contact The Old Homestead Press, 73 Fairfield Road, Bow, London E3 2QA, England.

Broken Arrow, the quarterly magazine of the Neil Young Appreciation Society, and *On a Journey through the Past*, a collection of writings from the magazine, edited by Alan Jenkins, published by the Neil Young Appreciation Society, Bridgend, Wales, 1994. This wonderfully informative and entertaining magazine has published 66 issues as of Feb. 1997. The book, *On a Journey through the Past*, includes "Welcome to Miami Beach," Mark Lyons' translation of the *Tonight's the Night* insert, interviews with Elliot Roberts, Joel Bernstein, Billy Talbot and Neil Young, histories of Crazy Horse and Buffalo Springfield, John Bauldie's "Helpless" essay, some very useful discographies, and other treasures. The listeners' poll I refer to often in *Love to Burn* appeared in *Broken Arrow* #58, 2/95. Another valuable reference tool is "A Chronological Listing of Neil Young's Copyrighted Songs," in #61. To order book or magazine, request information from NYAS, 2A Llynfi Street, Bridgend, Mid Glamorgan, CF31 1SY, Wales UK. Or: http://ourworld.compuserve.com/homepages/nyas

The following books are also referred to in *Love to Burn*:

"The Canadian Years" Neil Young, Don't Be Denied by John Einarson, Quarry Press (Canada) 1992, Omnibus Press 1993.

Neil Young, The Visual Documentary by John Robertson, Omnibus Press, London, 1994.

The Complete Guide to the Recordings of Neil Young by Johnny Rogan, Omnibus Press, London, 1996.

Neil Young by Brian Keizer, Boulevard Books, New York, 1996.

The Dark Stuff by Nick Kent, Penguin Books, London, 1994. The last chapter, entitled "Neil Young and the Haphazard Highway That Leads to Unconditional Love" is based partly on interviews Kent conducted with Young in 1989, 1990, 1991 and 1992. In one intriguing segment Young describes to Kent what can only be the epiphany that inspired him to write "Grey Riders" in 1985, except he gives Kent the impression that it happened a few days before this conversation in 1989.

The Rolling Stone Interviews, The 1980s, edited by Sid Holt, St. Martin's Press/Rolling Stone Press, New York, 1989, includes James Henke's 1988 interview with Young. There is also a book called *Neil Young: The Rolling Stone Files* which I have not been able to find, but I believe it contains most of the interviews with Young from that magazine.

Invaluable to me, but not available to the public, was a privately published collection of lyrics called *Neil Young Songs* an Austrian fan gave me in 1996.

4/01 (40180)